# The Fortune Flirtation

## Roman Heirs, Book 3

### Jenna Bigelow

*To my parents – please don't read Chapters 16, 19, the beginning of Chapter 20, Chapters 21, 23, 27, and the end of Chapter 36*

# CHAPTER 1

LUCRETIA FROWNED AT THE results on the abacus before her. A small sum of money—about ten denarii—was missing from her accounts. She hoped she'd just made a mistake with her accounting, but such an error was unlike her. As the proprietor of Ostia's second largest shipping business, she couldn't afford mistakes, even over a few denarii.

She had a sneaking suspicion as to where the money went, but she was loath to admit it to herself. Surely Marcus, her fourteen-year-old son, knew better than to pilfer from her accounts.

But it was the sort of thing a rebellious adolescent might do, and ever since his father's death last year, Marcus had been even more prone to such unruly habits. His great passion these days was chariot racing, and he was constantly betting on the latest races. To be fair, he did win more than he lost.

With a sigh, Lucretia pushed the wax tablet away and pressed the heels of her hands against her eyes to soothe the persistent throbbing in her skull. A thieving son was the last thing she needed.

A tap came at the door, and Lucretia lifted her gaze to see Dihya, her friend and colleague, poking her head into the back room of their two-room office. "Lucius Avitus Felix is here.

Again." Dihya's expressive mouth twisted in distaste. "Shall I tell him you're busy?"

Lucretia groaned. Lucius Avitus Felix was one of the richest men in Ostia and the owner of the city's largest shipping venture. He had been her late husband's perpetual rival, locked in a never-ending competition for who had the most ships, the best profit margins, the fastest shipments, the most sought-after products. Felix, somehow, had always managed to maintain a slight edge over Cornelius.

Now that his rival was dead, Felix had turned his attention to Lucretia. But he wasn't just trying to beat her. He was trying to remove her from the game entirely.

"I'll see him," she muttered. If he wanted to speak to her, he wouldn't leave until he did, so better to get this over with.

Dihya nodded and withdrew. Lucretia busied herself tidying her desk, pushing aside the abacus and neatening her stacks of paper. Her office was small, little more than a cell, with most of its space taken up by crates stuffed with records going back decades, to the very start of Cornelius's business. A few chests contained money for everyday expenses, though the bulk of her capital was stored at the temple bank, safeguarded by priests and the gods. On the corner of her desk, a lamp burned lavender-scented oil, diffusing a pleasant smell into the air and providing some extra light in addition to the single window cut high into the wall.

Lucius Avitus Felix entered her office. Tall and lean, he wore an ankle-length tunic of dark blue, which complemented his fair complexion and dark hair.

She chided herself for noticing such things. "Felix," she greeted him, gesturing to the chair opposite her desk.

He nodded to her and sat. "Lucretia." His eyes, the gray of a bleak winter morning, moved over her and their surroundings with dispassionate efficiency, as if cataloguing every detail to file away in his head for some future purpose. She hadn't given him much to notice—or so she thought.

His eyes fixed on her face. "You look tired."

Her eyebrows shot up, but she forced herself to moderate her expression. He wasn't usually outright rude, but everything Felix said and did was calculated several times over. So if he was being rude, it was likely to get a reaction from her.

She levelled her chin at him. "If there's something you wished to discuss other than my appearance, please get to the point. I'm busy."

He surveyed her for another moment, eyes flicking from her face to her left hand, where she used to wear Cornelius's ring. She resisted the urge to slide her hand beneath the nearest piece of papyrus.

"I've come with a proposition for you," he finally said. His voice warmed, losing its cool, clipped quality. "I would like to offer you something of great value." He even smiled at her, a charming mask settling over his face as if they were making conversation at a dinner party.

Lucretia tried to ignore the flip her stomach gave at his smile. She had always—guiltily—found Felix handsome, even when she'd been happily married to Cornelius. Felix's cold, scheming personality irked her, but she couldn't deny that his appearance didn't generate quite the same reaction. "And what is that?"

He leaned forward, bracing his forearms on the edge of her desk. "My hand in marriage."

She choked on a laugh, which made her cough. When she recovered her breath, she grinned at him. Triumph rose in her chest. "You are really so threatened by my business that you would tie yourself to me in marriage just so you can control my ships?"

She knew better than to think there was any romantic feeling underlying this ridiculous proposal. Once, several years ago, he had attempted a flirtation, but her quick rejection had ended any further overtures of that sort.

No, this proposal had a different motivation. In the year since Cornelius died, Felix had been steadily trying several different angles to induce her to sell her ships to him. First, a generous cash offer. Then an even more generous one.

When simple money didn't work, he became more persuasive, reminding her how difficult and time-consuming it was to manage a business operation like this. Surely she would prefer to devote her time and energy to raising her son or securing a new husband. Surely she didn't want the hassle and stress of managing a business.

While it could be stressful at times, this business was Lucretia's greatest chance at independence, at carving out a life for herself and Marcus where they were beholden to no one. Cornelius had given her a great gift in leaving the business to her, and she wasn't about to squander it. One day, her ships would be her son's legacy, and she was determined to make them as successful as possible.

Felix, composed as always, showed no discomfiture at her reaction. "I can give you security. A comfortable life. My house is twice the size of yours, if I'm not mistaken. Additionally, I have a summer residence at Baiae with sweeping water views. You and Marcus could spend as much time there as you wish. Speaking of Marcus, it could benefit the boy to have a stepfather to smooth his path as he comes of age. And you must be lonely without Cornelius. I could offer you companionship, should you wish it."

A blush stole across her cheeks at his last words. Did he mean social companionship, or was he suggesting companionship of a more...*marital* sort?

Either way, it was impossible.

"Of course, your ships would serve as dowry, as your father is no longer living and cannot provide you with one," he continued.

She raised an eyebrow. "If I were to divorce you, I would take everything back." And while she might legally retain ownership of her own property in marriage, her husband would become her legal guardian and would have to consent to any decisions she made. That would effectively give Felix total control over her holdings.

He nodded. "A risk I am willing to take—that I will give you no reason to dissolve our marriage. You would have complete freedom. You would not have to spend your days poring over account books or negotiating with suppliers. You could do exactly as you please."

"I *am* doing exactly as I please," she replied. "If you really think I would give up everything I've worked for just for the promise of a bigger house and some vacations to Baiae..." She shook her head. "I refuse your proposal."

His eyes narrowed, the charming mask slipping. "I have made you several generous offers, Lucretia, this last one being the most generous of all. I have treated you like a respected associate. But allow me to advise you that this will be my last offer. If you maintain your refusal, you will no longer be my colleague, but my adversary. And my adversaries do not last long."

That was true enough; for the last several years, Felix had dedicated himself to picking off competing shipping enterprises one by one, whether through undercutting their prices, overtaking their supplier relationships, swaying their investors, or simply convincing them to sell their ships. Lucretia was now the last major competitor in Ostia. If she folded, Felix would control the entire flow of goods into and out of the port city, which could have disastrous consequences if his greed took over.

So she would stand against him, if it came to it. She would risk whatever it took to maintain her independence, and she certainly wouldn't accept his offer of marriage.

"My refusal stands."

"Perhaps you wish to think about it."

She rose to her feet, a gesture of dismissal. "I trust you'll have no further reason to speak to me again."

A muscle pulsed in his jaw. In a quick, spare movement, he stood and cast her one long, dark glance before he turned for the door.

Lucretia waited until she heard the outer door to their office open and close before sinking back into her chair. She let out a long breath. She wasn't thrilled at the idea of having Felix for an enemy, but she owed it to Ostia—and possibly the entire Roman economy—to stand against him.

Felix walked away from Lucretia's office, passing through the Square of the Guilds where all of Ostia's commerce centered. He tried and failed to unclench his jaw. He had planned to return to his own office, on the opposite side of the square from Lucretia's, but now he was too irritated to get any work done. Better to take a brisk walk to work off his frustration.

Lucretia's calm refusal of his best offer rankled him. Who did she think she was playing with? She had to be the only woman in Ostia who would refuse a marriage proposal from him.

Unluckily for him, Lucretia was the only one he had any interest in marrying.

Purely for business reasons, of course. If he couldn't convince Lucretia to sell her ships to him outright, then he'd thought offering a lifetime of security and a respected stepfather for her son would sway her.

His proposal had certainly had *nothing* to do with the fact that thoughts of her had filled his mind ever since they first met years ago, when she was still married to Cornelius. Her shining auburn hair, her quick wit and delicate laugh. Her tempting figure, always hidden beneath a loose dress.

Five years ago, she had also refused him—though that proposal had been of a more prurient nature than the one he'd made today. His inelegant, fumbling advance had left him deeply embarrassed.

It had been a simple thing to quietly lust after her when she was nothing more than his rival's wife. But now, a year after Cornelius's death, Lucretia herself had become his greatest rival. A layer of regard had built—unwillingly—alongside his attraction to her. She had managed to maintain and even grow her husband's business. Somehow, she had convinced the captains of her ships to stay with her and had preserved Cornelius's relationships with merchants and suppliers from Massilia to New Carthage. It made him wonder if perhaps she had been more involved with the business during Cornelius's lifetime than Felix had realized, if her husband's key contacts were willing to trust her without batting an eye.

He hated the way he felt around her. Though he strove to avoid her, Ostia's small social circle threw them together more often than not. Whenever they were in the same room, his attention was drawn to her like a hapless moth to a flame. She scrambled his focus, rendering his other conversations a blur of half-understood words.

On a few occasions, in a particularly crowded room, they'd touched, and each brief moment of contact was branded onto his mind. There was the time her shoulder had brushed his arm when she'd stepped aside to make room for someone to pass. Then the time when her knee had bumped him as she'd risen from the dining couch. Most memorably, she'd once stumbled into him, jostled by someone behind her, and her entire body had pressed against his for one breathless, heated moment. Much as he resented his reaction to her, he hoarded those little moments like Croesus hoarded gold.

But Felix would not let Lucretia's allure blind him. She was standing in the way of his goal to monopolize shipping to and from Ostia, and he would find a way to remove her from his path.

As he made his way through the streets, leaving the colonnaded central square behind, a commotion down a side street caught his attention. He paused, glancing into the shadowy alley. It was just a group of adolescent boys, embroiled in a scuffle.

He made to keep walking, but the nature of the scuffle kept his focus. It didn't seem to be an ordinary, evenly matched brawl, but a three-on-one beating. The boy at the middle of it all was curled into a ball, trying to protect his face from the kicks and punches of the others.

Distaste curled in his stomach. Felix had occasionally been the victim of such torment as a child. If there was one thing he couldn't abide, it was an unfair fight. Nowadays, he visited the gymnasium twice a week to spar with his fists and had developed into a highly capable boxer, but as a boy, he'd been too often targeted for beatings, until his mother, Volusia, had removed him from school and secured private tutors.

Well, he was overdue for a training session, so dispatching these bullies would serve two purposes.

Felix strode into the alley and grabbed the closest boy by the neck of his tunic. He hauled him off the victim and shoved him toward the wall of the alley. The second boy turned to Felix with a snarl and aimed a punch, but Felix deflected the blow easily and rewarded the boy with a cuff to the side of his head that sent the boy reeling to the dirt.

The third boy took a step back, his gaze flicking between Felix and his two comrades, both attempting to drag themselves to their feet.

Felix narrowed his eyes. "Go."

The boy turned and ran. The other two stumbled after him, leaving Felix alone in the alley with their erstwhile victim.

The adolescent hauled himself to his feet, brushing dirt off his knee-length tunic. A few scrapes and bruises marred his arms and legs, but he didn't seem to be seriously injured. "Thank you," he muttered.

Based on the tenor of his voice, Felix put the boy's age at fourteen or fifteen. He was scrawny for his age, though, which was likely at least part of the reason he'd been targeted. Boys like his attackers loved an easy victim.

"I've been in your position more than I'd like to admit," Felix replied. "Not particularly enjoyable, is it?"

The boy shook his head, inspecting a scrape on his elbow with a frown. There was something about him that seemed familiar. Something about the coppery sheen of his hair tugged at a thread of recognition, but Felix couldn't place it.

"Do I know you?" Felix asked. "What's your name?"

The boy glanced up, meeting his gaze with hazel eyes that sent another pang of familiarity through Felix. "Marcus Cornelius."

*Cornelius.* "Lucretia's son," he realized out loud with a jolt. He had never actually met Lucretia's fourteen-year-old son, but now he clearly saw the resemblance. Marcus's hair was a few shades browner than Lucretia's rich auburn, but they had the same eyes and even the same pointed shape to their chins.

Marcus narrowed his eyes. "You know my mother?"

"Yes." *And I'm trying very hard to ruin her.* "My name is Lucius Avitus Felix."

Recognition dawned on Marcus's face. "I know you. Mother says you—" He bit back the words, flushing. "Never mind."

Felix could imagine the sort of things Lucretia would say about him. *Grasping. Greedy. Money-grubbing. Ruthless.* "You should get home," he said. "Before she starts to worry." He nodded to the boy, then turned and left the alley.

# CHAPTER 2

As soon as Felix left, Dihya reappeared in Lucretia's office, taking the chair he had just vacated. Their office consisted of two rooms, a front room where Dihya dealt with visitors, and a back room that served as Lucretia's private workspace. "What did he want this time?"

"You'll never believe it."

Dihya leaned forward, eyes lighting with interest. "Tell me!"

Dihya was the widow of Cornelius's former right-hand man. Both men had died in the same shipwreck a year ago, and she and Lucretia had bonded over their shared grief. Once Lucretia found her footing with Cornelius's business, it became clear she needed a trusted partner to help manage things. So, she'd hired Dihya.

The woman could read and write, and she knew much about the business already from her late husband. A freedwoman, she hailed from the province of Mauretania, on the African coast, and spoke Berber, which helped communicate with merchants and suppliers in that region. Of course, all Lucretia's contacts spoke either Latin or Greek, but Lucretia had noticed that letters written in Dihya's Berber script tended to get a faster, more helpful response. While Lucretia appreciated all of Dihya's wide-ranging skills, she had come to value her friendship and advice most of all.

"If you can believe it, he proposed marriage," Lucretia said. "With my ships as a dowry, of course."

Dihya's mouth dropped open. "And what did you say?"

"No, obviously!" Lucretia threw her hands up. "Even if I liked him—and I despise him—I'm never going to marry again. And I would certainly never marry a man whose sole desire in life is to take my business from me."

"I don't think that's his *sole* desire," Dihya said with an arched eyebrow.

"Stop that," Lucretia said in her sternest tone. Felix might once have harbored certain...*feelings* toward her. But those feelings, whatever they might have been, hadn't stopped him from trying everything in his reach to acquire her ships for himself. He grasped for power as greedily as Caesar Augustus, who'd been steadily consolidating his influence in the handful of years since the civil war.

Her stomach growled. "I need some sustenance after that conversation. Are you hungry?"

Dihya smiled. "If you mean Caeso's bakery, then I'm always hungry." Caeso operated a stall very close to Lucretia's office that sold freshly baked bread, honey cakes, and flatbreads with various toppings. Lucretia and Dihya often visited him when in need of a quick lunch or afternoon snack to get them through a long day.

They rose to their feet and left the office, Lucretia locking the door behind them. The day was pleasant, with a strong, cool breeze whipping at the edges of Lucretia's garments. Even several blocks from the harbor, she could smell the sea air on the wind. She used to love nothing more than to linger at the harbor's edge, looking out over the rolling waves as flecks of saltwater dampened her face. But after Cornelius's death, she only went to the harbor when business required.

They passed through the Square of the Guilds, where all of Ostia's merchants and shipping enterprises kept offices, and soon arrived at Caeso's stall. At certain times of day, his wares would attract long lines of people, but now, they were his only customers.

The young baker sat on a stool behind the wooden counter but jumped to his feet when he saw them. "Good afternoon, ladies. Always a pleasure to see you both." His wide smile lingered on Dihya, and Lucretia suppressed a grin of her own. She had lately noticed a certain rapport growing between Dihya and Caeso—lots of prolonged smiles and extra treats that somehow found their way into Dihya's hands.

Caeso was undeniably a handsome man, with broad shoulders, strong arms, and an easy smile. But Lucretia's stomach never fluttered when she saw him, and her eyes weren't drawn to linger on the planes of his face.

Her mind went back to Felix's visit. It irked her that she found him handsome, even as he'd issued a proposal in a bare-faced attempt to seize control of her ships. How unfortunate, that the only man to kindle such feelings since her husband's death was the one she found intolerably scheming and avaricious.

Lucretia returned her focus to the much more pleasant matter of purchasing an afternoon snack. "Hello, Caeso," she greeted the baker. She glanced over the items on display. There wasn't much left by midafternoon, only a few round loaves of bread and flatbreads topped with olives, which weren't Lucretia's favorite. "Busy day?"

He nodded. "Though I had a feeling you might be paying me a visit, so I took the liberty of holding a few things back." He reached beneath the counter and withdrew a platter of four hand-sized honey cakes topped with sliced figs and berries.

Lucretia let out a sigh of pleasure at the sight of the sweets. "Just what I needed."

"Has it been a trying day, then?" Caeso asked as he withdrew a clean cloth for wrapping.

Dihya shot a grin at Lucretia. "She's been proposed to."

Caeso's dark eyebrows rose. "Really? Are congratulations in order?"

"No," Lucretia muttered. "I rejected him."

"It was Lucius Avitus Felix. Do you know him?" Dihya continued.

"Yes, of course," Caeso said. "In fact, I supply the bread to his household. He's quite picky—only the finest flour—but then again, I suppose he can afford to be."

Dihya rested her hands on the wooden counter, leaning close and lowering her voice. Lucretia didn't miss how Caeso's cheeks flushed beneath his tanned skin as Dihya put her mouth within a handsbreadth of his face.

"Do you think you could poison him?" Dihya asked in a whisper. "He doesn't need to die…just make him a *little* bit uncomfortable."

Caeso cleared his throat, his gaze flicking from Dihya's eyes to her mouth.

"She's joking," Lucretia hastened to say. "We'll take two of the cakes, please." She handed over a few bronze coins.

Caeso broke away from Dihya and took the coins. He laid two cakes on the cloth, then added the other two, tying the cloth neatly around them. "Take them all. This late in the day, I'll probably not be able to move them."

"You're too kind," Lucretia said with a nod of thanks.

Dihya rewarded the young man with a gleaming smile as she hefted the package. "You're going to plump us up if we're not careful!"

Caeso's eyes swept over Dihya's body from head to toe, and his ears turned as pink as the berries atop the cakes. "I–I'm sure that won't be a problem," he stammered.

Lucretia took pity on him and steered Dihya away. "We'll be back soon, no doubt," she said to Caeso in farewell, and they turned back toward their office.

Once out of earshot of Caeso, Lucretia looped her arm through Dihya's. "Have some mercy on the poor man."

Dihya cast her a confused look. "What do you mean? Oh, I was only joking about the poisoning."

Lucretia shook her head with a smile. Dihya's obliviousness was amusing, as her mind was sharp as an arrow when it came to matters of business. "Of course."

Lucretia worked until late afternoon, drafting replies to merchants who wanted to know if she was interested in another shipment of lavender-flower honey from southern Gaul, or to alert her that a poor harvest in Hispania would drive up the price of olive oil.

Shipping ventures like Lucretia's depended on networking with merchants who didn't want the hassle of buying, crewing, and sailing their own ships. Instead, Lucretia took on the risk and expense of maintaining a fleet, and the merchants sold their cargo directly to her at a favorable price. Lucretia's ships then distributed that cargo throughout places like Gaul, Hispania, and northern Africa, returning laden with wares from those regions that would be transported down the Tiber to Rome for a handsome profit.

Cornelius had mostly concentrated in the western Mediterranean, and Lucretia had maintained that focus. Felix, on the other hand, concentrated on the eastern part of the sea, areas like Greece, Asia Minor, and Egypt. Those eastern regions yielded wares with higher profit margins and also traded with far eastern lands for luxury goods like silk and spices, which was how Felix had managed to accumulate so much capital.

Once the shadows lengthened, Lucretia set aside her work, bid Dihya goodnight, and returned home. The atrium of her house was quiet, lit with flickering oil lamps at this hour, and the scent of dinner cooking wafted from the kitchen. The last rays of sunlight glanced off the central pool, beneath where the atrium opened to the sky.

Now, she remembered the unpleasant matter from earlier—Marcus's thieving. She'd forgotten all about it after Felix's visit and the other demands of the day. But she had to confront Marcus, even if she already knew it would end in nothing but another argument.

With a sigh, she went to Marcus's room. The door was closed. She tapped gently on it. "Marcus?"

A grunt sounded from within. She took that as an invitation and eased open the door.

Her gangly son faced her with arms crossed over his chest, a scowl on his face. She noticed straightaway that he wore a different tunic than the one he'd worn this morning when he left for school. Her eyes flicked to fabric balled in the corner of the room—the old tunic, no doubt.

"What do you want?" Marcus snapped, drawing her attention back to him.

She frowned. "As if I need a reason to speak with my son?"

He rolled his eyes. Dirt streaked one of his forearms, and there was a scrape on his jaw. Her lips tightened. It wasn't the first time he'd come home with the signs of having gotten into a fight, and she'd chided him many times for engaging in violence. She held back from scolding him again, though. Better to focus on one infraction at a time.

"I was reviewing my accounts and noticed ten denarii missing." She fixed him with a steady stare. "Would you happen to know anything about that?"

He met her gaze for a moment, then his eyes slid to focus on something behind her. His jaw clenched in a mulish expression. "No."

Frustration rose in her chest, a hot, prickly tide. "Don't lie to me, Marcus."

He narrowed his eyes. "Are you accusing me of something?"

"You took that money. I don't know why, as your allowance is more than generous, but—"

"Search me, then." He waved an arm around the room. "If you think I've taken it, then surely you'll find it here."

She doubted that was true, as she would bet double the amount he'd taken that he'd spent it already. "Consider this a warning. If I notice anything else missing, I'll dock your allowance by that amount."

He shrugged again, an affectation of nonchalance.

Lucretia left the room, closing the door behind her. She crossed through the atrium, taking deep breaths in an attempt to ease the powerless frustration clogging her throat. Lately, talking to Marcus felt more like negotiating with a recalcitrant supplier than interacting with her son.

She paused in front of the ancestral shrine at the side of the atrium. Here, a collection of death masks were mounted on plinths, allowing the ancestors of the Cornelius family to keep watch over their descendants. The most recent death mask was her husband's. She gazed at his face, remembering a simpler time when they had been a happy family of three. When Cornelius was on a sea voyage, she used to take Marcus to the harbor to watch the ships coming in and out. He would crow with delight every time he spotted a new set of sails, asking eagerly if Papa was on that ship. The game never got old, even when Cornelius was gone for weeks at a time.

Those homecomings had been the best. Even now, she could feel the tight clasp of her husband's arms around her as he stepped onto the dock, could recall Marcus jumping up and down with excitement as Cornelius showed them the treasures he'd brought back from Syracuse or New Carthage or Melita.

Their marriage seemed strongest when they missed each other. After the joy of each homecoming faded, their interactions would inevitably turn stiff and uncertain, cordial rather than tender. But there was always another voyage on the horizon, and another joyous return.

Then, a year ago, Cornelius and his ship had not returned. Eventually, she'd received word of the shipwreck, the entire crew lost in an unlucky storm. After his death, Lucretia had not been able to set foot within sight of the harbor, the memories too raw and painful. But, as she became determined to keep his business running, she forced herself to, in order to inspect her ships and speak with her captains.

Now, she laid a hand gently atop Cornelius's mask. She sent up a silent prayer that he would watch over Marcus, impart some of his steadiness and maturity to their son.

But she felt no answering spark, no sense that Cornelius was listening. She withdrew her hand with a sigh. Perhaps his message was clear. Lucretia would have to deal with their son on her own.

# CHAPTER 3

L UCRETIA MUTTERED A CURSE as she gazed down at the two letters that had come for her. She was in her study at home, where she sometimes attended to matters in the morning before heading to her office in the Square of the Guilds. Since the room opened onto the sunlit atrium, her study at home had better light than her office, though it too was packed with boxes of records and correspondence.

Felix had been busy in the few days since she had refused his proposal. One of her investors now requested to liquidate his shares, and another had informed her he was selling his holdings in her business to another individual.

She had no doubt about who that other individual might be.

Felix was trying to pick off her investors one by one, either buying their shares outright or convincing them to liquidate. Luckily, these two held only minor stakes, so it wouldn't cause an immediate problem. But if it continued, things became far less certain.

Her fists clenched at his audacity. He was trying to destabilize her, to steal her business out from beneath her very feet.

She needed to get ahead of him.

Her largest investor, a friend of her husband's named Publius Calpurnius Lentulus, held nearly a one-third stake in her business.

If Felix got to Lentulus, that would create serious problems. She needed to make sure that didn't happen.

Lucretia donned a palla to cover her hair, then made her way into the streets. She walked the few blocks to Lentulus's house, where she was swiftly admitted into the atrium. Helvetia, Lentulus's wife, collected antique pottery and proudly displayed her most ostentatious pieces on plinths around the atrium. As Lucretia waited, she surveyed the closest one, a large water jug featuring a trio of libidinous satyrs.

Helvetia greeted her a few moments later. "Lucretia! How lovely to see you." Helvetia kissed her on both cheeks. She was a kind woman about ten years older than Lucretia's thirty-four years, with warm brown eyes and the beginnings of smile lines around her mouth.

Lucretia returned the greeting. "I hoped I might find Lentulus at home?"

"He is." Helvetia raised her voice to a pitch that made Lucretia wince. "Husband!"

The man poked his head out from the doorway to his study, a room off the atrium. "What is it? Oh, Lucretia." He emerged fully, joining them in the atrium. Lentulus was about fifty, a few years older than Cornelius had been, and his dark hair was now streaked with gray. He bent to kiss Lucretia's cheek. "Were we expecting you?"

"No," Lucretia said. "I'm sorry for the intrusion. I merely had a quick business matter to discuss."

Helvetia bowed her head with a smile. "Sounds extremely dull, so I will leave you to it." She left the atrium.

Lentulus conducted her to his study, where Lucretia sat opposite his desk.

"How is young Marcus these days?" Lentulus asked. "Is his Greek improving? I could recommend a good tutor."

Lucretia summoned a relaxed smile. "He is applying himself to his studies with diligence." Lentulus didn't need to know about Marcus's current unsavory habits.

"Good, good. Now, what can I do for you?"

Lucretia leaned forward. "We've spoken of Lucius Avitus Felix before—his efforts to consolidate trade in Ostia under his own influence."

Lentulus nodded. "He was forever a pebble in Cornelius's sandal."

"Lately, he has taken a more…specific interest in my holdings," Lucretia continued. "I've been made aware that he is approaching my shareholders, trying to convince them either to sell their shares to him, or liquidate them entirely."

"Ah." Lentulus's brows drew together. "I see how that would be concerning."

"So far, he has only managed to sway two of my smallest investors. Which brings me to the reason for my visit today. I have to assume he will soon approach you." She met Lentulus's steady gaze. "I hope you know how much I value both our friendship and our partnership. You were Cornelius's closest friend, and I've been honored that you've transferred your trust in him to me. I hope, that if Felix should—"

Lentulus waved a hand, cutting her off. "I'm sorry you've taken the trouble for a visit, Lucretia."

Lucretia took a breath, worry pooling in her stomach. Had she misjudged Lentulus? Was it possible that Felix had already gotten to him? Was he going to pull his support and leave her scrambling?

"There's no need for this," Lentulus continued. "If and when Lucius Avitus Felix approaches me, he will know in no uncertain terms that my loyalty remains with you. Even if I had never known Cornelius, and even if I didn't hold you in such great esteem, I understand that giving one enterprise sole control over commerce in Ostia can only have disastrous effects."

Lucretia released her breath in a relieved sigh. "Thank you. Your support is much appreciated." She could now reassure her other investors that Lentulus would stand by her, and no doubt that would help bolster their confidence in her.

Lentulus pushed back from his desk and stood. "Now, may I convince you to stay for a bite to eat? Helvetia will insist."

Lucretia smiled and rose to her feet, feeling lighter than she had in days. "Of course." Now, she only had to worry about what Felix would try next.

Felix left his office with a bounce in his step. The sun was shining, he'd just eaten a delicious lunch of flatbread stuffed with cheese and olives, and he was on his way to meet with Lucretia's largest investor. Swaying Publius Calpurnius Lentulus could be the crack in Lucretia's foundation that would send her enterprise crashing to the ground.

A figure emerged from the shadows of the portico that surrounded the Square of the Guilds, and Felix stopped short.

He frowned. "Marcus?"

Lucretia's son ambled up to him. "You said your name was Lucius Avitus Felix, right?" It had been a few days since the fighting incident, and the minor scrapes and bruises the boy sustained seemed to be gone.

Felix nodded, still frowning. "How long have you been waiting outside?"

Marcus deftly ignored the question. "I hear you box a lot at the gymnasium. You're supposed to be pretty good."

Felix liked to think he was more than "pretty good," but he didn't need to court the admiration of a fourteen year old. "What's this about?"

"I want you to teach me," Marcus declared.

"No," Felix said immediately. Despite his refusal, a stab of sympathy panged him. Usually, a boy's father or brother would teach him how to fight. Felix's ex-army stepfather, Maximus, had undertaken that duty, as Felix's father died when he was only nine. But Marcus had neither father, brother, nor stepfather to teach him.

Regardless, it wasn't Felix's place to educate the boy. *Especially* given that Marcus was the son of the woman whose business Felix was trying to dismantle.

Felix started walking down the street, hoping Marcus would take the hint and run off.

But Marcus followed, jogging every few steps to keep pace with Felix's longer, brisk stride. "Why not?" A slight whine entered his voice.

"Because if you're regularly getting beaten up in three-on-one fights, knowing how to box isn't going to help you. Boxing is inherently a fair fight, relatively speaking. You'd be better off training your legs so you can outrun them. Do some laps at the running track."

Marcus glowered at him as Felix made a sharp turn onto another street. "Is that what you did? Run away?"

Felix now regretted admitting to Marcus that he had once been the prey of bullies. "No, my mother hired a private tutor." He increased his pace, but Marcus kept up. "I'm surprised your mother hasn't done the same." Lucretia had never struck him as a neglectful parent, not that he had much occasion to think of her as a mother instead of a business rival or object of his unwilling desire.

"Can't tell her," Marcus said. "So you didn't learn to fight in school? Were you in the army?"

"No." Growing up, Felix wanted to follow in his late father's footsteps and become a statesman, which would have required at least ten years of military service. But at the age of seventeen, his mother finally told him the truth about his father's death: he'd been poisoned while governing one of the Gallic provinces, rather than dying of an illness as Felix had believed until then.

This revelation had thrown his plans into disarray. Suddenly, his dreams of becoming a praetor or governor or consul seemed pointless. Why serve the same system that had murdered his father?

So he'd turned to trade instead, investing in ship financing before slowly building his own fleet. He wasn't satisfied to be a simple merchant. Felix had spent his whole childhood and ado-

lescence dreaming of greatness, of honoring his father's legacy, so if he was going to pursue something, he'd be the best
at it. He'd still attain greatness, still honor his father, just in a
different way than he'd originally planned. One day, he could
hold the entire Roman economy in the palm of his hand, and
he didn't need to be a consul or governor or even a *princeps*
like Caesar Augustus to do it.

Felix fixed Marcus with a stern look. "And I didn't learn
to *fight*. Boxing is an art. It's as different from a brawl in
the streets as wine is from vinegar. Why were those boys
attacking you, anyway?" Given how annoying Marcus was
being at this very moment, it was distinctly possible he'd
deserved the beating.

"We made a bet on the races," Marcus said. "I won—of
course—and they wouldn't give me my winnings. They said
I must have cheated, which is stupid, and I told them that any
idiot would have known better than to bet on the Blues for
that race, as they've got a new driver who hasn't learned the
horses yet. That was when the punching started."

"I see." Felix had found himself in similar situations as a
boy—always wanting to be *right*, to demonstrate his intelligence and superiority even when it got him thrashed.

Marcus jogged a few steps and planted himself in front of
Felix, blocking his path. For a moment, the expression of
unyielding stubbornness on the boy's face looked very like his
mother—though Lucretia carried herself with a dignity that
her son lacked. "I still want to learn."

Felix attempted to sidestep him, but Marcus matched the
movement. Felix glared at him. "Get out of my way."

"Or what? You'll punch me?" Marcus put up his fists in such an amateurish manner that Felix almost groaned. It was no wonder the boy had become an easy target for bullies.

Perhaps it wouldn't hurt to give Marcus a few pointers. Just so he wouldn't get himself killed in his next scuffle. Felix swept out a hand to push Marcus's elbow down. "Someone can break your ribs if you keep your elbows up like that. And don't put your thumbs inside your fists."

Marcus adjusted his fists. He threw a wobbly punch and almost fell over.

Felix caught him by the shoulder. "Your feet are as important as your fists." He demonstrated a typical boxing stance with his right foot a step behind, knees slightly bent.

Marcus copied it. Felix gave him a light push to the shoulder, and the boy toppled, catching himself on his hands and knees.

"Practice that until someone can shove you without you falling over," Felix said. "Then you can come back. Now, I have a meeting."

"I'll practice!" Marcus shouted after him as Felix stepped swiftly around him. "I'll be back!"

# CHAPTER 4

F ELIX WAS GLAD TO find Lucretia's investor at home, and the man received him in his study. Publius Calpurnius Lentulus was a sturdy man with graying hair who surveyed Felix with a cool, reserved gaze. "I find myself quite busy this afternoon, so if you don't mind..." His fingers tapped the surface of his desk.

Felix heard the unspoken words beneath Lentulus's outward politeness. *Get to the point.* "Of course." He leaned back in his chair, affecting ease though it was clear the man had only received him out of the barest civility. "I understand you have a significant stake in the business of the late Gnaeus Cornelius."

"I have a significant stake in the business of his widow, Lucretia."

"Yes, of course," Felix said. "I am of a mind to expand my own holdings, and I would like to make you a generous offer for the purchase of your shares."

"No," Lentulus said curtly.

Felix blinked. "You haven't even heard my offer yet." Mentally, he increased by half the price he'd originally planned to offer.

"As you are so well-informed about my business holdings, I wonder if you also know that Gnaeus Cornelius was one of my closest friends. We served together in the fifth legion."

"Ah, the fifth." Felix racked his brain to come up with anything he knew of that legion, for once cursing his lack of military experience. "My stepfather was in the, er, third." In fact, he had no idea which legion his stepfather had belonged to, but it seemed a safe enough fib.

Lentulus ignored the remark. "I would never withdraw my support from Lucretia. It would be an affront to Cornelius's memory."

"With respect, sir, I find that sentimentality is rarely a good foundation for business decisions."

Lentulus's gaze hardened. "Perhaps not, but the fact remains that my holdings are as profitable as they ever were. Lucretia's management has not faltered." He rose to his feet, forcing Felix to rise also.

The dismissal was clear, and Felix knew it would be useless to push further. He inclined his head in a formal nod. "Thank you for your time."

He left Lentulus's house. The sunlight, which earlier had seemed like a beneficent omen, now made him squint uncomfortably, and sweat dampened the back of his neck as he walked through the streets.

Winning Lentulus would have been the keystone of his maneuvers against Lucretia. It should have been an easy victory—offer Lentulus more than the shares were worth, make a deal, and go on his way.

But Lentulus hadn't even heard the offer. His affection for Lucretia and her dead husband had outweighed any money Felix could tender.

The rejection rankled. Perhaps this was Lucretia's edge: people *liked* her, in a way they had never liked him. Cornelius, too, had been affable and well-regarded by everyone.

Felix never seemed to form those sorts of attachments with people. He was competent at maintaining business relationships, but having friends purely for social purposes seemed like a waste of time. He would much rather spend an evening haggling over the price of olive oil than socializing at a dinner party, though he forced himself to accept the occasional invitation, recognizing the valuable connections they could cultivate.

Well, if he couldn't beat Lucretia when it came to the connections she had built, he would have to take more drastic measures. He just didn't know what they were yet.

When his mind was fuzzy and he was faced with a problem he couldn't solve, he went to the gymnasium. The pain and physical suffering of a boxing round—whether against an opponent or a sand-filled leather bag—often jolted loose the wheels of his mind.

He traversed the few blocks to the gymnasium, a large building which also housed a bathing complex. There was nothing more pleasurable than sinking into a hot, steamy bath after a brutal boxing session.

Felix paid the small entrance fee, then went to the changing room to shed his tunic, leaving himself clad in a loincloth. He picked up a clean towel and also bound his knuckles in strips of cloth to protect them. Professional boxers wore metal knuckle casings to deal maximum damage to their opponents, but such vicious measures were not necessary for a hobbyist like Felix.

In the outdoor training area, a tall, elegant colonnade bordered a running track, with an open field in the center. In the field, men practiced javelin throwing and wrestling. Inside the shaded colonnade, there were spaces for weightlifting, bags hung for boxing, and benches lining semicircular niches for those who came to the gymnasium to socialize. The clang of heavy weights hitting the stone floor echoed through the colonnade.

Felix found an unoccupied boxing bag. He set down his towel and stretched to warm up, loosening his shoulders, back, and wrists. As he did so, he gazed around. On the exterior wall of the building that housed the baths, a large mural depicted the mythic runner Atalanta. Wearing a hip-length tunic that exposed one breast, she was rendered in motion, running with her feet barely touching the ground. Felix had often thought the mural was an ironic choice for the gym, where no women were permitted.

A thought struck him, and he straightened sharply from his sideways bend.

Lucretia was a woman, and like Atalanta, Lucretia was attempting to carve her own path in a world of men. Of course, he had always known Lucretia was a woman—he was painfully aware of it most of the time—but he had never fully comprehended how he could use that to his advantage.

Because he had just realized how to cut off Lucretia's operations from their very origin. Women were allowed to engage in business only with permission from a male guardian. In practice, this rule was loosely observed, but if her guardian should explicitly withdraw consent, then Lucretia would have to cease her operations.

If Felix could only contact her guardian…but he didn't know who it was. Lucretia's father was deceased, and as far as he knew, she didn't have any brothers. Perhaps she had an uncle or a distant cousin who had assumed the role after Cornelius died.

Thus, he first had to discover the identity of her guardian, and then persuade, bribe, or otherwise coerce the man into forcing Lucretia to cease her business endeavors. Then Felix could swoop in and buy up her ships, taking control of her lucrative merchant relationships and trade routes in the western Mediterranean.

His mind full of his fledgling plan, Felix finished stretching and approached the boxing bag. He landed one swift punch to the center of the bag. The impact radiated through his knuckles all the way up his arm.

Something about this plan felt uneasy, bereft of the satisfaction that usually filled him when he solved a nagging problem. Yes, perhaps it was unfair to target Lucretia based only on her gender, but business was business. If Felix was able to combine her mastery of trade in the western Mediterranean with his control over the eastern Mediterranean, he would be unquestionably the most powerful businessman in Ostia. And from there, he could expand north to Genua, south to Neapolis.

That was the path to true power—not through politics or statesmanship, like his murdered father. But through simple, cold money.

Atalanta had eventually succumbed to a man's trickery, and if Felix had his way, Lucretia would too.

# CHAPTER 5

"I HAVE GOOD NEWS and bad news," Dihya announced as Lucretia entered the office in the morning. "Well, mediocre news, not bad."

"Oh?" Lucretia slipped off the light cloak she wore to protect her dress from the dust and dirt on the streets, and hung it on a hook. "Mediocre news first, I think."

Dihya passed her a wax tablet. "A message from Publius Calpurnius Lentulus. He writes that Felix paid him a visit yesterday, attempting to convince him to relinquish his support of you."

Lucretia scanned the message. She had, of course, anticipated this; it was why she'd made sure to ascertain Lentulus's constancy. But the proof of Felix's audacity made her teeth clench.

Even though he hadn't been successful, this still required retaliation. She'd have to consider her next move. He couldn't be allowed to get away with this unscathed.

"And the good news?" Lucretia asked.

Dihya jumped to her feet with an excited bounce. "My daughter has a suitor!"

"Oh, that's excellent!" Dihya's daughter, Tadla, was fifteen, and Lucretia had often listened to Dihya fret over her marriage prospects. Dihya had feared that Tadla's pickings would be slim, without a father to negotiate her betrothal. Listening to Dihya's worries made Lucretia grateful she had no daughters, as Marcus would find his own bride when the time came and not for at least a decade at that.

"Who is the lucky man?" Lucretia asked. "Do I know him?"

"You do, indeed. He's none other than our favorite baker."

Lucretia's mouth dropped open. "Caeso? He's interested in—in Tadla?" She would have sworn Caeso's interest lay in the mother, not the daughter.

Dihya nodded enthusiastically. "I've told him all about how sweet and gentle she is. And her skills in weaving, cooking—she'll make him a good wife. And she couldn't hope to do better than Caeso. He seems like a kind man, doesn't he? He must make a good living from his business. And as a baker's wife she'll never go hungry." Her smile grew. "Not bad to look at either, is he?"

"No," Lucretia said with a chuckle. "Has he met Tadla yet?" Perhaps she had misjudged the hints of flirtation between Dihya and Caeso.

Dihya shook her head. "I've asked him to dinner tonight. He can meet her and see that everything I've told him about her is true."

"And how does Tadla feel about this?"

Dihya waved a hand. "She's nervous, of course—you know how shy she is. She says she doesn't want to get married, but what girl does? Once she meets Caeso, all her fears will be soothed."

"You're sure his interest is, well, serious?" Lucretia pressed. "He seems like a good man, but I didn't realize he was interested in…marrying." *I thought he was interested in* you.

A trace of doubt entered Dihya's gaze. "Do you think he's unsuitable for her? Have you heard things about him? I mean, does he have vices I should be worried about?"

"No, no," Lucretia demurred. "I haven't heard anything. He seems like a very kind, honest man." She smiled and clasped her friend's hand. She must have misinterpreted the warmth between Dihya and Caeso. All Dihya wanted was a good match for her daughter, and Lucretia was happy for them both. "I'm sure he'll make an excellent husband for Tadla."

Felix beckoned his secretary to sit in the chair before his desk. Siro, a slender man with sharp green eyes, was Felix's most talented and trusted employee. A freedman, Siro had innumerable connections to other freedmen in Ostia, who made up the bulk of administrative and bureaucratic roles. His associations had come in useful many times when Felix needed information—such as the identity of Lucretia's main investors, most recently.

"What have you learned?" Felix asked. A few days ago, he asked Siro to make inquiries about Lucretia's legal guardian. Siro had taken a pouch of coin to various government offices to see if he could persuade anyone to share the official records.

Siro withdrew a piece of papyrus and slid it across the desk to Felix. "A man named Manilius Cotta. I'm not sure of the relation to Lucretia, perhaps a distant cousin."

"We will need to find out where—" Felix began.

Siro held up a hand. "I'm told he lives inland, on an estate near Spoletium."

Siro was one step ahead as usual. Felix smiled. "How would you feel about a trip north?"

The secretary nodded briskly. "I can leave tomorrow. One thing first—no, two things." He withdrew the pouch of coin that Felix had given him to conduct his inquiries. "Didn't end up needing this. A bureaucrat owed me a favor."

Felix waved the pouch away. "Keep it for your journey." A less trustworthy man would have kept the coin without saying a word. "My mother and stepfather live in the vicinity of Spoletium. I'll write you directions and a letter of introduction. They'll be happy to host you for a night or two."

Siro bowed his head. "Thank you, sir. I'd be honored to accept their hospitality."

"What was the second thing?"

Siro secured the pouch back to his belt. "There's a boy skulking outside. Dressed too fine to be a beggar. I tried to shoo him off, but he said he knew you."

Felix groaned. *Marcus.* Well, he only had himself to blame; he had told the boy to come back. "Send him in on your way out, will you?"

Siro rose to his feet. "Of course, sir." He dipped his head and exited the study.

Felix had only a few moments to himself before Marcus entered the office. "Hello, Marcus."

Marcus immediately adopted a passable imitation of the boxing stance Felix had shown him. "Shove me."

With a sigh, Felix rose from behind his desk and came over to Marcus. He exerted gentle pressure against the boy's shoulder, and when Marcus didn't fall over, pushed harder. Marcus wavered, but held the pose.

"Good," Felix said.

Marcus's eyes lit up. Felix tried to ignore the gratified feeling that sparked in his chest. "Though you should bend your knees more. It will give you more leverage."

"So will you teach me?" Marcus asked.

Felix knew he should say no: spending time with Lucretia's son while trying to ruin her felt rather *complicated*. After all, Lucretia was his adversary. He shouldn't even be speaking to Marcus, let alone be giving him boxing lessons. But he had promised Marcus, and the boy had no father or brothers to teach him how to defend himself. Lucretia would never have to know.

"A few lessons," Felix said. "Just until you can hold your own without being thrashed. Meet me at the gymnasium tomorrow when you're done with school."

# CHAPTER 6

T HE NEXT MORNING, LUCRETIA was surprised to find the office empty, the door still locked, when she arrived. Dihya usually beat her there, eager to start sorting through the day's tasks and identifying matters that needed Lucretia's input.

Then, she remembered last night had been the dinner Dihya had arranged for Caeso to meet Tadla. Perhaps it had gone late into the evening, which could only be a good sign. She didn't begrudge Dihya the occasional late start, especially when it concerned Tadla's future.

An hour later, Lucretia heard the outer door of the office opening. She went into the front room, excited to hear all about the important dinner.

But Dihya looked terrible, with dark shadows beneath her eyes. Her curly dark hair was hastily braided, several tendrils escaping—far from her usual neat arrangement.

"Oh, Lucretia!" Dihya groaned. "Everything is ruined!" She collapsed into a chair and buried her head in her hands.

"Blessed Juno, what's wrong?" Lucretia went straight to her, patting her shoulder. "Is Tadla all right?"

"She's *humiliated!*" Dihya cried.

"By the gods, what happened?" Lucretia demanded. A tide of concern rose within her. She had never seen Dihya this distraught. Dihya had even borne the loss of her husband with stoic grief.

Dihya took a steadying breath. "I still hardly know. The meal was going well enough. Tadla barely said a word, so it was mostly me and Caeso talking. I was telling him all about how talented, how sweet she is. But I wanted to give them a chance to talk alone, to get to know each other. So I made an excuse to leave the table, and went into the other room." She pressed a hand over her eyes as if she could block out the memory of whatever had happened.

Lucretia lowered herself to her knees next to Dihya's chair, gripping her friend's hand. "Did he—did he try something with her when you were gone? I swear by Juno, I will burn down his bakery if he disrespected your daughter." Caeso had always struck her as most courteous and thoughtful in their brief interactions, but then again she didn't know him well.

Dihya shook her head woefully. "Dis, I can barely think of it without wanting to die. Or murder him. Or both." She twisted a lock of unbraided hair in anxious fingers. "He followed me into the other room. He said something about how grateful he was for the chance to get to know me better. And then—and then—he tried to kiss *me!*"

Lucretia's mouth dropped open. Maybe she hadn't been entirely wrong about a certain attraction between them. At least on Caeso's part. "Did you let him?"

"No, of course not!" Dihya gave her a scandalized look. "I slapped him and threw him out."

"Oh, Dihya." Lucretia stroked Dihya's hand. "I'm so sorry."

"I just don't know how he could have thought—I mean, the nerve of him!" Dihya spluttered. "To kiss *me*—his potential bride's *mother!*"

Lucretia hesitated. "To be quite honest, I had thought there was some attraction between you. It wouldn't have surprised me if he wished to court you, not Tadla."

"That's ridiculous," Dihya protested.

"Is it?" Lucretia raised her eyebrows. Matters of the heart must be Dihya's blind spot. She could read and write multiple languages, perfectly recall months-old conversations, and run calculations in her head without an abacus, but it seemed she couldn't figure out when a man was obviously interested in her. "I've seen you talk and laugh together when we visit his stall. More than I would think possible for something as simple as buying some bread. And the way he looks at you..." She gave a meaningful shrug.

"Of course I enjoy speaking with him. That's why I thought he would be a good match for Tadla."

"Do you find him handsome?"

"Of course!" Dihya said. "Or else I never would have thought of him for Tadla."

"With respect, I don't think it's normal for mothers to be attracted to their potential sons-in-law." Lucretia gave Dihya a searching look. "Is it possible there might have been some...confusion? A misunderstanding over what the dinner was about?"

"I don't see how there could have been," Dihya said. "I was quite clear. I told him all about Tadla."

"Did you explicitly say you wanted him to marry her? Did he clearly say he was interested in her?"

Dihya closed her eyes, brow furrowing. "Well…I'm not sure. But why else would I have invited him to dinner?"

Lucretia resisted the urge to roll her eyes. "He *likes* you, Dihya. He wants you, not Tadla."

"Impossible!" Dihya shook her head, adamant. "Everything we talked about had to do with my daughter. I told him how beautiful she was, how skilled in weaving, how good-natured she is…"

"And what did he say to all that?"

Dihya swallowed, the resolute expression fading from her face. An uncertain frown pulled at her mouth. "When I spoke of her beauty, he said there must be a close resemblance between mother and daughter. And when I mentioned her weaving, he said what a great teacher she must have had. And…" Her voice trailed off. "Oh no. *Oh no!*"

Lucretia bit back a laugh. "He was trying to flirt with you, I fear. And you would only talk about your daughter, so he worked with what he had."

Dihya uttered a word in her native tongue which had the flavor of an expletive. "There's no…there's no way."

"When you left the table, he must have thought you wanted him to follow you. I'm not saying he was right for trying to kiss you with no warning, but I think the poor man was dreadfully confused." A chuckle slipped out from Lucretia's lips, which caused Dihya to level a baleful glare at her.

"Don't laugh at me, Lucretia! This is the worst thing that has ever happened in my life!"

That seemed like rather an exaggeration, especially coming from someone who had formerly been enslaved, but Lucretia understood the sentiment and kept quiet.

"I thought my daughter finally had a suitor," Dihya continued. "A good man, able to take care of her. But it was all a lie!"

"Tadla may not have a suitor, but you might," Lucretia pointed out. "If you can bring yourself to think of him that way."

Dihya pressed her lips together. "He's practically a child!"

Now Lucretia let herself roll her eyes. True, Dihya was near Lucretia's thirty-four years, but Caeso was a grown man with his own trade. "I would put his age at twenty-five, if I had to guess. Do you like him?"

Dihya buried her head in her hands, her voice muffled. "It doesn't matter if I like him. I could never face him again."

Lucretia looped an arm around Dihya's shoulders. Perhaps it was better to let all this go, but her friend had a chance at love again and Lucretia wasn't about to let her waste it. "What if I went to speak with him? I could find out if it was truly a misunderstanding, and see where things stand between you."

Dihya raised her face. "You would do that?"

"I would do much more than that for you." Besides, she needed a distraction from her troubles with Felix, something that would bring joy, not worry and frustration.

A hesitant smile crept over Dihya's face. "All right. You can speak with him."

"Good." Lucretia gave Dihya's shoulders one final squeeze. "Besides, it's only self-interest on my part. If you fall out with him, I'll never be able to enjoy his baking again!"

# CHAPTER 7

THE NEXT DAY, LUCRETIA took a detour on her way to the office. She had two missions this morning, each important in their own way. Firstly, she had to see if she could mend things between Dihya and Caeso.

Secondly, she was going to disrupt Felix's operations. After learning of his attempt to sway Lentulus against her, she had decided on a tactic to indicate that such efforts would not be tolerated.

Caeso's bakery stall was on the way to the harbor, so she stopped there first. The breakfast rush had already passed, but even so, there were two people in line when she arrived. She waited patiently as they completed their purchases, then stepped up to the counter.

Caeso nodded politely to her. "Good morning, Lucretia." His brown eyes flicked anxiously behind her, no doubt expecting to see Dihya. The corners of his mouth pulled down slightly when he noticed she was alone. "What can I get for you?"

"A honey cake and a few moments of your time, if you please." No one else was in line behind her, so hopefully she had enough time to get through this conversation before Caeso's attention was called elsewhere. "I heard you had dinner with Dihya the other night."

He glanced away from her as he retrieved her requested delicacy. "Has she sent you to berate me? Believe me, I've done enough of that to myself."

Lucretia rested her hands on the wooden counter between them. "I think there may have been some confusion about the dinner."

His gaze snapped to hers. "Confusion?" He wrapped the honey cake in a clean white cloth and laid it on the counter before her.

"You see, Dihya intended you as a suitor for her daughter. She arranged the dinner for you two to meet."

Caeso's mouth dropped open. "Her *daughter?* Tadla is a child!"

"She's of age to marry. The same age I was when my parents were thinking of a match."

Caeso clenched his fists as if on the verge of punching himself. "Oh, how could I have been such an idiot? What must she think of me?"

Lucretia pressed her lips together against a smile. "Dihya had much the same reaction."

"Following her and kissing her like that—and what must her daughter have thought?" Caeso grimaced. "I must have offended the poor girl terribly."

Caeso's immediate concern for Tadla bolstered her good opinion of him. "I don't think Tadla has much desire to marry yet, so I wouldn't worry too greatly about her. I imagine she's somewhat relieved, in all honesty."

"I thought—I thought Dihya was flirting with me," Caeso stammered. "And she did keep going on about her daughter, but I assumed that's just how mothers are. I swear by Vesta, she never said anything about marrying her daughter!"

"I know," Lucretia said. "Dihya made some unfortunate assumptions. Though," she allowed her voice to take on a gently chiding tone, "I would caution you against kissing women with no explicit indication that they would welcome it. If you had been more circumspect, this whole situation may have been avoided." Though, to be fair, if Caeso hadn't acted so impulsively, how long might this whole miscommunication have lasted?

Caeso ran an agonized hand through his short dark hair. "You're right. I was so foolish. She gave me this odd look when she left the table. I thought she wanted me to follow her! I couldn't think what else she meant by it. Please, Lucretia, will you apologize to both of them on my behalf? I'm sure they don't wish to see me, but I must beg their forgiveness for how I acted."

"My hope is that you may be able to deliver such a message in person," Lucretia said. "Dihya asked me to come speak to you, to see if there really was a misunderstanding. I'll tell her of our conversation, and I believe she'll want to apologize to you as well. She should have been clearer about her intentions."

"Oh, if you could make that happen, I'd be eternally grateful," Caeso said. "I couldn't live with myself if she thought poorly of me. I really do like her—I mean, more than like her. I think about her all the time. She's the most beautiful woman I've ever seen. No offense," he added hastily, flushing.

Lucretia grinned. His infatuation was endearing. "None taken."

"I was sure there was no way she'd think of me like that," he continued. "Then she invited me to dinner and I thought, maybe she liked me too. Maybe this was my chance. But then everything went so wrong. Oh, Lucretia, if you could help me fix things with her, I'd owe you, well, *everything*."

"I'll do my best." Lucretia took out her purse to pay for the honey cake, but Caeso waved away her coins. She accepted the gesture with a grateful nod. Another patron had appeared in line behind her, so she bid Caeso farewell and continued on her way.

Time for her second mission.

Lucretia made her way from Caeso's stall to the harbor, shading her eyes as she gazed out at the water. A ship was slowly making its way in, sails furled as a neat row of oars dipped in and out of the water. Usually, she only came to the harbor when she was expecting one of her ships to return. But today, she had come to surveil Felix's ship.

She watched the ship until she was sure she recognized it as the *Proserpina*, one of Felix's vessels. Then, she headed to the nearby building which housed the office that dealt with import and taxation. She bypassed the man watching the entrance with a smile and a silver coin, then entered the first room she came to, a large space filled with clerks scribbling onto wax tablets. The clicking of abaci filled the air.

Lucretia glanced around, chin raised as she waited for someone to notice her. She carried herself as if she were expected, as if she had every right to walk into this room and survey their operations.

After several moments, a portly man in a rust-red tunic hastened up to her. "Are you lost, lady?" Thankfully, he wasn't one of the bureaucrats whom she'd met before. Today, it was better for her not to be recognized.

"No." She smiled sweetly, noting how his gaze softened as she did so. "I'd like to pass along some intelligence that the *Proserpina*—Lucius Avitus Felix's ship—is carrying unreported cargo. I heard some gossip at a dinner party and I felt it was only my duty to report it."

The man frowned. "Lucius Avitus Felix always pays his taxes."

"But can you be sure that he pays in *full*? I've been told it's very easy to conceal items of value among humbler cargo. I would hate to think he was depriving your office of its due."

"Well—I would never accuse a man like Lucius Avitus Felix—" the man stammered.

"I'm not accusing anyone," Lucretia replied. "Merely suggesting that you look into it." She dropped a small coin purse in front of the man, which he only barely caught, then turned and left the building.

She couldn't resist a smile of satisfaction. If Felix was going to go after Lentulus, then she would go after Felix's cargo.

This tip to the tax officials wouldn't *actually* harm him—provided he wasn't engaging in any illegal activity. Felix seemed scrupulous, so she doubted he had anything to fear from an audit of his cargo.

But it would be a nuisance, and Felix deserved a nuisance after his efforts to steal her investors out from under her. He needed to know that he couldn't get away with such schemes without retaliation.

However, she couldn't help wondering what Felix would try next. Perhaps he would try to go after her suppliers. She would have to write some letters, try to get ahead of him.

There was only one way he could truly destroy her, one great risk she'd taken to guarantee herself full autonomy over her business. As long as that secret remained hidden, she could face whatever Felix threw at her.

# CHAPTER 8

FELIX GROUND HIS TEETH as he surveyed Paulinus, the secretary standing before him. Siro was away to Spoletium in search of Lucretia's guardian, but Paulinus was a worthy, if slightly jumpy, second-in-command.

"What do you mean, the customs officials are holding my cargo?" Felix demanded. One of his ships had docked this morning, and Felix should already be well enmeshed in the work of selling its goods to the various merchants who would distribute them down the Tiber to Rome and from there throughout Italy.

It wasn't unusual for customs officials to make a cursory inspection of incoming boats, but Felix had managed to avoid undue hassle by virtue of always paying his taxes in full, along with a few well-placed bribes. But today, it seemed they were in a mood to be more thorough than usual.

Paulinus clasped his hands, fingers squeezing each other. "They say they have not yet finished their inspection."

"Did they say how long their inspection would take?"

Paulinus took a small step back, as if to distance himself from Felix's wrath. "A few days. Maybe a week."

"A week!" Felix barked.

Paulinus jumped, and Felix took a deep breath. This mess wasn't Paulinus's fault. "Do you have any idea why this happened?"

The secretary's glance flicked around the room, looking anywhere but at Felix. He stared intently at the striped jug of water that rested on the corner of Felix's desk. "One of the officials I spoke with hinted they'd received some sort of...tip that you might be importing unauthorized cargo."

"They didn't say from whom?"

Paulinus shook his head.

Felix had some ideas on that front, but it wasn't Paulinus's concern. He let out a tight breath. "I suppose we must let the officials do their work. Please alert me if you receive any further updates."

Paulinus nodded. "Of course, sir." He withdrew, leaving Felix alone.

Felix rose from his chair and paced his small office. He needed to sell this load of cargo in order to pay his captain and crew, not to mention finance another voyage. If his funds were delayed by a week, his sailors wouldn't get paid, and they could very well leave his service and find alternate employment. Then Felix would have to hire another crew from scratch, which would cause even more delays.

He did have significant capital stored at the temple bank, but he was saving that to fund his eventual expansion to new ports. He didn't want to dip into it unless he had no choice.

While this development wouldn't cripple his business, it was annoying and frustrating. And Felix didn't like being annoyed or frustrated.

Well, he supposed no one did, but he found it especially rankling given that he had a fairly good idea of who tipped off the authorities.

This had Lucretia's handprint on it. She had both the motive to frustrate him as well as the knowledge of how to do it. He pictured her weaseling her way into the customs office, smiling that intoxicating smile at whatever hapless officials she found, persuading them Felix's cargo needed investigation. They would have been powerless to resist her.

He clenched and unclenched his fists as he contemplated her treachery. Lucretia was probably sitting in her office at this very moment, a stone's throw away, smirking in satisfaction at what she'd done.

Before he realized what he was doing, he was out of the office, legs eating up the distance to Lucretia's headquarters on the other side of the Square of the Guilds.

He half-expected to be refused entry, but her dark-haired secretary, Dihya, allowed him into the front room with an air of stoic resignation. The woman curtly ordered him to wait while she went into the back.

Felix heard the murmur of two female voices—Dihya's Berber-accented Latin mixed with Lucretia's smooth voice—and then Dihya re-emerged. "She's busy."

"Busy turning the customs authorities against me?"

Dihya raised her eyebrows in a parody of innocence. "I'm sure I have no idea what you mean."

He glowered at her, prepared to wait as long as it took.

Luckily, Lucretia emerged from her office only a few moments later, surveying him with a cool gaze that made his skin crawl with awareness.

"I thought you were busy," he managed, forcing himself to focus on his annoyance with her and not the way he wanted to sink his fingers into the auburn curls tumbling over her shoulders.

Somehow, Lucretia had only become more alluring in the five years he'd known her. He had thought that women were generally supposed to decrease in appeal as the years passed, and he believed she was a few years older than him to start, but the opposite had happened. Lucretia the wife was beautiful, but Lucretia the widow wore a mantle of confidence that was as irresistible as her full-lipped smile.

"I am," she replied. "But I can't have you hovering about and distracting my second-in-command." She beckoned him, and he followed her into her private office, where she closed the door behind them.

She arched her delicate eyebrows at him. "Was it not clear after our last meeting that we have nothing further to discuss?"

Felix got straight to the point. "We didn't, until you made the customs officials hold my cargo on suspicion of smuggling."

Her calm gaze didn't waver. "I think you mean, until you tried to steal my investors out from under me."

He stepped close to her, until he could smell the lavender perfume that clung to her skin. Lavender was one of her key imports from southern Gaul. "I warned you when we last spoke, we are now adversaries."

"As an adversary, I am entitled to take action against you, then." Since he had stepped closer, she had to tip her face up to look him in the eye. "Did you expect me to roll over and let you do as you please?"

That sentence sent all sorts of disconcerting images flying through Felix's mind. Lucretia on her back, creamy skin bared...He blinked in an attempt to clear his head. "No," he admitted unsteadily.

She took a step toward him, and their bodies brushed. Heat crept over him, a pleasurable itch that he wanted to assuage and prolong at the same time. Ever since she refused his clumsy advance five years ago, he had been trying to bury his desire for her, like a forgotten coal in an empty hearth. But the spark remained, and now it was ready to burst back into flame.

"Are you ready to declare a truce?" she asked, her voice somehow sultry despite the mercenary subject matter. "Restore balance to shipping in Ostia. I will continue my trade in the western Mediterranean, and you can have the east."

Felix struggled to focus on her words and not the sensations her proximity was arousing. He was no stranger to stirrings of lust, but when they related to other women, such feelings were easily ignored, like a gentle summer breeze.

His reaction to Lucretia, however, was a maelstrom, winds howling and whipping, destructive and powerful. This must be one of Venus's cruel tricks, to make him long for the one woman he had to destroy.

Her lips parted as she awaited his answer. His body urged him to kiss her, to taste that sweet mouth, but there was categorically no way she would welcome an advance from him, and he didn't fancy ending this encounter with a slap.

The thought of Lucretia's horrified reaction if she discovered his feelings toward her doused his desire and cleared his head. "No truce," he finally managed, voice rasping. Before her allure could ensnare him again, he turned and fled the office.

# CHAPTER 9

*Five years ago*

FELIX SURVEYED THE CROWDED dining room from its periphery, the red-painted wall at his back. He had just settled into Ostia a week ago, and this was his first social outing—a dinner party hosted by an acquaintance of his mother. He knew no one else in Ostia, so this would be an important step in making connections, building alliances, and identifying his enemies.

The sweet scent of perfumed oil from several lit candelabra mixed with the savory aroma of food, as appetizers circulated on trays borne by slaves throughout the mingling guests. In the opposite corner of the room, a musician strummed a cithara, its notes blending into the hum of conversation and laughter.

His gaze flicked over the assembled people, trying to glean what he could from their interactions. He pinpointed a few married couples, as well as one couple flirting who definitely weren't married to each other. Then there was a small group of women talking amongst themselves, and a corresponding group of men. The women kept glancing over at the men, and Felix suspected they were complaining about their husbands.

A throat cleared next to him and a female voice spoke. "Excuse me, sir, but this is a dinner party, not a chariot race."

Felix blinked, pulling himself out of his analysis, and looked to his left. A woman—a *beautiful* woman—regarded him with a raised eyebrow and a slight smile. She wore a dress of emerald green, belted at the waist with a thin gold chain. Her hair gleamed bronze in the flickering lamplight. A red carnelian necklace encircled her throat, echoing the color of her hair. Her hazel eyes commanded Felix's attention—pools of inviting warmth he would be happy to drown in.

As soon as that ridiculous sentiment occurred to him, he chided himself. Women, as a rule, did not catch Felix's notice like this. Of course, he could appreciate a woman's beauty. But he was not the sort of man to be rendered weak-kneed and bewildered by a pretty smile or tempting figure.

She'd spoken to him, and he had to say something back. What had she said, something about a chariot race? "Beg pardon?" he managed.

Her smile grew, bringing further light to her eyes. That smile seemed to warm him all the way down to his toes. "You're watching the party like my son watches a chariot race. Trying to figure out who's taking the lead, who might be about to make a move for a better position, who's on the verge of crashing."

A prickle of discomfort crept over him at how quickly she had assessed the direction of his thoughts. "I'm new to Ostia," he said in defense. "I was merely trying to get the lay of the land."

"I see," she said, taking a sip from the wine cup held in her delicate fingers. "I thought you looked unfamiliar. My name is Lucretia."

He nodded to her. "Lucius Avitus Felix."

"Where have you moved here from?"

"Rome," he answered. Was she the most beautiful woman he'd ever seen? His brain attempted to flick through the faces of other women he knew, eager to compare her to her peers, but suddenly his mind was blank, hers the only face he could conjure.

"Ah, the big city. Ostia must seem like a sleepy little village in comparison." The noise in the room behind them—which Felix had momentarily forgotten existed—swelled as a burst of laughter rang out from another cluster of people, and Lucretia stepped closer to him to hear his response. The folds of her dress touched the fabric of his tunic, and he felt the whisper of contact like a flame.

Dis, what was wrong with him? Or was this how other men felt around those they desired? He'd often noticed that he didn't have quite the same interest in pursuing carnal pleasures, either with women or with men, as others of his set. As a younger man, when his peers were extolling the skills of this or that popular courtesan, Felix had found more interest in his studies. And now he simply didn't have time for such indulgences. At the end of a long day spent negotiating with shipbuilders or meeting with artisans to get the best price on their wares, all he wanted to do was fall into bed on his own.

But this woman cast his celibacy into doubt. Suddenly, he became acutely aware of what he'd been missing.

Lucretia tilted her head, waiting for a response, and he struggled to turn his mind back to what they were discussing. *Rome…Ostia…sleepy little village…*

"On the contrary," he replied. "Ostia has a certain energy that Rome lacks. The merchants and sailors, hailing from all over the world…Rome feels stagnant by comparison." Rome, while large, was full of politicians and social climbers, and Ostia's single-minded focus on commerce and trade was refreshing.

Someone passing too close jostled Lucretia from behind, and she stumbled forward a step, colliding with him. For one brief, delicious moment, her body—her warm, soft body—pressed against him from shoulder to hip. The banked desire kindled by the mere sight of her flared to life. A tingle of heat spread over his skin, an unaccustomed, restless feeling.

The gallant thing to do would have been to gently catch her arm and help her find her feet. But Felix's mind was too addled by her proximity to act, and by the time he'd mastered himself, she had already separated herself with a murmured apology.

"I will leave you to your surveillance, Lucius Avitus Felix." She inclined her head. "I must rejoin my husband." She swept away, her brilliant green skirts trailing in her wake.

The word *husband* sent an unpleasant but absurd pang through him. Of course she was married. She appeared to be in her late twenties, perhaps a handful of years older than him, and she had mentioned a son.

Felix watched as she went up to the cluster of men and slid between two of them, effortlessly inserting herself into their group. The man to her right rested a possessive hand on the small of her back. Felix's gaze snapped to his face.

That man was Gnaeus Cornelius, proprietor of a prominent shipping business here in Ostia. If Felix hoped to ever achieve unquestioned dominion over commerce in Ostia, Cornelius would have to fall.

And this woman—the only one to ever catch Felix's attention in this way—was his wife.

He appraised the way Lucretia and her husband interacted as the conversation took place around them. When she spoke, Cornelius angled his head toward her with a deferential nod, prompting the rest of the men to listen to her. But the hand he'd placed on her back had fallen after only a moment, and they stood next to each other without touching.

Felix detected affection and mutual respect borne of a years-long marriage, but no great passion or adoration.

Well, that was nothing surprising. It was like that with most married couples of his acquaintance—except his mother and step-father, who still behaved with stomach-turning ardor after nearly fifteen years of marriage. But their marriage was the exception, Felix gathered, and he had little desire to entangle himself in matrimony to a woman he would come to only tolerate. Maybe, if he ever met another woman who stirred the feelings Lucretia had, who made him forget his surroundings and stumble over his words…maybe then he'd consider marriage.

Felix kept his distance at that first dinner party. The social scene in Ostia was not large, so he saw Lucretia again, with and without her husband.

Both she and Cornelius were universally well-liked, though while Cornelius was more reserved, Lucretia was open and generous with her laughter and smiles. Any time there was a new guest at one of these parties, Lucretia never failed to figure out a way to draw them into the conversation, make them feel included. She was witty without being cruel, friendly without being simpering.

He realized that was exactly what she'd been doing when she approached him at that first party. She'd noticed him standing off to the side, not speaking to anyone, so she'd engaged him. A kind, welcoming thing to do. He'd been too stupefied with desire at the time to recognize it. Now every time he saw her doing the same thing to another newcomer, a spike of jealousy twisted in his chest.

He expected his interest in her to fade over time, but each time he saw her, he still had that disconcerting reaction to her presence. They occasionally exchanged words, never anything more than small talk, but he found himself always managing to position himself within earshot of her at the dinner table. He struggled to take his eyes off of her face, always laughing and animated, and more often than not his food grew cold on his plate as he drank in the sight of her.

It was just an infatuation. Perhaps he was overdue for one, as he'd never experienced this before. But it was damned inconvenient. How could he make conversation about the price of olive oil and the cost to ship it from Greece to Egypt when Lucretia was in his line of sight, nibbling a slice of fruit or chuckling at someone else's joke?

He should simply distance himself from her: stop attending the same parties, or at the very least stop sitting within view of her. But that was easier said than done.

"Hello, Felix," she greeted him, smiling, at a dinner party about three months into their acquaintance. "Are you settling in well to Ostia?" They were in the atrium of their host's house, as guests were still arriving, milling around before the formal meal began.

He returned the smile, though the expression felt awkward on his face, like an ill-fitting pair of sandals. "The sea air is a vast improvement."

"My husband finds it so invigorating he spends every other month at sea," she replied, an acknowledgement that Cornelius was absent that evening. "Perhaps you should try it." A teasing lilt entered her voice.

Was she criticizing him for not joining his ship captains on voyages to other ports? "I trust my captains."

Her eyebrows drew together. "As does Cornelius." Her voice lost its softness.

He realized she thought he was disparaging Cornelius's management of his business. "I only meant—I'm sure you wish he did not spend so much time away." He cursed his idiocy. He had not meant to spend their first real conversation in months talking about her husband and how much she must miss him.

She gave a graceful shrug. "My son Marcus keeps me more than busy when his father is away."

So was that an admission that she *didn't* pine for her husband? "You must be lonely often."

"I could say the same of you. You live alone, do you not? Are you lonely, Felix?"

That question had never occurred to him. "I—well—" He didn't know the answer to her question, but as he stammered, a wild impulse seized him. Maybe there was one way to fix this inconvenient attraction. Surely, if he were to bed her—the thought alone sent a flare of heat through him—he would no longer be so enraptured by her. A married woman who'd already given her husband a son, and whose husband was often away for weeks or months at a time, might easily welcome the attentions of another.

The idea seemed rational and insane at the same time.

"If I was lonely," he said, the words spilling from his mouth like grain from a split-open sack, "would you permit me to pay you a visit, when your husband is away?"

Felix had never attempted to seduce a woman before, and he instantly realized he'd made a misstep.

Her full lips parted for a moment in the barest flicker of surprise, before a cool mantle of politeness blanketed her. "I have found that I am quite capable of entertaining myself. But—" She put a hand on his shoulder and spun him around.

Her touch made his heart race, and he fought to concentrate on what she was saying.

"That lady over there…" She nudged him toward a dark-haired woman wearing a pair of heavy emerald earrings. "…is generally welcoming of visitors, as I understand." She gave him a formal nod, then slipped away to join another conversation.

Felix stared after her. Embarrassment crawled up his skin, and he wished the stone floor of the dining room would open up and swallow him down to the underworld.

The rational part of his brain insisted there was nothing to be embarrassed about. He'd never felt embarrassed after a business proposition being refused, and surely this wasn't much different.

But the creeping discomfiture remained. He gave himself a shudder, attempting to shake it off, and released a long breath. He could already think of a dozen ways he might have approached the matter differently. *Anything* would have been better than what he'd just done—baldly asking her if she'd sleep with him after never sharing more than small talk with her.

*Idiot.*

Even so, he sensed that even the most suave overture would have been rejected just as soundly. He would not be so impolite as to press his suit a second time. Lucretia did not want him, so the matter was closed.

# CHAPTER 10

*Present day*

Aftter Felix stomped off, Lucretia attempted to return to work, but the encounter lingered in her mind. She took a deep breath, inhaling the traces of the scent he'd left behind, something herbal and fragrant that clung to his clothing. Perhaps thyme, or sage?

She had never seen him so ruffled. Usually, he was the very picture of cold equanimity. But perhaps that was only when he had the upper hand. All it took was one little incursion into his affairs to rattle him. She allowed herself a smile at the memory of it.

But in that moment at the end of their conversation, it seemed that something other than annoyance flustered him. His pale skin had flushed, and heat sparked in his gray eyes.

An answering thrill, strange and unbidden, lit in her own belly. Her mind flashed back to that evening five years ago when he had propositioned her, somehow bumbling and aloof at the same time. His interest then had been evident but restrained. She was no stranger to men noticing her, and there was no harm in enjoying some light flirtation. But she didn't wish to engage in adultery, so Felix's advance had been easy to refuse.

She couldn't deny his appeal, with his dark hair, lean body, and sharply chiseled features, but she found him too withdrawn for her liking. Yes, he observed all the niceties at social occasions, but there was something distant in his manner that suggested he had no true interest in the people he engaged with.

Today, however, his remote façade had cracked—just a bit, but enough to spark thoughts of what might have been. What if she had, hypothetically, accepted his austere attempt at seduction? Would bedding him have burned away his coldness, stripped off his dispassion?

Before she could dwell on such thoughts, Dihya poked her head into the office. "*He* was in a good mood." Smug sarcasm edged her words. "I take it your plan worked?" Lucretia had told Dihya of her intention to hold up Felix's cargo.

Lucretia smirked. "Indeed. Speaking of plans—I talked to Caeso this morning."

Dihya came toward Lucretia's desk, fingers twisting a fold of her dress. "And?"

"I believe it was a genuine miscommunication," Lucretia said. "He was quite apologetic, and he feared he'd upset Tadla as well."

Dihya waved a hand. "I didn't tell her exactly what happened, but she was relieved to hear that he won't be coming to court her again."

"He wishes to apologize face to face. I told him I would see if you were amenable." Lucretia paused. "Personally, I think you should let him do more than apologize."

A flush darkened Dihya's golden skin. "Are you sure? I mean—is it quite proper?"

"Who cares about proper?" Lucretia said with a laugh. "You're unattached, and there is a young, handsome man who desires you. A great deal, from what I gather." She grinned. "He said you were the most beautiful woman he's ever seen."

Dihya's flush intensified, and she mumbled a denial.

"I'm not saying you need to marry him," Lucretia continued, "but don't turn your back on this opportunity."

Dihya glanced down. Her thumb brushed the finger on her left hand where her wedding ring used to sit. Lucretia's own ring finger tingled in sympathy. For months after Cornelius's death, her hand had felt empty without the ring. She used to feel jolts of worry that she'd lost it somewhere, until she remembered that it was sitting in the jewelry box in her bedroom, never to be worn again.

"I never imagined…being with anyone else." Dihya lowered her voice, as if speaking of something forbidden, and sat heavily in the chair opposite Lucretia's desk.

Lucretia reached across to take her hand. "I understand, of course. But your husband wouldn't want you to be alone forever, would he?" Lucretia didn't know much about Dihya's relationship with her late husband, but it had always seemed like a practical match, in which the two respected each other, at least.

Dihya gave her a half-smile. "If I was the one who died, I'm certain Severus would be married again by now."

Lucretia chuckled. "Yes, men do seem to need a wife more than women need a husband, don't they?"

Dihya lifted her eyes skyward in exasperation. "They are rather hopeless. What about yourself, Lucretia? If there was someone interested, would you pursue it?"

Lucretia considered for a moment. Perhaps she was being hypocritical by urging Dihya toward a flirtation, when like Dihya she had never truly considered what it would be like to be with someone else. "I think I would," she finally said. "I'll never marry again, but I wouldn't deny myself a…pleasurable dalliance."

Dihya raised an eyebrow. "Does that apply to Lucius Avitus Felix?"

"Felix!" Lucretia exclaimed. "Of course not. Don't be ridiculous."

Dihya glanced toward the door. "I overheard your conversation. And I see the way he looks at you. The man is desperate for you. I half-expected him to try to take you atop your desk."

Those words sent a flood of unsettling images through Lucretia's mind. Papers fluttering to the floor, the splash and clatter of an overturned inkwell, a lean body pressing her into the hard surface of the desk…"I would never—with *him!*"

"Of course not," Dihya said. "But if you ever did decide that you desired a *pleasurable dalliance*…I think you'd find a willing participant without much effort."

Lucretia shot her friend a glare. "Enough of this. I must return home. I want to meet Marcus when he gets home from school. See you tomorrow."

She bid Dihya a hasty goodbye, gathered up her things, and left the office, trying not to feel like she was fleeing an uncomfortable conversation.

She had timed her departure well, for she arrived home just before Marcus.

"Hello, sweetheart," she greeted him in the atrium. "How was school today?" At least today, he didn't look as if he'd been in a fight. And no further money had gone missing from her accounts.

He grunted something unintelligible and turned toward his room.

Lucretia took a hasty step forward, desperate to recapture his attention. "Would you like to attend the games tomorrow? I hear there should be an interesting fight." Lucretia herself had little interest in gladiatorial combat, but for some reason it was the sort of thing young men enjoyed. Cornelius used to take Marcus regularly, but it had been a long time since Lucretia did anything with her son, just the two of them.

Marcus sidled away from her. "I was going to go with my friends."

"Oh." Disappointment welled up, but she smiled. "Well, have fun. You'll have to tell me how it goes."

Marcus retreated to his bedroom, and this time, Lucretia didn't try to stop him.

Felix pushed a cup of wine and a plate of figs and cheese toward Siro, recently returned from his travels to Spoletium. "What have you learned?"

Siro, still dusty from the road, took a long sip of wine. "I spent several days asking around at all of the estates surrounding Spoletium, seeing if anyone could direct me to Manilius Cotta. A few people recognized the name but weren't sure where to find him. Finally, I found someone who directed me to an estate, but it was empty apart from a few slaves. They told me the master was traveling and they weren't sure when he would return. I thought of staying, but I wasn't sure how long it would take, and I knew you would be eager for news. Your family was most hospitable but I didn't wish to overstay my welcome."

Felix nodded. "Thank you. Perhaps another trip is in order. And perhaps I should go myself. This matter may require some delicacy, and besides, I owe my parents a visit."

"Your parents did mention when I saw them that they were quite eager to see you, sir," Siro said. "Would you like me to identify some suitable dates?"

The matter was important, but not critical, and Felix was expecting some shipments in the coming weeks that he wanted to be in Ostia to oversee—especially to make sure that Lucretia didn't try to meddle with his cargo again. "Leave it with me. I'll arrange it when the time is right."

A touch of guilt itched at him; forcing Lucretia to surrender her business by convincing her guardian to withdraw his consent still didn't quite feel fair. But the law was the law, he reasoned, and pushed the guilt aside.

# CHAPTER 11

"**I** PUNCHED SOMEONE!" MARCUS crowed as he met Felix on the steps of the gymnasium. "Look." He held out his knuckles, reddened and bruised.

Felix inspected his hand, then looked over the rest of him. There didn't seem to be any significant damage—no other bruises or bloody wounds. "What happened?"

For the last several weeks, Felix had been meeting Marcus at the gymnasium to train. The boy had been steadily improving in his boxing technique, and Felix had been making him run laps and lift weights as well. It was early days, but Felix could see the beginnings of muscle filling out Marcus's lanky frame.

In the back of his mind, he knew it was wrong to meet with Marcus like this, without Lucretia's knowledge, but he told himself he was going to be at the gymnasium anyways. If Marcus happened to show up at the same time, well, that was merely a coincidence.

"Two boys tried to steal my coin purse after school. I pretended to give it to them"—Marcus mimed handing over a purse with his left hand—"and then punched one of them in the nose!" He dealt a quick jab with his right hand. "They were so surprised they didn't even run after me."

"Well done. Perhaps it's time we try some sparring." There was a peculiar satisfaction in watching Marcus improve, and Felix realized the last time he'd felt this way was while building his shipping business years ago. He had used an initial loan from his mother to purchase a stake in a merchant ship. When the ship completed its journey and sold its cargo, he'd been paid back with significant interest, which he'd used to acquire a ship. Sail to Greece, stock it with cargo, return to Rome, sell for a profit, invest in more expensive cargo, repeat until he could buy another ship. And then another, and another...He might not wear the imperial purple, but he was building an empire of his own.

He had never expected that teaching Marcus how to box would elicit similar feelings, but Marcus's progression from a hapless, scrawny adolescent to someone who could land a solid punch lit a fire of pride inside him. Like the day he'd looked out over Ostia harbor and noticed that four out of the five ships docked there were his own.

The fifth, of course, had been Lucretia's.

"I get to punch you?" Marcus asked, distracting Felix from his thoughts. "What if I hurt you?"

Felix snorted. "I think I'm more in danger of stubbing my toe on the gymnasium steps."

Marcus scowled, but followed him into the gymnasium.

They trained for about an hour, until Felix could tell Marcus was growing frustrated by his inability to land a punch on Felix. Then, they washed off and headed home. Marcus's house was in the same direction as Felix's, so they walked together, cutting through a slanting alley for a shortcut.

The alley was so narrow that if Felix stretched his arms out, his fingertips would brush both sides. It reminded him of the fight he'd interrupted when he first met Marcus, the bullies who had cornered him in an alley just like this one.

"Stop a second," Felix said. "This could be useful." He gestured to the enclosed space. "A bully is never going to fight you out in the open. And fighting in such a restricted space has its own challenges as well as benefits."

Marcus glanced around. "Oh?"

"A wall can be a weapon," Felix explained. "If you can use someone's own momentum to shove them into it, that could incapacitate them as easily as any punch."

He began to demonstrate, and Marcus watched with interest.

Lucretia couldn't hold back a smile as she walked to the harbor to oversee the arrival of one of her ships. Dihya and Caeso had straightened out their misunderstanding, and things seemed to be progressing between the two—so much so that Lucretia had noticed Caeso escorting Dihya to their office this morning, as if the two had spent the night together. So far, Dihya had been private about the details, which Lucretia respected, but all signs pointed to a blossoming relationship.

Lucretia's enlightened self-interest had also paid off: Caeso kept finding excuses to drop off any unsold loaves or pastries at their office at the end of the day, and he no longer accepted any payment from her when she visited his stall. She was happy for her friend; Dihya deserved all the joy she could find with Caeso.

Passing the mouth of a crooked passage between two build-ings, Lucretia stopped short. Something caught her eye, a flicker of pale green fabric that was unsettlingly familiar. She spied two figures further down the alley. One was taller than the other, and the smaller one wore the pale green tunic that had caught her attention.

She knew that color…knew that fabric. It looked exactly like the fabric she had woven and dyed with her own hands when Marcus had outgrown his last batch of tunics.

She squinted, struggling to make sense of what she saw in the shadows.

When the taller figure aimed a punch at the smaller person's jaw, Lucretia's feet carried her toward them at a run before her mind could process what was going on.

When her brain caught up, she reached for the small knife she carried for household tasks. She wrapped her fingers around it, took aim, and let it fly—straight at the center of the attacker's back.

The man moved to the side, and the knife struck him in the upper arm before clattering to the dirt. The man yelped and clapped a hand to the bleeding wound, turning to see what had assailed him.

Lucretia darted forward, picked up the knife, ready for another strike—but froze as she saw Felix standing before her, Marcus at his back, wide-eyed. Confusion ripped through her. Was it possible that Felix's schemes to unseat her had gotten even darker? Was he trying to kidnap or harm her son in order to force her to hand over her ships?

Her heart pounded, hands unsteady. She thrust out the knife, pointing it directly at Felix's throat. Felix flattened himself against the alley wall, hands up.

"Lucretia," he gasped. "What are you doing here?"

"You don't ask the questions," she snarled.

"Mother!" Marcus exclaimed. "Stop it!"

She cast a quick glance at Marcus, assessing his condition. She couldn't see any blood, and he didn't seem to be injured.

"It's not what it looks like," Felix said, still holding his hands up and eying her knife. Blood oozed from the small wound on his arm, darkening the sleeve of his tunic.

"What it *looks* like," Lucretia said, striving to keep her voice from shaking, "is that you're trying to murder my son."

"I certainly am not!" Felix said, somehow daring to sound outraged.

"Put the knife down!" Marcus shouted. "We were just practicing!"

"Practicing what?" Lucretia demanded, keeping her focus on Felix.

Felix lifted his hands higher, as if that could intensify his surrender. "I have been teaching Marcus how to box."

Lucretia blinked. "You...what?"

"It's true!" Marcus said. "I–I heard that Felix was a good boxer, so I asked him to teach me."

"You've never shown an interest in boxing before," Lucretia said, her mind still struggling to catch up. Marcus wanted to learn to box? And somehow Felix had ended up teaching him? Though there was clearly still something she didn't understand, her immediate terror eased just a bit, as it seemed that Felix wasn't actually trying to harm Marcus. "I would have gotten you a real teacher if you had asked."

"I'll have you know, I'm an excellent instructor," Felix said. "Marcus's skill increases by the day."

She glared at him and thrust the knife even closer to his throat. "Now is not the time for your arrogance." She turned to her son. "Marcus, please go home. I wish to speak with Felix in private."

Marcus frowned. "But—"

"*Go. Home,*" Lucretia hissed. She hated speaking to Marcus in such an imperious manner, but she needed to get to the bottom of this and didn't want him to see her threatening Felix more than he already had.

Marcus sighed, rolled his eyes, and left, throwing one last glance back at them as he exited the alley.

Lucretia returned her focus to Felix. "How long has this been going on? I will gut you like a fish if you lie to me." In truth, this knife was much too small for any gutting, but the sentiment still made Felix's face turn satisfyingly pale.

"I don't know, a month?" A bead of sweat formed on Felix's temple. "We meet at the gymnasium a few times a week."

Her jaw clenched. Marcus had been going behind her back for an entire month. He didn't necessarily know the depth of her contention with Felix, but he had to know they were competitors.

"How did it start? Did you seek him out?"

"He—" Felix bit back the words. "We met by chance."

Lucretia had sensed there was something Marcus wasn't telling her, which was why she wanted to interrogate Felix in private.

She stepped closer, pressing the tip of the knife into the hollow at the base of his throat. "Tell me the truth."

Felix swallowed, the movement pressing his pale skin against the knife. He hesitated a moment, then something in his expression gave way, and words tumbled out. "I came upon him being beaten up by a group of boys. I intervened to drive them off before I knew he was your son. The next day, he came to ask me to teach him how to box. So he could defend himself. That's all it was—Marcus will confirm this story. I expect he was too embarrassed to say it earlier."

Shock made Lucretia's arm waver, and she had to renew her grip on the knife. "I-I knew he'd been getting into fights…"

"Not of his own instigation," Felix said. "He's being targeted by boys who like an easy win."

"Who are these boys?" she demanded. "Did he give you any names? I will go to their houses—"

"He's of an age where he should fight his own battles," Felix said. "His mother intervening will only make things wor—" He broke off as she rotated the knife, causing the point to dig into his skin.

The gentleness in his tone made her teeth grind together. Who did he think he was, to be giving her parenting advice? As if he knew Marcus better than she did.

"I'm sorry," he choked out. "I knew it was a bad idea, but I was only trying to help him. I was the target of bullies too."

Lucretia narrowed her eyes. It was difficult to think of Felix as a child, much less one who was bullied, rather than the aloof, assured master of trade he was now.

There was only one thing further she had to hear from him before she could truly relent. She withdrew the knife slightly, to give him some breathing room, and watched his face carefully. His reaction to her next question would tell her everything she needed to know. "I know some men…" Her stomach churned at even the thought of what she was suggesting, and she struggled to find the words. "Boys his age…"

"If you truly think me capable of that, then kill me now." His voice was low and fierce.

She met his eyes, gray as storm clouds. In all of their dealings, no matter the enmity between them, Felix had never lied to her. He had always been forthright to a fault, whether propositioning her at a party or informing her that he was going to do everything in his power to destroy her business.

Now, when it mattered most, she believed him…much as she might want an excuse to make him bleed.

She lowered the knife. Felix clapped a hand to his wounded arm, wincing. The danger was past—in fact it had never really existed in the first place—but Lucretia's breath was still choppy, and her knees shook. She took a step away from Felix, bracing herself against the opposite wall of the alley.

Felix reached for her, as if to steady her, but she shied away. "*Don't* touch me." The last thing she needed was support from the man who had been spending time with her son behind her back. It was clear that Marcus liked Felix, even regarded him with a respect he'd never shown her. It felt like a betrayal, like a knife twisting in her gut.

"I didn't mean any harm," Felix said.

She shot him a scorching glare, even as she felt like she was about to vomit. "You will stay away from him. I will speak with him myself and forbid him from seeing you, but if he should disobey, you are not to engage with him."

"I fear that will only make him—"

She raised a hand, and Felix broke off. She was not here to listen to his opinions on how to raise her son.

"Very well," he conceded. "I will have nothing further to do with him."

"Good. Now leave."

Felix left the alley, clasping a hand to his bleeding arm. She felt no remorse for wounding him. In fact, it had been extremely satisfying.

She took a deep breath, still in the grip of the terror and rage that had come upon her when she thought Marcus was in danger. She leaned back against the wall, attempting to find steadiness in its cool solidity.

But anger still pulsed through her, prickly and scorching. She was angry at Felix, of course, but there was an undercurrent of resentment toward Marcus as well. And beneath even that…she was angry at herself.

She must have done something wrong for Marcus to go to Felix of all people with his problems instead of her. Even though Marcus didn't know the extent of her rivalry with Felix, he'd still preferred to confide in a stranger instead of his own mother.

Maybe she'd been too focused on her business. She often put in long hours at her office, after all. She'd thought Marcus was of an age where he appreciated some independence, but perhaps she should have been more mindful. Paid more attention.

It had been different when Cornelius was alive. Then, he'd been the one who wasn't there—either out for the day at the office or away for weeks on voyages. Lucretia had spent nearly all her waking hours with Marcus, except for when he started attending school. She'd *known* him, then.

Now, it felt as if she didn't know him at all. He'd turned into a surly, secret-keeping stranger. The pain of it sat heavy and aching in her chest.

And then there was Felix. Marcus might be able to plead some plausible ignorance of how things stood, but Felix knew exactly who Marcus was. She couldn't help but believe he'd had some sort of ulterior motive. He must have been nurturing this strange friendship with Marcus in the hopes of finding out something that could further his efforts to destroy her.

Rage flared. She needed to exact retribution, both for this as well as Felix's continued attempts to stymie her trade activities. Just last week, he had stolen one of her most trusted captains by offering a ridiculous wage.

It was time to enlist the help of a force more powerful than herself: the gods. Lucretia believed she was in good standing with all the important deities. She observed all the proper rites, paid for regular sacrifices each month, and donated to the upkeep of various temples. She directed most of her piety toward Neptune, god of the sea, and prayed every day for the safety of the men who crewed her ships. Now, it was time to make good on that devotion.

She was going to put a curse on Felix.

Lucretia emerged from the alley and walked to the nearest temple, outside of which she purchased a thin sheet of lead roughly the size of her hand along with an iron nail. She borrowed a sharp stylus from the seller, with which she inscribed a careful message on the surface of the lead.

*From Lucretia of the Cornelii to the divine Neptune. I ask that you visit your wrath upon Lucius Avitus Felix so that he ceases in his efforts against me. In return, I will fund the sacrifice of three fine pigs, the fattest that can be found, in honor of your majesty.*

She read the message over. For a moment, she wondered if she should be more specific about exactly what kind of "wrath" she was requesting, but decided to leave it up to the god. It wouldn't do to be too prescriptive.

When she was satisfied with the wording of her curse, she rolled the lead sheet into a tight scroll and hammered the nail into it. She handed the curse seller an extra bronze coin for his help, then walked toward the harbor.

The curse felt heavy and smooth in her hand. She had never cast a curse before, and she held the item gingerly, as if it were already imbued with Neptune's power.

Curses were supposed to be deposited somewhere deep, like the bottom of a well or buried in the ground. The sea had to be deep enough, Lucretia reckoned, and it seemed more likely that it would catch Neptune's attention this way.

When she reached the harbor, she walked out onto the furthest dock. The waves lapped gently at the side of the wooden structure, and the sun was just beginning to set, casting a fiery glow over the water. She tightened her fingers around the curse, drew back her arm, and threw it as hard as she could into the sea.

When the tiny scroll of lead disappeared beneath the waves, Lucretia released a breath. It was done. Now, she had only to wait for the gods to do their work.

# CHAPTER 12

ELIX'S ARM THROBBED AS he returned home after the incident with Lucretia. His steward's eyes widened when he beheld the wound, but Felix waved off his help. He wanted to be alone.

In his bedroom, he shed his bloodied tunic and dabbed a wet cloth against the wound, wincing. He was lucky her aim hadn't been better. Even her small knife could have seriously wounded or killed him if it struck the wrong spot.

The image of her, fierce and vengeful, stuck in his mind as he cleaned his arm. There had been a moment where he actually feared she was going to slit his throat. He could still picture the fury in her eyes, the hardness of her jaw as she questioned him. If his answers had been anything less than satisfactory, he had no doubt she would have killed him for harming her son.

He had known from the start it was wrong to see Marcus without his mother's knowledge. But he had done it anyway, his sympathy for Marcus outweighing his better judgment. This was what happened when one was guided by emotions, not logic—the result was a near-death experience in an alley and a bloodied arm.

He should never have come between Lucretia and her son, not that he meant any harm. Their business feud could continue, but Marcus should never have been part of it.

And poor Marcus: Felix regretted disclosing the truth of his bullying to Lucretia. It was clear the boy hadn't wanted his mother to know, but telling the whole truth had seemed like the only way to stop Lucretia from dismembering him. He wanted to apologize to Marcus, to explain himself, but he knew Lucretia would have his balls if he made any attempt to communicate with the boy.

But perhaps an apology was still in order, if not to Marcus directly.

Felix summoned someone to help bind his arm, as he couldn't tie a bandage one-handed. Then, he found a blank wax tablet and a stylus. Ignoring the throbbing in his arm, he wrote:

> *Lucius Avitus Felix to Lucretia of the Cornelii: I wish to reiterate that I truly meant no harm, though I recognize it was wrong of me to have any interaction with your son without your knowledge. Please accept my apologies. Marcus is lucky to have you as a mother.*

He read over the note. He felt as if there should be more to say, but those few lines seemed to be all that was appropriate. He couldn't, after all, tell her how magnificent she'd looked, eyes blazing fierce as Minerva, as she threatened him. Couldn't admit how his pulse had raced as she pressed her knife to his throat, both with fear and an unwilling excitement at her proximity.

He found himself wondering if the wound would scar, if he would forever be marked by her.

If it did, if he was, he didn't think he would mind.

He snapped the wax tablet shut. Gods, he was pathetic. Lusting over a woman who despised him. He needed to get ahold of himself.

When Lucretia returned home after casting her curse, she went straight to Marcus's bedroom and tapped on the door.

"Go away." Her son's voice, low and curt, sounded through the door.

"Could we please talk? I know what happened earlier—"

"I don't want to talk," he snapped, bitterness edging his voice.

Lucretia flinched. In all of their arguments, he had never sounded so hostile. She debated pushing the issue, forcing him to face her, but relented. Perhaps it was better to give him some space.

"Very well," she replied. "I'll have your dinner brought to your room."

She paid a visit to the kitchen, asking for Marcus's dinner to be delivered to his room and hers to her study, then spent the rest of the evening alone.

In the morning, a letter from Felix arrived. She read over the short missive. She hadn't expected an apology, and her eyes lingered on the neatly inscribed sentences. Despite wanting to believe the worst of Felix, his words did seem genuine.

*Marcus is lucky to have you as a mother.* She didn't need reassurance from Felix, but his words partially quieted the thorny, uncertain part of her that feared she was making mistakes.

Now that she had some distance from the events of yesterday, she questioned if she had overreacted. The image of the blood staining Felix's arm was vivid in her mind. Never before had she caused someone physical harm, and much as she told herself he deserved it, her conscience prickled.

But Felix wasn't her concern—Marcus was. She still couldn't believe he had gone behind her back like that. Yesterday's anger had cooled, leaving melancholy in its wake.

Her heart ached for him. If Cornelius was still here, would Marcus have gone to him? Maybe Marcus thought that she, as a woman, couldn't understand.

And maybe he was right. Lucretia, after all, had never dealt with the sort of violence boys inflicted upon each other. To her, the simplest solution was to speak to their parents and see the perpetrators disciplined. But yesterday Felix had said that would only make things worse, and he seemed to know from experience.

Clearly, Marcus had been seeking help and guidance she couldn't provide. So she had to figure out a way to give that to him that did *not* involve interaction with her greatest rival.

When Marcus returned home from school, Lucretia was waiting in the atrium, so he couldn't avoid seeing her. He stopped short, a surly set to his jaw.

Lucretia cleared her throat and held out a plate of walnut-stuffed dates—Marcus's favorite. "I want to apologize," she said without preamble. "I fear yesterday got out of hand."

His eyes flicked up to hers in surprise. She realized he must have expected her to scold him, not apologize. He approached and took the offering of food.

"I will look into a boxing teacher for you," Lucretia continued. "A real professional. Would you like that?"

Marcus surveyed her for a moment, then gave a slow nod. She expected him to retreat to his room, but he paused. "He's not so bad, you know," he said, then turned down the hallway toward his room, popping one of the dates into his mouth.

*Not so bad* was practically a ringing endorsement from Marcus. But then again, Marcus didn't know how Felix was systematically working to undermine her business operations. And her business was Marcus's legacy. If Felix succeeded in dismantling it, Marcus would lose his rightful inheritance.

Her mind returned to that confrontation in the alley. The Felix who only cared about himself would have immediately offered up the knowledge about Marcus being bullied. But yesterday, he'd hesitated, only revealing it after multiple threats. He'd done his best to preserve Marcus's confidence, until he had no choice.

Could she have been wrong in her initial assumption that Felix had only helped Marcus in the hopes of gaining something he could use against her? It seemed difficult to believe of someone like Felix—cold, avaricious, money-minded above all else.

But maybe, there was a small, kind part of himself he kept carefully hidden behind his aloof façade. A part that would help a struggling boy for nothing in return, that would spend what had to be hours over the course of weeks teaching him how to box so he could defend himself. Maybe she had been slightly, marginally wrong about Felix.

Just a tiny bit.

# CHAPTER 13

T HE NEXT DAY, LUCRETIA woke to winds howling and rain pummeling the tile roof of her house. She dressed and made her way into the atrium, where rain poured into the impluvium, the pool beneath the opening in the roof. The rain fell with such force that water splashed from the pool onto the stone floor, dampening her sandals.

Lucretia eyed the water level of the pool. If this rain continued, they'd have to keep a diligent watch to make sure it didn't flood. It had been a long time since Ostia had seen a storm of this intensity, and she hoped it would pass quickly.

The ships in the harbor would be tossing at their anchors, and any ships at sea nearby would have to navigate carefully to make sure the wind didn't push them into the rocky coasts that surrounded Ostia.

A shiver ran through her as she imagined facing a storm like this while at sea, at the mercy of the wind and waves. It reminded her too much of Cornelius's death. She had spent many nights with her mind conjuring the chaos and terror of his final moments.

A crack of thunder made her jump, and lightning flashed. Lightning always made her think of the gods.

A horrible thought struck her. *The curse.*

Was it possible—could this storm be Neptune's handiwork?

She put a hand against one of the columns in the atrium and swallowed hard as the awful possibility loomed in her mind. What if she had made a terrible mistake? This storm could capsize any ship, could send dozens of men to their deaths.

When she wrote the curse, she'd envisioned something like a cargo of rancid olive oil or a load of spices that were too poor quality to be sold. Not death or injury. But to a god, a few dozen human lives lost must seem as inconsequential as swatting a fly.

She took a deep breath and tried to be rational. Perhaps the storm was just a storm. Maybe she was presumptuous to think Neptune would conjure something so powerful solely in response to her curse.

But as morning turned to midday, the storm didn't relent. Marcus stayed home from school—to his delight—as frequent flashes of lightning lit the sky. The atrium pool eventually overflowed, forming puddles on the floor.

Lucretia's stomach was in knots all day. Each crack of thunder or howl of wind made a fresh stab of guilt spear her as she imagined what it would be like to be at sea in a tempest like this. She attempted a few prayers at the household shrine for the safety of any sailors caught in the storm, but she worried the gods would find her requests disingenuous after the curse.

Toward twilight, the winds eased, and the rain softened from a downpour to a steady drizzle. Lucretia went to bed, but sleep eluded her. Visions of ships sinking and men sucked beneath the waves haunted her.

At some point in the middle of the night, the rain finally ceased. The silence felt ominous after a day of constant noise.

Lucretia rose, exhausted, in early morning. In the atrium, water pooled on the floor, and she had to hold her dress up to her calves to avoid soaking it. She gazed up at the dawn sky through the opening in the roof, finding it blue-gray and cloudless.

She hauled open the heavy front door to see what things were like outside. Bits of debris littered the street, and puddles of water had formed in many spots. The streets would be a muddy mess soon as people began to go about their business.

Guilt still plagued her, its grip tight and unrelenting around her chest, and she had no appetite for breakfast.

*What's done is done. Move past it. For all you know, no one was harmed last night.*

Her internal exhortations were fruitless. There was only one way to relieve her self-condemnation: she had to go to Felix and find out if any of his ships were even expected to be in the vicinity yesterday. She could breathe a sigh of relief if the answer was no. Then, she would make a large sacrifice to Neptune and ask humbly for her curse to be disregarded.

She covered her hair with a long palla of pale yellow and ventured into the muddy streets. She had never been to Felix's house, but she knew where he lived. The hour was early enough that she expected to find Felix still at home, rather than at his office, and this matter was too important to wait until later.

She picked her way along the driest bits of street. Patrician women used litters to ferry them around without having to dirty their feet, which would have come in very useful on a day like today, but such indulgences were above Lucretia's more moderate station.

When she reached Felix's house, a servant showed her into the atrium. She waited, shifting from foot to foot. She didn't relish being here, but for the moment, Felix was the only person who could ease her anxiety.

Lucretia glanced around as she waited, evaluating Felix's house. She'd expected to see more outward manifestation of his wealth: things like piles of shining coins spilling out from behind each door, rattling underfoot wherever he walked, or a larger-than-life statue of himself cast in solid gold.

Instead, the house was surprisingly understated in its elegance. A mosaic spread beneath her feet, the geometric patterns intricate and perfectly symmetrical. That alone would have cost a fortune to install. Slender columns surrounded the atrium, their carved capitals painted in blue, yellow, and red. A glimmer of gold paint shone at their edges, but it was just the barest touch, enough to draw the eye without overwhelming. Between the columns stood slender bronze candelabras, the oil lamps unlit at this hour. Stone planters held flower bushes around the perimeter of the atrium, lending the space an airy, natural feel.

Lucretia wondered what the rest of the house was like. Did all the rooms feature this restrained sophistication?

She debated sneaking a look at a few more rooms, but Felix appeared before she could be so brazen. A white bandage showed beneath the short sleeve of his tunic, and the sight of it sent another pang of guilt through her. In the past day, she had become the sort of woman who slashed someone with a knife, cast a curse on that same individual, and now might have condemned innocent men to a watery grave.

Felix paused several paces away from her and eyed her with trepidation. "Are you armed?"

She recognized that he was attempting to make a joke, but she was not in the mood for humor. "Are you expecting any ships in the near term?"

He frowned, a line appearing between his dark brows. "I was…but I received word this morning of a wreck at the coast a few miles south, after yesterday's storm. I have reason to believe it's one of mine, based on the timing and location."

At the word *wreck*, the ground lurched beneath Lucretia's feet. Spots appeared before her eyes. She flung an arm out, blindly seeking one of the columns that lined the atrium. Instead, her hand encountered warm, firm flesh. Felix's shoulder. He had crossed the distance between them and grasped her arm for support.

"Lucretia? Are you well?"

"It's my fault," she gasped, all the breath driven from her lungs. "I-I did this."

His arm circled her waist, holding her up as her knees verged on buckling. Gently, he guided her to a bench against the wall. She collapsed into it. He stood in front of her, staring down at her with mingled concern and confusion. "Do you require a physician?"

She shook her head, struggling to regain her breath.

Felix clapped his hands, and a servant appeared instantly. "Some wine for the lady," he requested, and the woman hastened off.

She didn't deserve to drink his wine, didn't deserve any consideration after what she'd done. "I did this," she repeated, trying to find the words for her confession.

Felix crossed his arms over his chest. "I doubt that."

"You don't understand." She gripped the metal arm of the bench. "When we parted the other day, I...I was so angry with you. I p-put a curse on you. Asking Neptune to punish you."

"A curse." He considered her for a moment, as if she'd just confessed to preferring dates over figs. "And you believe the storm was Neptune doing your bidding? Targeting one of my ships?"

She nodded.

He chuckled.

"Don't mock me!" she snapped.

He sobered. "Forgive me. But I don't believe this storm was anything more than unfortunate happenstance."

"How can you be so sure?" She desperately wanted to believe him.

"If you had any idea how much money I've spent glorifying Neptune, you would know there's no way he'd forsake me just because *you* asked him to."

She swallowed hard. "But the timing...and Ostia hasn't had a storm like that in years..."

"Lucretia." He spoke her name as if the syllables were precious, tender, and the anxiety suffocating her eased—just a bit. His voice, usually so clipped and cutting, softened. "Sometimes a storm is just a storm." He seated himself on the bench next to her, and she became acutely aware of the lean span of his body only a handsbreadth from hers.

"And sometimes it's the wrath of the gods," she murmured. "Do you know...are there any survivors?"

"My secretary is assembling a crew to see if anything may be salvaged." Felix hesitated. "Shipwrecks do not usually have survivors."

She swallowed hard, picturing Cornelius's body washed up on a beach somewhere. "I must go. I must see it for myself."

"See it—? You mean, you want to go to the wreck?"

She nodded. "I have to face what I've done."

"You've done *nothing*!" Felix took a tight breath. "Besides, you have no way to get there. You don't even know where it is."

Lucretia rose to her feet, muscling through the unsteadiness in her knees. "You said it's a few miles south. I can follow the coastal road."

"You don't mean to walk!" Felix spluttered.

She faced him, summoning the coolness that usually got her through her encounters with him. "Do you have an alternative?"

He stared at her, eyes narrowed and jaw clenched. She met his gaze as evenly as she could despite the turmoil inside her.

Something seemed to give way in his expression, and he sighed. "I was planning to ride down there to assess the situation, while my secretary gathers men. I suppose my horse can carry another."

"I would be most grateful."

Felix breathed something that sounded like it contained a curse, then sent for someone to ready his horse.

# CHAPTER 14

*A* FEW MILES TURNED out to mean an hour crammed onto a horse's back, arms wrapped unwillingly around Felix's waist. If the storm was indeed her fault, this must be part of her penance.

"I'm still surprised you ride," Lucretia said, raising her voice over the wind as the sturdy brown horse slowly traversed the winding coastal road south of Ostia. "I assumed you have your minions carry you in a litter everywhere you go."

Felix gave a dismissive shake of his head. "My stepfather is a horse breeder. There was no way I could have grown up without being at least a mediocre horseman."

He was more than mediocre, Lucretia had to admit. She knew little of horses, but the ease with which Felix managed the beast was evident in his relaxed posture and loose grip on the reins.

For her part, she felt dreadfully unsteady, as if any unexpected movement might tip her off the side of the horse. She had to cling to Felix much tighter than she wished, digging her fingers into the fabric of his tunic. The unpleasant proximity also allowed her to notice his smell, something woodsy and lightly spiced. It was the same aroma she'd detected in their brief moments of nearness before.

Now, she recognized the fragrance as marjoram; his clothes must be stored with sprigs of it. Marjoram hailed from the eastern regions where Felix concentrated his trade, so it made sense that he preferred it—just as she liked to perfume herself with Gallic lavender.

Lucretia couldn't help breathing deeply as they traveled, allowing the calming, herbal fragrance to fill her lungs.

She had never been this close to Felix before, with multiple body parts pressed tight, jostling against each other as the horse trotted. Then again, she hadn't been this physically close to *anyone*—save a rare perfunctory hug from Marcus—in a long time. Since Cornelius died. And their marital relationship had been waning for several years before his death. They had still been friendly and companionable, but the ardor of their early marriage had long since dwindled by the time Cornelius was taken from her.

Now, with Felix's lean body beneath her hands, a hesitant tendril of sensation sprouted within her. It spiraled through her, sparking tingles where their bodies met.

Lucretia tamped it down hastily. Perhaps this inappropriate craving was her mind's way of distracting her from the guilt and self-reproach that had consumed her for the past day.

Finally, Felix drew the horse off the main road, down a dirt path that led toward the shore. They had been stopping to ask anyone they passed for word of a shipwreck. A wreck was an exciting event, so news had spread with speed, and they easily received directions as they got closer.

The path sputtered to a halt at the top of a rocky cliff overlooking the water. Felix stopped the horse, hopped down, then reached up to help Lucretia. She didn't allow herself to enjoy the press of his hands around her waist as he supported her to the ground, but heat flared where he touched her nonetheless.

"It must be down here." He walked over to the cliff, looking down.

Lucretia followed him, then drew in a sharp breath when she saw what lay below.

A small, sandy beach stretched between the cliffs and the sea, and it was littered with wooden wreckage. Out at sea, a rock formation jutted from the water, sharp and unmoving against the rolling waves. The ship must have run up against that in the storm, then sank with its debris washing up on shore.

Between the splintered chunks of wood lay a different sort of wreckage, made up of rounder, softer forms. *Bodies.*

"Divine Juno," she breathed, shuddering.

A moving figure below caught her attention, and for a moment her heart leaped, thinking it was a survivor. But the figure moved quickly from one body to another, then paused to investigate a half-broken crate of something.

A scavenger, come to see what profit they could scrape from others' misfortune.

"That's my property!" Felix snarled as the figure yanked out an amphora, remarkably unbroken. "Stay here," he snapped to Lucretia.

He hurried forward, and for a moment Lucretia thought he meant to jump off the cliff. Then, she saw the narrow, steep path that wound its way down the rock face to the beach.

Felix was the last person she would take orders from, so she followed him. She hiked up her skirts in one hand, using the other

to brace herself against the rock to her right. She watched
Felix's steps carefully, matching the position of his feet, until
her toes touched the sandy beach.

Felix dimly registered that Lucretia had ignored his command
to stay behind, but he paid her no mind as he hastened down
the cliffside path. If she wanted to risk breaking her ankle, so
be it.

He made it to the beach and started toward the scavenger,
long strides eating up the sand. "Unhand that cargo!"

The other man froze, but didn't drop the sealed amphora
he'd extricated from the broken crate. "Piss off," the man
growled. "I have as much right as anyone to salvage."

"This ship and all its contents belong to me." Felix squared
his shoulders. The man was bulky, but shorter than Felix. A
fight would be bloody and vicious, but Felix would do what
was necessary to protect his cargo. "If you abscond with so
much as a splinter of wood, I'll have you prosecuted for theft."

The man's eyes slid to the side, assessing the surrounding
terrain. Felix could tell he was preparing to run, and Felix
gathered his own legs beneath him.

"Unless your name is Caesar Augustus, you've got no excuse
to be so high and mighty, cocksucker." The man bolted.

Felix leaped after him—but a retching sound from behind
pulled him up short.

Lucretia was on her knees next to one of the bodies, vom-
iting into the sand.

"Infernal Dis," Felix hissed. He cast one look at the man fleeing with the amphora—*his* amphora—then hurried to Lucretia's side. He knelt next to her in the sand, strategically putting himself between her and the body to block her view. "Lucretia?"

"Leave me—" Her stomach heaved again. "Alone. Go chase your precious cargo."

Felix looked again for the scavenger, but he had disappeared from view further down the beach. He would no doubt be back, with others, but Siro and a crew of men wouldn't be far behind now. They would secure the remaining cargo and arrange for it to be transported back to Ostia. "It's nothing."

Lucretia wiped her mouth, hand shaking. It unnerved him to see her like this. For all the years he'd known her, she had always displayed the utmost poise and self-assurance, which had only intensified since she'd taken over Cornelius's business. Seeing her like this—undone, her composure shattered—rattled him to his core.

"I deserve this," she said hoarsely. "This is all my fault."

He grasped her elbows and helped her to her feet, then took firm hold of her shoulders, forcing her to look at him. "For the last time, *this is not your fault*. Storms happen. I know that. These men knew that. Your husband knew that."

Pain flashed in her eyes at the mention of Cornelius. He sensed that was the root of her violent reaction: this wreck must bring up all sorts of unpleasant memories of his death.

Felix softened his voice. "Every man who takes to the sea knows what he is risking. They have judged it a worthwhile gamble. You are not responsible for their deaths."

She looked deep into his eyes, and Felix forced himself not to look away. Staring into the warm hazel depths of her gaze was like sinking into a hot bath after a grueling bout of boxing. Heat caressed every muscle, soothing aches he didn't even know he had.

Gods, she was dangerous. Even sandy, distraught, and vomit-flecked, she could still enrapture him without a thought.

As she looked at him, some of the frantic tightness in her gaze seemed to ease. "Do you really think so?"

"Yes," he murmured.

She broke their gazes, and he released her shoulders, stepping back from her.

"What will happen to them?" She gestured at the bodies on the beach.

"My men will transport them back to Ostia along with the cargo that can be recovered. Those who resided in Ostia will be returned to their families. For the others, I will see funeral rites held."

She gave a small nod of approval. "And what of those they leave behind? Wives, children who depended on their income?"

Felix frowned at her. "As I said, they knew the risks. They should have money set aside for such an occurrence as this."

She fixed him with a dissatisfied look.

He sighed. "I suppose I could dedicate a small fund for the widows."

"Good."

"Now, I need to collect any cargo that can be easily moved and put it in one spot, so it's easily defensible in case more scavengers arrive before my men. You can wait for me over there." He gestured to a shady spot next to the cliff.

She shook her head. "I can help move things."

He glanced at her dubiously, but thought better of arguing when he saw the determined light in her eyes. "Very well." He pointed toward a few barrels on their side. "Roll those over here. I will attend to the crates."

She nodded, and they got to work.

# CHAPTER 15

L UCRETIA'S ARMS BURNED AND her back ached as she helped Felix assemble his cargo. His diligence was admirable; a lesser man might have thrown his hands up and declared the entire ship a loss. But Felix was determined to salvage anything he could. It was just for the sake of profit, but somehow, his efforts made it seem like the crew's deaths would not be in vain.

She painstakingly avoided looking at the corpses that littered the beach. To her, each one had Cornelius's face.

Nevertheless, Felix's steadfast assurance that none of this was her fault helped ease her guilt. She chose to believe him, though she wasn't sure why he had been so insistent on the matter. After all, it was in his interest for her to crumble and fall.

Thankfully, the next people who arrived at the beach were Felix's men, led by his secretary Siro. They rigged a system of ropes and pulleys on the cliff and hauled the cargo up piece by piece, loading it onto carts to be taken back to Ostia. The bodies, too, were ferried up the cliff and stacked onto a cart, covered respectfully with a wide tarp.

By the time the operation finished, the sun's lower rim was just sinking beneath the horizon, casting a blinding red glow on the water.

Felix wiped a bead of sweat from his brow. If he was sweating, she must look a thousand times worse. Moisture dampened the neckline of her dress, and she didn't even want to think about what her hair must look like.

"It's getting late," Felix said. "I'm afraid we won't be able to return to Ostia tonight. Too risky to undertake a journey with all this cargo in the dark. We will secure lodgings in the town nearby. We can eat, rest, and return to Ostia tomorrow morning."

Lucretia opened her mouth to protest—she didn't want to sleep in a strange inn with only Felix for company—but her stomach emitted a loud whine. She flushed. Her body seemed to be forcing her to admit that she was hungry, thirsty, and exhausted both physically and emotionally. A meal and a bed would do her good. "Very well."

"Marcus will be all right without you?" Felix asked, untying his horse's reins from the tree they'd been secured to.

"Marcus is not your concern," she replied, "but he will be well looked after by the household. I doubt he'll even notice I'm gone." She intended the words as a joke, but they took on a bitter edge.

Felix checked the fastening of the horse's tack. "Boys that age are often swine. I know I was. Don't take it personally."

"Your mother must have the tranquility of Vesta. I shudder to imagine what you were like as a boy." He must have been insufferable. "Please pass on my admiration to her."

Felix gave a short chuckle. "I will. Now, let's ride ahead and find a place for the others. Hopefully there's a tavern with a stable big enough to house our goods, along with the men."

He lifted Lucretia into the saddle. After climbing up in front
of her, he guided the horse back onto the road, and they headed
for the nearest town.

The towns along the coastal road saw their fair share of travelers,
so they had no issue finding a bustling tavern happy to take their
coin. Felix's men would have to sleep in the stables, guarding
the cargo, but Felix managed to secure a room for himself and
Lucretia.

Lucretia wished Felix would offer to bed down with his men,
but he showed no indication of such nobility.

She put the issue from her mind while they saw the cargo safely
transferred into the stable. Then, they ate—her first real meal all
day, as she'd been too anxious that morning to eat breakfast.
The bread was fresh, though the grain was coarser than what
her kitchen used at home. No meat or fish was offered, but she
enjoyed the warm, thick lentil stew. The wine, too, was good,
though heavily diluted with water.

With the aid of a full belly and several cups of wine, it became
easier to view today's events through a more moderate lens. She
could accept that the storm was a coincidence, and that the men
whose lives were lost knew what they risked. She still planned to
revoke her curse when she returned to Ostia, but she no longer
felt those men's deaths weighing heavy on her conscience.

Felix, somehow, had been instrumental in relieving her guilt.
It would have been so easy for him to play on her fears, to twist
them into something even greater, something that would truly

crush her. Instead, he had reassured her, helped her break free from her anxiety.

She thought back to Marcus's words about Felix: *he's not so bad, you know.* Maybe her son was wiser than she realized.

After the meal, she and Felix climbed the rickety staircase to the second floor of the tavern, where their room awaited.

Lucretia surveyed the small, lumpy bed pushed against one wall, then gave Felix a pointed look.

He met her gaze. "I'm not going to offer to sleep on the floor, if that's what you're waiting for."

"That would be the polite thing to do in this circumstance, I believe."

He raised an eyebrow. "Neither of us are married. We have no honor to protect. Two unmarried people may share a bed without cause for concern."

She glared at him. His nonchalance irritated her. She would never admit it, but the thought of sharing a bed with Felix sent a tingle of nervous agitation through her. "Then maybe *I* will sleep on the floor."

"I'm sure the mice would love your company."

He was infuriating. Any man of quality—any *good* man—would balk at the thought of a woman sleeping on the floor if there was an alternative. But Felix only cared for his own comfort.

She let out a tight breath and sat on the bed. It groaned under her weight. Perhaps the issue of who slept where would become inconsequential, if it collapsed beneath them.

She decided to change the subject, so it didn't seem like she was admitting defeat. "Do days like today make you question if it's all worth it?"

Felix crossed his arms and leaned against the wall. "Of course it's worth it."

"Men died today, Felix. For your profit." Lucretia noticed that despite his insistence that there was nothing wrong with sharing a bed, he wasn't exactly rushing to sit on the bed with her.

"Men die every day. My work doesn't just fill my own coffers. Rome relies on the goods we import."

She smoothed her hand over the scratchy wool blanket. "What would it take to make you give up this campaign against me?"

"There is nothing you could offer me."

"You know there is room for both of us to be profitable in Ostia."

He nodded. "But I don't just want to make a profit in Ostia. I want to control trade in all of Italy. Genua, Neapolis, Sicily…maybe further."

She scoffed. "One man could never do so much alone."

"I would employ trusted associates to manage operations in each port. People like you, with a thorough understanding of how things work."

She raised an eyebrow. "Are you offering me a job?"

"Would you take it?" The corner of his lip twitched—a shadow of a smile.

She grimaced. "I would throw myself into the sea before I became your employee."

His smile materialized, sardonic and thin, for only a moment before it disappeared. "It may take longer than I'd like, but you know I will prevail, Lucretia. I have more capital at my disposal than you. You cannot beat me."

She met his cool gaze. He wasn't bragging or blustering, but stating a fact as calmly as if telling her the current hour. Her lips tightened. He might be right—he certainly believed he was—but she couldn't let him see that she feared she agreed with him.

"And after you conquer trade in Italy, what then?" she asked, a sarcastic bite to her words. "I expect you'll raise an army and usurp Caesar Augustus himself?"

"No," he said shortly. "My father was a provincial governor. I have no desire for that sort of power."

"Your father was a governor?" She'd sensed Felix came from a good family in Rome, but she hadn't realized his father had achieved such a high position. How intriguing that Felix chose to pursue trade, rather than statesmanship.

"Yes. He died when I was nine."

"I'm sorry," she murmured.

She expected the conversation to end there, but to her surprise, Felix opened his mouth, then hesitated, as if considering his next words.

"Until I was seventeen," he finally said, "I believed he'd died of an illness. I spent my childhood studying history and rhetoric, preparing to follow in his footsteps, to honor his memory. Then, my mother told me the truth." His features tensed.

Lucretia found herself leaning forward, drawn into this tale of his past. "The truth?"

"He'd been murdered," Felix said, his voice clipped. "To cover up a scheme of corruption in the province."

She drew in a sharp breath. She could imagine the sort of turmoil that must have caused, to have something he'd believed for so long turn out to be a lie. "You must have been angry with your mother for keeping that from you."

"A little, at first. I came to understand why she waited to tell me. I wouldn't have been able to understand, as a child. But it made me rethink everything I'd planned. What was the point? My father worked his whole life to attain greatness, one of the highest positions in the Republic, and what did he get for it?" Felix waved a dismissive hand. "He was killed for his sense of honor. For trying to do the right thing."

The pieces were beginning to come together, shedding more light on why Felix was so driven, so relentless in pursuit of his goals. "So you turned to trade instead."

He nodded. "I realized I'd been striving toward a dream that didn't exist. Honor doesn't matter. Dedication to the Republic certainly doesn't matter—look at how things are now. Our republic is vanishing by the day. But whether we have consuls, or a king, or a *princeps*, money will always be the most important thing."

He wasn't wrong. One only had to look at the state of their government to see that. Caesar Augustus, after all, had achieved his current position through leveraging his vast personal fortune. He'd used it to raise armies and buy loyalty, and now, though he'd nominally returned power to the Senate after the civil war, no one questioned his supremacy.

"I see," she murmured.

Felix's gaze dropped to her lips, then slid over the rest of her body before quickly moving away. He uncrossed and re-crossed his arms, shifting from foot to foot.

Those little movements—those trifling hints of unease—gave her a tiny kernel of an idea. A brazen, shameless, preposterous idea. But one that could potentially be her last hope.

"What if there was something I could offer you that you want even more than dominion over Ostia?" She sat straighter on the bed, giving her back a slight arch. "Something money can't buy?"

His gaze flicked up to meet hers once more. "I'm listening."

She knew Felix had desired her once, and in recent encounters, she sensed his attraction remained. She noticed the lingering glances, the moments where his aloof mask splintered. Perhaps it was time to use that to her advantage. But it would have to be managed carefully. She couldn't allow him to have her without being completely certain she would get what she wanted.

Lucretia rose to her feet. In the small room, that movement alone put her within arm's length of Felix, where he still leaned against the wall.

He tried to back up, but there was nowhere for him to go, which resulted in him flattening himself against the wall.

She allowed her mouth to curve into a smile. "Don't worry, Felix. I'm not armed this time."

A hint of color came to his cheeks. "You hardly need a knife to be dangerous, but you are downright terrifying with one." He swallowed. "Tell me what it is you believe I want."

She moistened her lips. Even that small movement drew his eye. "Me. That's what you want, what you've wanted for several years. Am I mistaken?"

He swallowed again, as if his mouth kept going dry. "You are not."

A flare of triumph lit within her, but she kept it subdued. She hadn't won yet. "So, on those grounds, I believe we can come to an arrangement. You want me. I want you to stop targeting my business. Need I elaborate further?" She kept her voice mellow, with just a hint of sensual promise.

His mouth opened, his breath coming faster. "Are you really suggesting…what I think you're suggesting?"

She nodded.

"Say it. So there's no…confusion."

Lucretia stepped closer to him, until just the fabric of their clothing brushed. "I will give you carnal access to my body, in exchange for a truce. If you want to expand to Neapolis or Genua or Olympus itself, I won't stop you. Just leave me in peace in Ostia while you do it."

He drew in a ragged breath. "Carnal access…indefinitely?"

She chuckled. "No." She considered for a moment, calculating how much sexual access to her body was worth. "A week."

"A month," he countered swiftly. Despite his flustered state, he was ever the negotiator.

"Two weeks. Do we have a deal?" She pressed her body against his.

A groan rumbled in his chest. His hands skimmed down her body, coming to grasp her hips. Despite the mercenary nature of her proposal, heat sparked where he touched her. He frustrated her to no end, but she *liked* his hands on her.

"Lucretia," he whispered. "I want you, yes, but I don't want you like this."

She turned around, pushing her bottom into his hips. "Like this, then?"

His fingers tightened on her hips, gripping her so hard it was almost painful. "Dis, woman. You're going to kill me."

"Tell me this isn't worth a truce." She could feel him hard against her, and the sensation sent a shiver through her. She'd forgotten the unique delight of feeling a man's arousal, thick and insistent, pressed into her, and the pleasure of it came flooding back.

"Lucretia," he rasped. "I want you freely, or not at all." Despite his words, he didn't relinquish his grip on her hips.

"If you've ever lain with a slave or a courtesan, you have no grounds for such nobility."

"Well, I haven't."

She half-turned, as far as she could without breaking his hold on her. "Then who have you lain with?"

He somehow managed to meet her gaze evenly, despite the lust swirling in his storm-gray eyes. "No one."

Surprise made her go rigid, and he released her. "What do you mean, no one?" she demanded.

He shrugged. "I've been busy."

"Busy," she spluttered. "So you've never…with anyone?"

"No."

"That's impossible."

A half-smile quirked his mouth. "I assure you, it's not."

"Your father never…never took you to become a man?" It was common, almost universal for a father or older brother to take an adolescent to visit a courtesan when they reached a certain age, to initiate them into the ways of the flesh.

"I don't think bedding a prostitute is what makes one a man. Besides, my father died when I was nine," he reminded her. "And my stepfather cared more about making sure I knew how to ride a horse. As opposed to any other kind of riding."

Lucretia took a step back, surveying him as her mind recalculated what she thought she knew about him. She had never really contemplated how Felix spent his nights, but she had subconsciously assumed that as a bachelor, he made free use of Ostia's hardworking population of courtesans. The thought that he might be celibate—*virginal*, even—had never entered her mind.

"So when you tried to flirt with me five years ago…you wanted me to be the first." Something strange and warm lit within her that he'd thought of her that way. It suddenly put his interest in a different light, made it seem more meaningful than simple lust.

His lean shoulder rose and fell in another shrug. "I found you very beautiful, and I wanted to sleep with you. It was no more complex than that."

"Have you approached other women since?"

He hesitated a moment. "I suppose not. As I said, I've been busy."

"So I'm…" *The only woman you've ever wanted to sleep with?* She cut herself off before she voiced those words, her mind still working through the implications. For all this time, while he had been working to undermine her, he had been…lusting after her?

His jaw tensed. "I have been quite successful in setting aside any inconvenient feelings. Don't make the mistake of thinking this gives you any power over me."

"You are so determined to be in control of everything," she murmured. "It must be quite lonely."

"Not really," he said. "Piles of money are excellent company."

She snorted, then broke into a chuckle. A moment later, Felix joined her in a full-throated laugh. It was the first time she had ever heard him truly laugh. The sound was rusty at first, as if rarely used, but soon grew rich and deep.

Out of all the ways she had envisioned this strange day ending, laughing with Felix had to be the most unexpected.

# CHAPTER 16

F ELIX LAY AWAKE IN the small bed next to Lucretia. Night had long since fallen, and noise from the tavern below had slowed hours ago. The room was nearly pitch black, only a sliver of moonlight filtering through clouds and the tiny window.

He had never shared a bed with someone, and he couldn't wrap his mind around the fact that it was Lucretia here in bed with him. Lucretia, his greatest rival and deepest desire. Lucretia, who had made him an extremely salacious—and tempting—offer but a few hours ago.

For a moment, he considered reneging on his stubbornness and taking the floor, as she'd wanted him to do. Being in a bed with her, after everything that happened earlier, was torture. His fingers remembered what it felt like to sink into the softness of her hips. And his cock certainly remembered being pressed tight against that warm, round bottom of hers.

Lucretia finally knew of his longstanding desire for her, the fact that she was the only woman he'd ever truly wanted. She hadn't reacted with the disgust he'd once anticipated. She'd merely been surprised—possibly shocked—at the extent of his inexperience.

She rolled over in the bed next to him, bumping him with her leg. He froze, worried the contact would wake her, but she only let out a little sigh and relaxed against him.

He envied her comfort. But she'd spent the majority of her adult life sharing a bed with her husband, so this probably felt normal to her.

On the other hand, he felt as out of his depth as an elephant in the Alps. Even the dull, accidental touch of her leg against his made his cock twitch and harden. He took a deep breath, willing the desire to dissipate. He was no stranger to self-pleasure, but it seemed ill-advised to take himself in hand while sharing a bed with her.

He forced his mind to think of anything but the woman slumbering next to him. He latched on to the image of the broken bodies on the shore earlier. The gruesome scene did help dispel his ardor, but it also made him think of Lucretia's reaction. She had been truly affected by the loss of those men, and they weren't even her sailors. She had a good heart. Unlike himself, whose first instinct had been to think of the denarii and sestertii lost today.

She moved again in the bed, inching closer to him. Then a soft, warm arm flung out, catching him across the shoulders. Her fingers grasped onto him, and her head nestled against his chest.

Felix exhaled a long, slow breath, debating whether he should wake her or try to move her.

He settled for the latter option and gently slipped a hand beneath the arm that stretched over his body, attempting to disentangle her grip. Her limp fingers gave way easily, and then he only had to slide his shoulder and arm out from beneath her head.

As he did so, she shifted, and he paused. The position left her head cradled in the crook of his arm, the way he imagined one lover might hold another. Propped on his forearm, he stared down at her face, trying to assess if she was about to wake. In the dark, he could hardly make out her features, but he knew them well. Delicate nose, round cheeks, full lips. Long neck, elegant collarbones...He stopped himself before his assessment ventured lower.

A shadow lay across her cheek and lip, and he realized it was a curl of hair, escaped from the braid she'd bound her auburn locks in before bed. With his free hand, he dared to brush the curl out of the way. His fingertip grazed the skin of her cheek, softer than the silk he imported from Serica. He couldn't resist brushing the back of his fingers over her cheek. She was beautiful even in the dark, when all he could discern of her was the feel of her skin, the gentle sound of her breathing, and the warmth of her body.

For the umpteenth time in the last few hours, he cursed himself for refusing her proposal. If he had only agreed, he could have had her three times over by now. He could finally know what it would feel like to slide into the tight embrace of her body, to lose himself inside her.

He had refused for two reasons. Firstly, the cost of agreeing to a truce was too high. He wouldn't abandon his ambitions simply for the sake of a—likely explosive—tryst or three.

Secondly, he meant what he said to her: he wanted her freely, or not at all. He didn't want to feel like she was only lying with him to get something in return. He wanted her to *want* him, as much as he wanted her.

She stirred again, and something warm covered his hand where it still rested on her cheek. When he realized it was her fingers clasping his, he froze. The rhythm of her breathing changed, and her now-open eyes glinted, catching whatever scrap of light hid in the dark room.

"Felix," she breathed, voice slurred with sleep.

"Forgive me," he whispered. "I didn't mean to wake you. You were moving in your sleep." He wanted to untangle himself from her, but her hand was still holding his against her face.

"Yes, I do that," she said with a sleepy laugh. "It used to annoy Cornelius to no end. Now do you wish you'd slept on the floor?"

"No."

She chuckled. "You are so stubborn." She moved to sit up, and he dropped his hand from her face, straightening up as well.

He could sense her in front of him, but in the dark couldn't tell how close she was.

Until she put her hands on his shoulders. He twitched at her touch, instinctively moving away, but her fingers tightened on him. Then, something warm and soft pressed against his mouth.

Her lips, he realized, with a jolt of bewilderment that nearly toppled him.

This time, he succeeded in jerking away. He was breathing hard, shock and desire coursing through his body in equal measure. "My earlier decision is not open to being persuaded."

"I'm not trying to persuade you." Her voice was deliciously husky, as pleasurable to his ears as her touch was to his body. "I just wanted to kiss you."

"Oh." His mind went blank, like a wax tablet rubbed free of writing.

"May I?"

"Well—yes, I suppose."

Her warm mouth covered his again, and an aching fire spread over him. He wound his arms around her waist, drawing her body flush against his. She leaned back, bringing him with her, as she lowered them both to the bed.

This had to be a dream, he decided as his body settled over hers. But the lumpy mattress, rickety bed, and mouse scratching in the corner were not the stuff of dreams. She was all too real beneath him, solid and warm, her knee hiking up to make room for him between her thighs.

He knew he must be a clumsy kisser, so he let her take the lead, tentatively matching the movement of his lips to hers. She twined her fingers in his hair and opened her mouth, allowing her tongue to trace over his bottom lip.

His hand gripped her thigh, and his hips angled against hers of their own accord.

"Oh!" she gasped, mouth breaking away from his. "Felix, you have no idea how good that feels."

He moved against her in the same way, and heat licked up his spine. "I think I do."

"Don't stop." Her voice was low, urgent.

He obeyed, his cock throbbing and hard as marble. He rocked against her, and she let out a breathy moan, clasping her legs around his hips. Sensation built and tightened, sharp even through the layers of fabric separating them. Finding pleasure against her this way felt wilder, fiercer than when he was alone in his bed with his hand, a summer tempest in comparison to a spring rain.

She was moving too, squirming her hips against his as she matched his rhythm. Her breathing turned harsh and unsteady.

"Don't stop," she said again, this time a desperate plea rather than an instruction.

He was far past the point of stopping. He pressed into her even harder, following the instinct of his body. "Lucretia," he gasped. "I'm going to—"

And then she was moaning, nails digging into his shoulders as her body writhed beneath him.

*Fuck.* He wasn't entirely sure what a woman's climax looked like, but by the gods he hoped that was it, because he had no choice but to follow her over the edge.

# CHAPTER 17

T HE NEXT MORNING, FELIX rode at the head of their small group alongside Siro as they journeyed back toward Ostia. Lucretia, to his relief, was no longer riding with him on the horse, but sat in one of the carts laden with the salvaged cargo. Out of sight behind him, but impossible to get out of his mind.

They hadn't spoken last night or this morning. After what happened, Felix had scrubbed his tunic, laid it to dry, and returned to bed, grateful the dark hid his nakedness from her. By then, Lucretia had rolled over, facing away from him. He couldn't tell if she was asleep or not. He thought not, by the shallow rhythm of her breathing, but he behaved as if she was. Perhaps she was as unnerved as he was and wished to pretend this encounter had never occurred.

Exhaustion finally overtook him, and he slept until the sun's rays woke him in the morning. Lucretia was absent from bed, having already gone downstairs to find something to eat in the tavern. It was a relief they didn't have to exchange awkward, stilted words…though there would have been an undeniable pleasure in waking next to her, in seeing her auburn hair spread over the pillow, the sunlight threading it with gold.

But she'd been gone, and they hadn't spoken a single word.

Now, on the road to Ostia, Felix squinted up at the scant clouds dotting the sky, hoping the sun's brightness would chase away the confusing specter of last night.

"If I may, sir…" Siro said as they passed farm after farm. "How did the lady come to be with us yesterday? I was rather surprised to see her. Given that you are not exactly…friends."

*Not exactly, indeed.* Felix briefly explained the events which led to Lucretia accompanying him to the wreck.

"She *cursed* you?" Siro bristled, casting an outraged glance back at where Lucretia rode in the cart. "The nerve of that woman. Such things are not to be trifled with."

"I believe she intends to undo it when we return."

"She had better. All the more reason for you to find a way to eliminate her. Speaking of which, have you fixed a date to travel to Spoletium?"

Felix sighed. He'd been putting off the trip to search for Lucretia's guardian. The whole journey would take at least a week on horseback, and he didn't particularly enjoy traveling. No doubt in his absence, Lucretia would think of another way to strike at him. Though at least curses were perhaps now off the table.

"I must look at the calendar when we return to find a suitable date," Felix replied.

Getting to Lucretia's guardian could be the most effective way to remove her from his path. But as his mind ran over the events of yesterday, he couldn't help wondering if there was a way to get everything—or at least almost everything—he wanted in one fell swoop.

He wanted Lucretia; he'd known that since meeting her, and it had become an unquestionable hunger as of last night. And he wanted to broaden his influence over trade throughout the Mediterranean.

He had believed the only way to attain the latter goal was to start with Ostia, to attain total control here and then expand. Which required removing Lucretia, his last remaining rival.

But in one of their conversations yesterday, Lucretia had given him another idea. *You know there is room for both of us to be profitable in Ostia,* she'd said, and she was right.

Perhaps he could afford to leave her be in Ostia, and turn his focus to other port cities. Start acquiring a few shipping operations, finance more ships, and expand from there. Lucretia could keep her trade in Ostia unchallenged.

That avenue also opened up the very tempting prospect of being able to accept her proposal—or at least, negotiate a modified version.

His nobler hesitation yesterday had been that he didn't want her to feel obliged to sleep with him. He wanted her to want him.

And last night proved that she did.

He turned to glance back at her. She sat primly in the cart, one arm resting on a barrel. Their gazes met, and he turned quickly back to the front. There was something knowing in her gaze now, something that recalled their intimacy of last night. He might never be able to look at her again without thinking of what they'd shared. No matter what happened from here, she would always be a part of him.

When Lucretia returned to Ostia in midafternoon, Marcus was just setting his school bag down in the atrium.

He frowned, glancing through the open front door at the group of riders and carts moving off. "Where have you been?"

She couldn't blame him for his accusatory tone; after all, she had been gone overnight with no word or notice. "I'm very sorry, sweetheart. It was an unexpected trip, and we were detained overnight."

"Was that Felix with you? I thought you hated him. I thought we were never supposed to speak with him again." No wonder he sounded so peeved—she must look like a terrible hypocrite, forbidding Marcus from associating with Felix and then turning around and spending a day and night in his company.

"I don't *hate* him." She explained briefly about the shipwreck and the events which had led her to spend the night in a coastal town with Felix—though chose to leave out their sleeping arrangements.

"A shipwreck? Why couldn't I have come?"

"It was very gruesome, Marcus," she chided. "Men died."

He huffed but abandoned the subject. "Can I have ten denarii?"

She granted the request, pleased that he asked this time instead of stealing from her. After she gave him the money, he disappeared. Lucretia spared a few minutes to freshen up after her travels, then went to her office to catch up on anything she'd missed while away.

Dihya was there, of course, and jumped to her feet when Lucretia entered. "Where have you *been*?"

Lucretia sighed and, once again, relayed the broad strokes of her unexpected journey with Felix.

"And you spent the night with him?" Dihya demanded. "In the same bed?"

"He was too snobbish to take the floor!"

"Well, did anything happen?"

Lucretia hesitated. It would be easy to lie and say that they'd been perfectly proper, but Dihya was her friend. "There may have been some...touching. And..." Lucretia closed her eyes and spoke so fast the words ran together. "I may have attempted to get him to agree to a truce by offering carnal favors."

"You *what?*" Dihya's face displayed a strange mix of outrage and delight.

"He said no," Lucretia added. Well, not precisely *no*: he'd said *I want you freely, or not at all.*

"Blessed Juno," Dihya breathed. "What has gotten into you lately, Lucretia? You went from cursing Felix to running off with him and trying to barter your body."

"I don't know," Lucretia admitted. "But please, let's forget about it. It will not happen again."

"Do you want me to try another curse on him?" Dihya asked. "I have the ear of some African gods who would love to get their hands on a wealthy Roman, no doubt."

"No more curses," Lucretia said sternly.

"All right," Dihya said with an unconvinced shrug, but she permitted Lucretia to change the subject to other matters.

Lucretia worked until darkness fell, then pushed away from her desk with a tired sigh. Dihya had already left after Caeso came to collect her.

This time yesterday, she'd been gingerly climbing into bed with Felix. And then, a few hours later, not so gingerly rutting against him.

The events of last night still seemed hazy and dreamlike. But her body responded at the thought of it, and the residual pleasure sparking in her core was all too real.

She tried to explain it as simple lust. After all, she'd been widowed for a year, and even before that, her marital relations with Cornelius had been infrequent at best. But she'd grown proficient at satisfying her own urges over the years.

No, somehow it was *Felix* her body wanted. The thought boggled the mind. Felix, her cold, scheming rival. Felix, who wanted nothing more than to destroy her.

Felix, who had never desired any woman but her.

There was something seductive about his single-minded interest, paired with his inexperience. Why was she so tempted by the thought of being his first?

She couldn't afford to think of him that way. He was still her rival, still plotting against her. If she allowed herself to soften toward him, to *want* him, it could only weaken her ability to strike back at him.

Her business—and her independence—had to come first. Last night meant nothing, and they would never speak of it again.

# CHAPTER 18

"WHAT ARE YOU DOING here?" Lucretia demanded when Felix showed up at her office the next morning. Dihya hadn't yet arrived, so there was no one to hold Felix off from striding straight into the back room.

He raised an eyebrow. "That's rather a rude greeting."

Lucretia rose to her feet and folded her arms across her chest. "In recent memory, your visits have either been to propose marriage or harass me about taking very reasonable action against you. So which is it this time?"

The angles of his face somehow seemed to intensify as he looked at her, giving him a shrewd look. "More similar to the former than the latter."

"If you think another proposal—"

He held up a hand to silence her. "Not an offer of marriage. Rather, a counter-offer to what you proposed at the tavern."

She blinked, taken aback. The memory of her brazen proposition rushed through her, warming her cheeks, but she strove to mask her embarrassment. "You refused. And to be honest, I'm not sure what I was thinking when I made that offer."

"Are you open to hearing a counter-offer?"

She knew she should demur and send him on his way, but despite herself, she was curious. What did he mean, a counter-offer? "I suppose."

He took a step closer, and she steeled herself against the heat sparked by his proximity. Her mind flashed back to that night, the feel of his body on top of her, pressing into her. He'd been as close as one could be without actually being inside her.

"In exchange for a truce, I accept your offer of a carnal relationship," he said. "In addition, I would like your consent to apprentice your son."

Her mouth fell open, thrown by the unexpected request. She couldn't even dwell on her surprise at his acceptance of the bargain she wasn't sure she still wanted to make. "Marcus? Why?"

"I would consider it practice for when I have a son of my own one day. That's all."

Lucretia surveyed him. She had a feeling there was more to it than that. After all, Felix had gone out of his way to help Marcus, even as he was trying to undermine her. He seemed to like Marcus, and Marcus had even gone so far as to say "he's not so bad" about Felix at one point. Which was high praise from her son.

It might not be the worst thing for Marcus to find a mentor in Felix. It still rankled that Felix had developed a rapport with him without even trying, but she had to think of what was best for Marcus.

Lucretia considered. Logically, this offer seemed to have no downsides for her. She would get freedom from Felix's scheming, a mentor for her son, not to mention the chance to...

She tore her mind away from the prospect of the *carnal rela-tionship* he offered. She could not go around making decisions based on lust. If she was to consider this, there would need to be parameters.

"How long would this continue?" Lucretia asked. "I offered you two weeks in our last conversation."

He contemplated for a moment, his gaze raking over her. "I propose an indefinite term. Any of us, including Marcus, may dissolve the agreement at any time."

*Indefinite.* Her mouth went dry at the thought of an indefinite carnal relationship with Felix. The last time they'd discussed this, she'd treated her body as a tool to be bartered. But now, after that night, she recognized the mutual pleasure that could be found in such an arrangement. This was no longer about offering herself in payment, but instead it had become something with an intriguing sense of balance.

"I'll put your offer of mentorship to Marcus to see if he agrees," Lucretia said. "For the rest, I have one amendment." She swal-lowed and met his gaze. Was she really about to agree to this? "I don't want to be your lover. I want to be your teacher."

This way, at least, she could maintain some distance, some control. Simply becoming lovers was too nebulous, dangerous in its latitude. Where these things were concerned, she sensed boundaries were important. She could allow herself to enjoy it—to enjoy *him*—but only within the limits she would set.

Heat flared in his gray eyes, turning them to smoldering charcoal. "Are you qualified to teach such things? As far as I understand, you've only been with one man. I may be better served with a more experienced instructor."

Her eyebrows shot up, indignant. "I was married to Cornelius for fifteen years. Assuming we had relations an average of eight times a month during that time, that is a total of…" She paused, working out the numbers in her head.

"One thousand, four hundred and forty times," Felix finished.

She glared at him, irritated that he'd solved it before her. "Which is one thousand, four hundred and forty times more than you, if I'm not mistaken." Her calculations were inflated, given how often Cornelius had been absent and how their relations waned in the last years of their marriage, but Felix didn't need to know that.

A smile twitched at the corner of his mouth. "I concede, and accept your amendment."

Dihya arrived, escorted by Caeso, just as Felix departed. "What did *he* want?" Dihya questioned, looking after Felix with a suspicious glower.

Lucretia leaned against the wall beside Dihya's desk. Her mind whirled as she tried to comprehend what she'd agreed to. How had they gone from rivals to her agreeing to teach Felix the ways of the flesh in exchange for a truce? It was insanity.

But during that conversation with Felix, it seemed to make perfect sense.

"He gave some more thought to the arrangement I proposed after the shipwreck." A shiver of nerves ran through her. What would Dihya think of all this? "He wants to apprentice Marcus. In exchange for a truce and…a carnal relationship." Lucretia left out the part about Felix's lack of experience; it didn't feel right to share something so personal about him.

Dihya let out a ringing laugh. "So you're really going to do it?"

Lucretia glared at her. "This is not a laughing matter."

Dihya didn't restrain her chuckles. "I should have known it would take a business proposition in order for you to consider sleeping with someone new."

The enormity of what she had agreed to finally sunk in. Sleeping with Felix? Being intimate with him? "I'm already regretting this." She pressed her hands to her eyes. "I should back out. Never mind the truce, we'll just have to think of something else—"

"No!" Dihya grabbed Lucretia's hands, forcing her to open her eyes. "You're unattached, and there is a young, handsome man who desires you. You don't need to marry him, but don't waste this chance." Dihya raised an eyebrow. "Sound familiar?"

Lucretia let out a resigned sigh. Those were her exact words from when she'd convinced Dihya to give Caeso a chance. "Your memory can be extremely irritating."

Dihya smiled smugly. "Trust me, it will be worth your while. I have a feeling Felix is good in bed."

Lucretia flushed. "How could you possibly sense such a thing?"

Dihya lifted one shoulder in a shrug. "Men like him—those who come off as being so aloof and reserved—my theory is they let it all out in bed." Her smirk grew. "I bet he'll be a wild lay."

"Dihya!" Lucretia's cheeks burned. She didn't want to admit that Dihya might have a point. Despite Felix's inexperience, and despite the fact that they hadn't even shed their clothes, there had indeed been something…wild…about their brief encounter at the tavern. "Is Caeso like that?"

"Well, unlike Felix, Caeso is *nice*. But when it comes to bedding..." A knowing smile grew on Dihya's lips. "Let's just say the man knows what he wants and has no qualms about taking it. Do you have any idea how strong hauling sacks of flour and kneading bread makes a man?"

Lucretia let out a shocked laugh.

"If I'm wrong, you have an escape," Dihya reassured her. "Remember, Caeso supplies the bread to Felix's household, so if he's bad in bed, we'll just poison him!"

That evening, Lucretia broached the subject of Felix's proposal with Marcus. His agreement, after all, was requisite. But she had to frame the matter carefully, as he couldn't know of her *other* involvement with Felix.

At dinner, she slid a plate of honeyed walnuts toward him, which was a fail-safe way to get his attention. "Lucius Avitus Felix came to see me today," she informed him as he shoved a walnut into his mouth. "We've been discussing some business matters. You know we are competitors."

"Which is why you hate him," Marcus said through a mouthful of walnuts.

"I don't *hate* him. But he is ambitious, and he wants to control trade in all of Ostia. To that end, he's been undertaking efforts to sabotage my business."

Marcus listened to this in silence, perhaps putting the pieces together of why she'd been so angry when she discovered his association with Felix.

"But we have recently reached an agreement. A truce. As part of that, he has offered to apprentice you. You will learn a great deal from him, I'm sure."

Marcus's nose wrinkled. "I don't want to learn about ships. I want to learn *boxing*."

Lucretia sighed. "I imagine Felix will be happy to continue that facet of your education. If he does, will you agree to apprentice with him?"

Marcus considered for a moment, chewing contemplatively on another walnut. His admiration for Felix must have outweighed his disinterest in ships, for he nodded. "Fine."

"Good." Lucretia kissed him on the forehead, ignoring how he shied away. "I'll let Felix know."

"Wait a moment." Marcus frowned at her. "A week ago, you nearly murdered Felix. Then two days ago, you went to see a shipwreck with him. Now today, you want me to apprentice with him?" He gave her a suspicious look. "And apparently he's been trying to sabotage you this whole time?"

Lucretia hesitated. "I told you, we agreed on a truce."

"But why would he agree to such a thing?"

*Because he really, really wants me.* "The terms are not your concern." Too much sharpness entered her voice, and she instantly regretted her tone.

Marcus's gaze shuttered. "Fine. Whatever." He dumped the remaining walnuts onto his plate and set about devouring them.

Lucretia watched him in silence, her chest tight. Why couldn't one conversation with him go smoothly? At least he had agreed to be mentored by Felix. She hoped Felix's influence would do him good.

# CHAPTER 19

L UCRETIA FELT AS IF she were walking on air as she arrived at Felix's house by the light of a brilliant sunset. Earlier that day, she'd visited the temple of Neptune, where she paid for the sacrifice of three chickens in exchange for revoking the curse. Coupled with the fact that she no longer had to worry about Felix trying to sway her investors or pay off her crews, a weight seemed to have lifted off her chest.

At the direction of his steward, she entered Felix's dining room. The dining room was smaller than she expected, but then again, Felix was not one to host a crowded dinner party. The walls were painted not with elaborate frescoes, but in the most modern style, which featured a rich red background sparsely decorated with painted architectural details, like slender columns and elegant candelabra. Lucretia usually found such décor rather flat, but seeing it in Felix's stylish house, she had to admit there was a certain striking quality to the minimalist painting.

Felix was seated on one of the low couches that surrounded the dining table. He rose to greet her with a stilted nod. "Lucretia."

"Felix." A spike of awkwardness sliced through her good humor. How was she supposed to treat him, her rival turned paramour?

Felix seemed of a similar mind, as evidenced by his stiff greeting and silence once she joined him on the dining couch. They reclined facing each other, stretching out with their feet pointing away from the table, leaning on one elbow.

"Marcus is amenable to your offer of apprenticeship," she said to break the silence.

"Yes, you said in your note," Felix replied. Lucretia had sent him a note yesterday to apprise him of Marcus's agreement and arrange this time for dinner.

"On one condition," she added.

"I should have known your son would be a shrewd negotiator."

"He stipulates that the boxing lessons should continue. And you should know he has little interest in learning our trade, so you may not find him the most enthusiastic apprentice."

Felix nodded. "I can work with that. And I agree to his condition."

"Good. He did display some suspicion about how we arrived at this agreement. I hope it doesn't need to be said that the details of our arrangement must remain completely secret."

"Did you think I was likely to tell Marcus I'm engaging in a carnal relationship with his mother?"

The words *carnal relationship* sent a shiver down her spine. "I hope not."

Felix turned to the food laid out before them—a vast amount for only two people. "Are you hungry? I wasn't sure what you preferred, so I asked the cook to make a bit of, well, everything."

She surveyed the spread. There was indeed some of everything here. Raw oysters, scarlet-red lobster, juicy sausages, fruit from figs to pears, and even a cheesecake.

"Are we expecting others?" she asked with an arched eyebrow.

He chuckled. "Not tonight." He began to make himself a plate, and she gestured for him to make her one too, which he piled high with a bit of everything.

It was customary for a servant or two to wait upon the dinner service, to pour wine and remove empty plates, but tonight, the dining room was empty. Felix had clearly planned for privacy.

They ate in silence. Lucretia tried desperately to think of something to say, something safe and mundane, but her mind could only conjure memories and sensations from the last time they'd been alone at night. Heat gathered in her core, spreading in tingles over her skin, and her appetite—for food, at least—abruptly diminished.

Felix ate in measured, almost delicate bites. She remembered that about him from the dinner parties they found themselves at together; he tended to eat without the messy gusto that other diners displayed. Each bite was carefully calculated, speared, and eaten with precision.

Again, her mind went back to their moment of passion. He had been anything but delicate or precise then. His movements had been powerful, hungry, almost desperate. As if his appetite had overwhelmed him, reducing him to nothing more than greedy lust.

There was a smug satisfaction in seeing him so changed from his usual scheming aloofness, knowing that she had been the cause of such a shift. She wanted to do it again, wanted to see him undone and lost to passion.

"Does the food not please you?" Felix asked.

Lucretia realized she'd been staring down at her plate without actually touching it. "It's excellent." She decided to jump straight into this strange thing they were embarking on. She sensed he was waiting for her to bring it up, not wanting to rush or pressure her. "I was merely giving some thought to our curriculum."

A slow, wolfish smile spread over his face. "What is our first lesson to be?"

"Anatomy, I think." Her stomach gave a flutter.

"How academic."

"Am I correct in assuming you've never seen a woman unclothed?"

"Not the bottom half."

That made sense; entertainment at dinner parties or other gatherings often featured scantily clad dancers, so it was not unthinkable that Felix would have glimpsed plenty of breasts despite his celibacy.

"Are you ready to begin now?" he asked.

Lucretia could tell he was trying to maintain his usual restrained, indifferent tone of voice, but she detected a current of eagerness hiding just beneath the surface, a slight tension behind the syllables. Despite the nerves twisting in her stomach, she was eager too.

Now was as good a time to begin as any, so she nodded. "If you're finished eating."

He slid his plate away with quick finality. "One thing first." He rose from the table, went to the door, and called out to whatever servant was lurking in the corridor. "Bring some more lamps, please."

A flush heated her cheeks as Felix returned to the table. The mention of lamps somehow made her fully comprehend what they were about to do—even though it was all her idea. She was going to bare herself to him. To let him look at her, in a way even Cornelius hadn't done. Of course, Cornelius had seen all parts of her over the course of their marriage, but she had never intentionally *displayed* herself to him.

Two servants brought a pair of tall oil lamps, the metal stands elaborately worked in a pattern of twisting vines. Felix instructed them to place the lamps directly between him and Lucretia, after which they lit the lamps and departed without a word.

Lucretia's heart thumped once they were alone again. An answering pulse throbbed between her legs. Divine Juno, was she really about to do this?

She swallowed hard, mouth gone dry.

Felix glanced at her. "Are you nervous?"

"No." The breathiness to her voice belied the denial.

"You don't have to do this, Lucretia."

She knew that. This had, after all, been her idea from the very beginning. But the prospect his words evoked—the idea of getting up and leaving—made her realize how much she wanted this. She wanted his gaze, wanted his hunger.

Before she could reason herself out of it, she straightened up on the couch, pivoting to face Felix, and gathered a fistful of her dress to draw it up to her knees. One foot rested on the floor, the other sank into the surface of the plush couch, her knee bent.

Felix leaned closer, as if drawn to her by an invisible string. His intense focus was both gratifying and daunting. She hoped whatever expectations he had formed in his mind over the years, he wouldn't be disappointed.

She continued raising her dress, baring her thighs. Finally, she drew the fabric up to her hips, revealing everything to his hungry gaze.

He exhaled, and she realized he'd been holding his breath. His gaze lifted briefly to her face, and the tentative reverence in his eyes gave her a surge of confidence. She lay back against the pillows behind her, allowing her legs to fall open.

She trailed her fingers over herself, luxuriating in the sensation that sparked. A muscle pulsed in Felix's jaw.

"Is this how you imagined it?" she asked, voice husky.

He cleared his throat. "I did not think it would be so...pink."

She blushed. It was pink because she desired him. Having her need laid bare like this should be embarrassing, but it was impossible to be abashed with him looking at her like that, naked lust etched in every plane of his face, his fists clenched tight at his sides as if he had to restrain himself from reaching for her.

Lucretia drifted her finger to the apex of her quim. "This is the place that gives the greatest pleasure."

His eyes tracked her movement. "I see."

"And this..." She moved her fingers down, between her folds. "Is where, er..." She couldn't find the words, so instead, she slipped one finger inside. Her channel was already slick with wanting.

Heat flared in his gaze. "I see," he said again, voice hoarser this time. "Is it not strange for the two to be so far apart?"

"It does take some finesse at times, to find pleasure with a man."

"Fascinating," he murmured. "May I touch you?"

Lucretia nodded. She expected him to go straight for her center, and she braced herself for a surge of sensation.

Instead, he laid a hand on her lower leg, near her ankle. He brushed gently upward, following the curve of her calf. She shivered when his hand passed over the underside of her knee, unexpectedly ticklish. His mouth twitched at her reaction.

His hand moved slowly upward, the touch lightening until it was just the tips of his fingers grazing the inside of her thigh. She couldn't help shifting beneath him, her body searching for more sensation.

Then his fingers reached the curls on the edge of her sex. She caught her breath, holding it as he delicately explored her folds. His brow furrowed in concentration.

There was a heady mix of power and vulnerability in letting him touch her like this. Even though she was meant to be the teacher in this encounter, she was completely exposed to his gaze and his touch. She couldn't hide her desire, the elemental fact that her body wanted him.

He glanced at her face. "Is this hurting you? You look uncomfortable."

She exhaled and tried to relax her face. "No."

He kept his gaze on her face as he trailed his fingers lazily up and down her folds. "Then it's giving you pleasure, and you find that uncomfortable."

He was a little too perceptive, despite his inexperience. "I just—it's been a while since someone…touched me," she admitted.

"But this pleases you?" He stroked her once more.

"Yes." Her breathing was quick and shallow. "But it would please me better if you touched higher. The spot I showed you."

"Here?" His index finger brushed the nub above her folds.

She bit back a gasp. "Yes."

"Show me how to touch you. Show me what you like." The words hovered between a request and a command. He moved his hand aside.

She acceded, finding the right spot and moving her fingers in a circular pattern. "Like that."

He touched her again, copying the movement.

She reached down to adjust the positioning of his fingers. "Here. Press harder."

He obeyed, finding a slow, firm rhythm that made lust creep over her skin in a demanding itch. "Will this make you come?"

"You're rather ambitious for your first endeavor."

"It's not my first endeavor. I believe I was quite successful the other night."

He had indeed been successful that night in the tavern, but that had been something of an accident. She had merely been enjoying the hard, thick feel of him against her before being overwhelmed by a sudden climax. To do this intentionally, without the shield of midnight and strange surroundings that made everything feel less real, was another matter. "That was different."

"Was it? Well, I find that I usually excel at whatever I turn my *hand*—" He briefly increased his pressure in a way that made her gasp. "To. I'm sure this will be no different."

She managed a breathless chuckle. "Don't get your hopes up." He would no doubt be insufferably smug if he succeeded in satisfying her, so she determined to remain as cool as possible, to not let him know what his touch was doing to her.

But remaining cool was a herculean feat when he was touching her like that. She had made the mistake of showing him exactly how she liked to be touched, and he was diligent enough to match it almost perfectly. The slight variations in rhythm only heightened the sensation, reminding her that someone else—*Felix*—was the one giving her pleasure.

She let out a long, slow breath, forcing herself to keep the rising tide of pleasure at bay. There was no way she would climax so easily. Not for him. Not like this.

*Definitely not*, she decreed, even as the muscles in her thighs tensed and her feet flexed.

He stopped—and she just barely suppressed a cry. Her core throbbed, desperately seeking the sensation he'd been giving her.

With his other hand, Felix traced her opening. "May I enter you?"

"Yes," she breathed. In that moment, she wanted nothing more than him inside her, filling her.

He hesitated briefly, then eased a finger in, her slickness guiding him. She drew in a sharp breath, and he paused. "Does that hurt you?"

She shook her head, unable to manage words.

"So warm," he murmured. "So soft." He sank in further, pressing deep, and she bit back a moan.

His other hand resumed stroking her, rubbing gently as he thrust in and out. Something in the avid way he was *focusing* on her brought her even higher. He was intent, thorough, and meticulous in pleasuring her, as if nothing else existed in his world but her. She was at once a tool for him to practice upon, as well as his greatest desire.

Never before had anyone lavished her with such single-minded concentration. Cornelius had been a generous lover, but his attentions had always had the aim of increasing his own enjoyment. Felix, on the other hand, worked her with the devotion of a scholar decoding a foreign tongue.

Pleasure coiled inside her, drawing tight like overspun thread about to snap. She grasped onto something—anything—to distract her from the inexorable wave on the verge of overwhelming her: the plush pillow beneath her, the clench of her fingernails into her palms, the scent of perfumed oil from the burning lamps next to them. It smelled like marjoram, that herby fragrance she'd noticed on Felix before.

He paused again, and she bit her lip. "You're twitching," he said. "What does that mean?"

"It means—it means—" If she spoke any more, she would end up begging for him.

He surveyed her with a mix of dispassionate analysis and carnal greed that made her muscles give another spasmodic twitch around his finger. "I believe I understand."

His thumb returned to her apex, stroking in unrelenting, methodical circles. Lucretia knew she was lost, vanquished by his slow, deliberate pleasuring, and she abandoned her efforts to hold the pleasure at bay. The thread snapped, and she gasped his name as spasms wracked her body from head to toe.

Her hand shot down to grip his, holding him tightly in place as her body writhed against his fingers. She wrung every last bit of pleasure from him, then collapsed back on the couch, chest heaving as shivers ran over her.

Felix gently withdrew his finger from inside her. "I did warn you, I am rarely unsuccessful."

There was that insufferable smugness. But lying limp on the couch, every muscle heavy with satisfaction, she couldn't even summon the will to be annoyed by him. "You show great promise as a student."

He grinned, then examined the liquid coating his finger before wiping it with a napkin. "You are a most accommodating teacher."

She managed to gather her legs beneath her and heave herself to a sitting position, drawing her dress back down to cover herself. Her quim felt tender, little spasms still sparking with every movement. She reached for her abandoned wine goblet and drank deep, her throat parched.

Felix watched her like an owl stalking a mouse. "There is another part of your anatomy you haven't yet elucidated," he said when she returned the goblet to the table.

She arched an eyebrow. "Oh? I thought I was very thorough."

"These." He reached out to touch her collarbone, tracing his finger down until it brushed the hollow between her breasts, just visible above the neckline of her dress.

Her nipples tingled, sending an answering pulse through her quim. She smoothed her hands around her breasts over the dress, squeezing and lifting them. "You want to see these?"

His pupils dilated. "Yes." The word was a hiss, a plea.

She allowed her hands one more luxurious pass over her breasts, thumbs brushing her nipples. "But you said you were already acquainted with what a woman looks like there."

A muscle clenched in his jaw. "I want to see what *you* look like there," he ground out.

"We are all generally the same, I believe, apart from nominal variations. There's no point in extending our lesson to that region." Her nipples had stiffened, and she circled her fingers around them, drawing his attention. A groan rumbled in his throat. She delighted in toying with him like this, returning some of the frustration he'd given her—and that frustration was evident in the large protrusion tenting his tunic.

Her quim gave another little pulse at the sight of it. She hadn't been able to fully appreciate his size and shape during their last encounter, and now she reached for him, wanting to feel his length in her hand. If she could desire him this much after achieving climax only moments ago, she could only imagine the lust that must be running rampant inside him.

He batted her hand away with a chiding sound. "If I can't touch, then you can't, either."

She shot him a glare laden with as much pique as she could muster. There would be time for all this later. Perhaps it was better to end this encounter here. "Then I suppose we're done for the evening."

She rose quickly to her feet, which caused her head to spin. She stumbled, arms flailing out.

Felix caught her around the waist, holding her steady as her dizziness dissipated. But as her balance returned, a new kind of unsteadiness took hold, born of being held in his arms, pressed tight against his body.

"Are you all right?" he murmured.

"Just a dizzy spell," she replied. His arousal was still evident, an intriguing stiffness against her stomach.

His hold on her loosened, but he didn't release her. "When can I see you again? Tomorrow?"

His eagerness gratified her. In that moment, she wanted nothing more than to say yes, to find herself right back here in no more than a day's time.

But she felt unmoored by this encounter, shaken by the effect he had on her. Some distance would help her approach their next meeting with more circumspection.

"Next week, I think," she said, stepping away from his tempting embrace. "I'll send a messenger when I've identified an ideal date."

He nodded, some of the lust receding from his face to be replaced by a layer of detachment. "Very well. I will bid you good evening, then."

She waited a moment, expecting him to see her out, but when no offer was forthcoming, she gave him a small nod and left the room.

# CHAPTER 20

I T WAS IMPOLITE TO let Lucretia leave without escorting her to the front door, but Felix had no other choice. His current state of painful, demanding arousal was not fit to be seen by his staff.

After she left, he closed the door to the dining room, threw himself down on a couch, and yanked up his tunic to get at his throbbing, unsatisfied cock. He let out a hiss as his fist completed the first hasty stroke. He'd been hard from the moment she started pulling up her dress, at the first glimpse of her delicately curved calf. The sight of her quim, thatched with reddish curls, had made him ache.

And then when he actually touched her—a groan rumbled in his throat at the memory. He'd been on the edge as soon as his fingers delved between her legs, exploring her most intimate places. The experience had made him question if it were possible to climax without a single touch.

Unfortunately, it hadn't happened, which was why he was now almost out of his mind with lust. He couldn't even remember when they had set their next meeting for. Or had they set it at all? There might have been a mention of a messenger to confirm the date…

He could figure that out later. Now, he had only one concern, and that was relieving the delicious, agonizing pressure in his groin.

He tightened his grip on himself, stroking up and down. She'd wanted to touch him, and by Mars, he had no idea how he'd summoned the self-control to deny her. He only knew he'd enjoyed the look on her face, peeved and petulant.

This was far from the first time he'd pleasured himself to the thought of her, but it was the first time he'd done it moments after touching her, after having his finger palm-deep inside her, the heady smell of her permeating his mind. He could still feel her muscles spasming around him. *Fuck*, what would that feel like on his cock?

The thought was too much to withstand. The pressure swelled and burst in a sweet, wracking release.

He collapsed back onto the couch pillows, fumbling at the table for a napkin to clean himself. His hands shook, his breathing choppy as he struggled to recover from the explosive climax. He heaved a deep breath. This arrangement with Lucretia was either the best or worst decision he had ever made. Only time would tell.

"You're late," Dihya said with a gleeful chuckle as Lucretia entered their office the next morning. "Sleeping in?"

Lucretia blushed. Maybe she had lingered in bed this morning, just a bit. Maybe she had closed her eyes and recalled Felix's touch on her last night, his focused, studious attention. Maybe she had

pleasured herself to the thought of what might have happened if
he hadn't pushed her hand away at the end of their encounter…

"I'm not late." She kept her words firm, as if strength of tone
could change the reading on the water clock.

Dihya twirled a stylus between her fingers. "You can make up
for it by telling me *everything*."

"I will do no such thing!" Lucretia protested. "I've never asked
you for the intimate details of your nights with Caeso, have I?"

Dihya rolled her eyes. "Caeso and I have a *normal* relationship.
He's not my greatest rival whom I've convinced to tumble me in
exchange for a business truce."

Lucretia groaned.

"Please," Dihya wheedled. A significant look entered her dark
eyes. "If I'm to be a boring married woman soon, I need something to sustain me."

"Boring married—?" Lucretia's mouth dropped open as she
comprehended Dihya's words. "Are you saying Caeso has asked
you?"

Dihya jumped to her feet, her hands giving an excited, girlish
flutter. "He has. Last night!"

"Oh, how wonderful!" Lucretia threw her arms around Dihya.
Then she pulled back, schooling her face into an expression
of mock-concern. "He knows he's marrying you, right? Not
Tadla?"

Dihya laughed, tears of happiness gleaming in the corners of
her eyes. "This time, we're quite clear on the matter."

Lucretia waited several days before contacting Felix again. She wanted to see how Marcus was getting on with him; if the apprenticeship portion of their bargain was not making Marcus happy, then she would have to break off their arrangement.

Marcus visited Felix each day after school, not returning home until sundown. Three days in a row, he returned sweaty and exhausted, with reddened knuckles.

"Are you spending all of your time at the gymnasium?" Lucretia asked after the third day, as they shared an evening meal together. "Felix is supposed to be teaching you about trade."

"We talk about that in between," Marcus replied, amid ravenous bites of duck leg. "If I lose, I have to listen to him explain something. Like how the weather affects the olive harvest, or how to tell a real gemstone from glass."

"Do you lose often?"

Marcus grimaced. "Most of the time. For now."

"I still don't like the thought of Felix punching you." She now trusted that Felix would never hurt her son, but it still seemed like an unnecessarily violent pursuit.

"It's not punching," he said with a disdain that reminded her too much of Felix. "It's *boxing*."

Lucretia had no idea what that was supposed to mean, but Marcus seemed to be enjoying himself, so she set the matter aside.

"He said one day I might be able to come with him to visit some of the ports he trades with," Marcus continued, excitement quickening his words. "Like Athens, or Alexandria."

"No," Lucretia said immediately, a reflex before she'd even fully absorbed his words.

Marcus frowned. "Why not? I thought you wanted me to learn."

Her mind flashed back to those lifeless, broken bodies on the beach. She could never countenance endangering Marcus's life in such a way. "You can learn on land. There's no need to take such a foolish risk."

His frown intensified into a scowl. "Traveling by ship is faster and safer overall than by land. Just because a few people get unlucky—"

"A few people, including *your father*," she snapped.

He flinched, then glared at her. "If Felix invites me on a voyage with him, I will go."

"You will *not*. Not without my consent." She had little time left to use that power, as all too soon Marcus would come of age and be his own man. But for the time being, he was still her child.

He rolled his eyes and uttered an infuriatingly cool "We'll see."

Lucretia let out a tight sigh. This conversation had started so well, and she'd ruined it with one word. Besides, it wasn't even a real issue; the voyage was only hypothetical at this stage. Marcus seemed to be enjoying spending time with Felix, and he'd been excited at the prospect of a voyage. She'd been too quick to quash him, driven by her own fears rather than any rational risk.

"I will consider it," she conceded. "*If* Felix should actually invite you to join him one day."

He ignored her capitulation, reaching across the table to load his plate up once more.

# CHAPTER 21

SINCE IT SEEMED MARCUS was not suffering from the arrangement, Lucretia sent a messenger to Felix to arrange a date a few days later. In the intervening days, her mind ran rampant with all of the things she could teach him. Playing this role with him thrilled her. She had never thought of herself as much of a temptress, her experience being confined to the marital bed, but somehow Felix made her feel as powerful as a siren.

She arrived at Felix's house in late afternoon on their appointed day, and joined him in the stylish, understated dining room. Once again, the table was laid with an obscene variety of foods. "You needn't go to such trouble," she chided him as she sat beside him on the couch. "Marcus is the glutton, not me."

"All boys his age are gluttons," Felix said. "And you're worth the trouble."

His gaze met hers as he said that, and her stomach fluttered. She pushed aside the sensation and looked over the spread. She pointed to a few platters which appeared to house dishes containing onions and garlic. "I advise avoiding those."

He frowned. "You don't like them?"

"I fear they will impede our lesson today." At his questioning glance, she clarified: "Kissing."

"Ah." Was it the low light, or was there a flush coloring his cheeks? "I see."

"Or perhaps we could undertake our lesson before eating."

"Yes," he said immediately.

His eagerness made her smile. She rose to her feet and beckoned him to stand also. A standing kiss was safer; if she let him kiss her on the couch, she had no doubt they'd end up much too entangled in each other.

She stood with an arm's length of space between them. "Now," she murmured. "Show me how you would kiss me. I'll correct you as needed."

He stepped closer to her, surveying her mouth as if it were an arithmetic sum he needed to solve. She moistened her lips.

A kiss should be nothing after what they'd shared, and they had kissed that one time at the tavern. But kissing was for lovers, and theirs was a more mercenary arrangement.

He placed his hands firmly on her shoulders, as if to anchor her in place. Then he bent his head and pressed his lips to hers in a quick, hard push before withdrawing.

She couldn't help being relieved that he wasn't as naturally skilled at kissing as he had been at making her come.

"Was that good?" He already looked smug.

"Mediocre." She delighted in the outrage that filled his face at her assessment.

"Mediocre?" he demanded. "I kissed you, didn't I? It was a success."

Lucretia rolled her eyes. "Kissing is more than a binary of success or failure."

He crossed his arms, shoulders rising in affront. He looked like a cat that had unexpectedly gotten wet, vexed and indignant. "So what am I meant to do?"

"Firstly, you don't need to pin me down as if I'm a chicken you're trying to catch. Embrace me, don't restrain me."

"Embrace," he murmured, as if taking mental notes.

"Secondly, a kiss should be a brush of lips at first. Let the pressure build naturally. And go slower. You kissed as if you were trying to win some sort of prize for speed."

He shot her an offended glare, but nodded. "I am ready for a second attempt."

"Proceed."

This time, he slid his arms around her waist, pulling her into him. "Does this classify as a suitable embrace?"

His body was warm and lean. Her curves pressed into him in all the right places, kindling heat between her legs. "Yes," she breathed.

"Good." He trailed one finger up her neck, tipping her chin toward him. The brush of his finger on her sensitive throat made her shiver convulsively. A trace of smugness returned to his face at the movement. Then he leaned down and brushed his lips against hers, the barest touch before retreating.

"Yes," she whispered. "That, again."

He did it once more, then moved his lips to her cheek. She felt him exhale in a warm rush against her skin as he dragged his mouth over her jaw to tickle her earlobe.

Another round of shivers ran over her, shooting from her ear to settle in a throbbing cluster between her legs. "I didn't instruct you to involve the ear," she managed.

"But you like it." His voice was low and rough in her ear.

She gave a sigh of admission, and he returned his mouth to hers. He kept the kiss feather-light, teasing, and she couldn't help seeking more from him. She pressed her mouth harder against his, allowing their lips to tangle. He let out a harsh groan when she sucked his bottom lip into her mouth.

His arms tightened around her, and they stumbled several steps until a wall against Lucretia's back stopped them. Now, she delighted in feeling pinned by him, trapped between his body and the wall with no escape.

She broke off from their kiss with a gasp, struggling to catch her breath. "Here," she panted, bringing a hand to her neck. "Kiss me here."

He obliged, grazing his lips along her throat. When she shuddered, he paused in that spot and kissed harder.

"Oh!" The hard pull of his lips made her think of his mouth between her legs, tongue working her into a frenzy. That would have to be another lesson at some point.

She hooked her leg around his, drawing their bodies even closer together. His arousal pressed against her, tempting and insistent. It would be so easy to draw up her skirt, pull aside his tunic, and let him slide deep inside her.

She took a deep breath, fighting to keep her head amid the tingly kisses and nibbles he was giving her neck. A hasty coupling against a wall wasn't what he deserved for his first time. She would approach that with more patience and finesse at a much later date.

But for now, she needed *something*, or else she'd dissolve in a pool of unfulfilled lust. "Perhaps a review of our last lesson is in order," she gasped.

He lifted his head from her neck and gave her a crooked grin, eyes lighting with avidity. "Indeed." He slid his hand between her legs, his other arm still wrapped tight around her waist.

Her knees almost gave out at the first heady touch, even dulled by the fabric of her dress and not quite in the right spot, and she had to grasp his shoulders to steady herself. "A little further down."

He adjusted his position, watching her face carefully. "There," he said in satisfaction when her eyes fell shut in pleasure.

She nodded. He stroked her slowly, moving in wide circles with the flat of two fingers. The slow movement, coupled with the barrier of her dress, quickly became more frustrating than pleasurable, and she shifted against him. "Lift my dress," she said, impatience sharpening her words.

He gave a low, dark chuckle. "Only if you let me remove it entirely. I want to see your tits. And touch them."

The thought of his hands on her bare breasts sent a shock of pleasure through her, making her quim twitch. Last time, she had refused, finding it fun to toy with him.

But this time, she wanted it too badly to deny herself.

He gave her another slow, teasing stroke. "Take off your dress, Lucretia."

"Fine," she hissed.

Triumph filled his face, and he stepped back to give her room. She untied the sash at her waist, then shrugged out of the loose dress, kicking it aside.

"Should have brought more lamps," Felix murmured as he surveyed her top to bottom. His hungry gaze lingered on her breasts, the nipples rapidly hardening.

"Touch me," she demanded.

He slid his palms over the undersides of her breasts, feeling their weight in his hands. Then he squeezed gently, allowing his fingers to sink into her flesh. His hands were warm, so warm, and her back arched, pushing more of her against him.

His fingers circled her nipples, then brushed over the stiff pink peaks. She drew in a sharp breath as tingles of pleasure raced through her. He paused, as if evaluating her reaction, then did it again.

"You like this almost as much as the other place," he said, continuing to toy with her nipples.

"Almost," she agreed, voice unsteady.

"What about both at the same time?" One hand left her breast and found its place between her legs. The touch of his fingers on her bare flesh, coupled with his other hand teasing her nipple, made her shudder and bow against him, head braced against the wall behind her.

"You're soaked," he whispered roughly in her ear. "I can only assume that's a good thing. Is it, Lucretia?"

The sound of her name rasping on his lips as he pleasured her almost undid her. "It's—it's a good thing." The words were mangled and barely intelligible.

"What does it mean?"

She sensed he knew exactly what it meant, but he wanted to toy with her. To make her admit that she wanted him. "It means—"

She broke off in a gasp as he slid one finger gently inside her.

"Tell me what it means." His voice deepened to a growl.

"It means I want you," she confessed. "It means I like the way you touch me."

He let out a sigh of satisfaction and rocked his finger inside her. "Would you climax from this alone?"

At that moment, she felt as if she could climax from the touch of a feather, but even so, she shook her head. "It's pleasurable—very much so—but not enough on its own."

"I see." His words somehow managed to have both the carnality of a man with his finger deep inside her as well as the attentiveness of a scholar learning from a sage. "So I should focus here, then—" He withdrew his finger and found the throbbing spot at the apex of her quim. "If my goal is to make you climax."

"You should," she breathed.

In response, he resumed the same rhythm she had shown him last time—quick, tight circles. She dug her fingers into his shoulders, letting him support her as the pleasure built.

"Oh," she moaned. "Oh, Felix, I'm going to—" The wave crashed over her, and she became senseless to everything but the flames of pleasure consuming her.

"Yes," he growled as her body rippled and writhed against him.

As it left her, she sagged, legs no longer capable of supporting herself. "I can't—"

He slid his arms around her, catching her by the waist. "I've got you. Don't try to stand."

Somehow, he swept her legs out from under her and carried her to the couch. Dimly, she registered a moment of surprise at his easy strength, as his body wasn't as bulky with muscle as some men were. But that must be a byproduct of his boxing practice, despite the overall leanness of his frame.

He laid her gently on the couch, and even went so far as to place a pillow beneath her head. "Thank you," she mumbled.

He brushed a curl of hair away from her cheek. "Are you cold? I can fetch your dress."

She shook her head. She was anything but cold, molten pleasure still seeping through her in waves of heat.

Heavy satisfaction suffused her, which made her realize he'd experienced no such resolution. Last time, he'd stopped her from touching him, and it had been rather fun to leave him unsatisfied. This time, however, she didn't want to end this without feeling her hand wrapped around his cock.

Once she caught her breath, she hauled herself into a sitting position, weary muscles protesting the movement. "You're getting very good at that," she said. "Perhaps a reward is in order. Lie back."

He gave her a look hot with hungry anticipation, along with a trace of incredulity, as if he didn't really believe this was about to happen. But he lay back, positioning a pillow beneath his shoulders and clasping his hands behind his head so he could still look at her.

Lucretia brushed her hand over the protrusion of his arousal through his tunic. "Is this all for me?"

A shudder went through him at the light touch. "Yes."

"Have you thought about me doing this before? Lifting your tunic, sliding my hand up…" She did exactly as she said, feeling the muscles in his thighs tense as she passed over them. "Wrapping my fingers around your cock?"

"Yes," he hissed as her hand found his arousal. "So many times."

The admission that she was the object of his fantasies thrilled her. She gave him a long, slow stroke. "Did you do this after I left last time?"

He gave a hoarse, strangled chuckle. "Barely a moment after the door closed behind you."

She laughed. Perhaps that explained why he hadn't walked her to the door. She'd taken it as a minor discourtesy, but maybe he'd just been beside himself with lust. "I like that. I like the thought of you pleasuring yourself while imagining me."

"It happens with mathematical regularity."

The fact that he was still able to conjure words like "mathematical" meant she hadn't yet achieved her aim of rendering him stupefied with pleasure. She increased the firmness of her grip, which made him gasp, and sped up until she drew a groan from his lips. "Tell me what you like. Faster? Slower?"

"Anything," he rasped. "Anything. Just—just touch me."

*I can do that.* She kept going, maintaining a steady rhythm. He released one hand from behind his head and grabbed a fistful of the couch cushion, knuckles whitening.

"Is this like you imagined it?" she murmured as she worked his cock.

"Better," he panted. "Your hand—so soft."

With her other hand, she cupped her breast, allowing her thumb to swipe over her nipple. Tingles shot through her, everything more sensitive after her climax. "I liked it when you did this earlier."

His pupils dilated, and he let out another groan.

"You're getting close, aren't you?" she asked, almost contemplatively.

He hissed something that might have been a "yes," and then a garbled plea of "don't stop."

She didn't, and continued her rhythm of firm strokes. A moment later, a tremor rippled through him. He moaned her name. His hand shot out to grip her wrist, clutching almost painfully as the climax roared through him.

A matching thrill made her heart speed up as she watched him. She drank in the sight of him, shuddering and lost to pleasure, like the finest wine.

When it subsided, he collapsed back against the pillows. His fair skin was flushed, dark hair in disarray with a sheen of sweat on his forehead. He looked thoroughly shattered, and pride swelled in Lucretia's chest. There was a singular satisfaction in doing that to a man, especially one as self-assured and controlled as Felix.

She found a clean napkin on the table and used it to gently wipe him and her hand.

"Come here," he mumbled, the words slurred and indistinct. He clumsily moved over to make room for her on the couch.

She lowered herself down next to him, laying her head on his chest. He wrapped his arms around her.

"Stay the night," he whispered in her ear.

She froze. That was the sort of thing that lovers did. Not people in a transactional relationship, who had negotiated an erotic education in return for a business truce.

This arrangement had no future. Even if they enjoyed each other for a month, or two, or six, it would come to an end eventually. Felix would no doubt marry some eligible maiden, and Lucretia had no desire for another husband.

So despite the considerable pleasure they could find with each other, maintaining some distance was paramount.

"No," she breathed. "I must return to look after Marcus."

"Of course." His voice betrayed no regret at her rejection. "Let's eat, and then I will have my steward escort you home."

# CHAPTER 22

Felix sat heavily on a stone bench, jaw aching. Marcus collapsed beside him and gulped down a cup of water. The boy had been steadily improving at boxing and had just managed to deal Felix a wicked blow to his jaw—though Felix had returned the favor with a strike to the shoulder that sent Marcus reeling into the dirt.

Though Lucretia had consented to boxing lessons being a part of Marcus's apprenticeship, Felix didn't fancy incurring her wrath if he were to permanently damage her son. He tried as best as he could to avoid sending Marcus home with any significant injuries like a broken nose, but sometimes he couldn't avoid a split lip or bruised knuckles.

"You're getting better," Felix said, rewarded by the way Marcus's face lit up.

"Really? I still feel like an elephant clomping around."

"Your strikes are getting faster and more precise. You're starting to build some muscle too."

Marcus flexed his arm experimentally, then winced, likely due to the soreness in his knuckles. "Thanks."

"Now, while we rest, tell me what you remember of how ship financing works."

Marcus took another gulp of water, perhaps to buy time as he thought. "One person gives another person money. To pay for a ship and transport goods."

"Right. And what happens when the goods are sold?"

"The lender gets paid back with a lot of interest. So they make more than they lent. But..." Marcus's brow furrowed. "If something bad happens—if the goods are lost at sea or something—the shipper doesn't have to pay back anything. So it's risky for the lender. They could lose their entire investment."

Felix nodded. "But quite profitable if they have good luck." Maritime financing was how Felix had gotten his start. Then, once he built up capital, he'd purchased ships of his own and slowly grown his operations.

"I mentioned to my mother that you said I might be able to join you on a sea voyage some time," Marcus said, unwinding the linen wrappings from his knuckles. "She wasn't happy. She said it was too dangerous. She always worries!"

"Mothers are meant to worry." Even at this innocuous mention of Lucretia, a little thrill ran through him.

Marcus's mouth twisted in disdain. "It's annoying. I'm nearly a man. I don't need a mother anymore."

Felix winced. If Lucretia ever heard him say something like that, her heart would break. He fixed the boy with a stern look. "I'm a man, and I still need my mother. Do you know when I was starting my business, I consulted her on nearly every decision? And I'm fairly certain my stepfather's horse-breeding business would be nowhere if not for her." While Felix's stepfather had an aptitude for horses, his business acumen left something to be desired. "She even solved my father's murder."

"Murder?" Marcus jumped to his feet. "Your father was *murdered?*" He seemed more fascinated than horrified.

Felix nodded. "Regrettably."

"Oh, that's not *fair.*" Marcus slumped back onto the bench with a dejected sigh. "I *always* have the parent with the most interesting death. Everyone else's dead parents are from illness or childbirth or something stupid—but my father died in a shipwreck!" His eyes shone with pride. "But murder—well, I think that beats shipwreck."

Despite the grim subject matter, Felix couldn't hold back a chuckle. His father had died a long time ago, and Felix was at peace with the loss. And even though Cornelius's death was much fresher, Felix suspected the boy's "ranking" of deaths was a way to cope with the loss. "I suppose it does."

"But how was he murdered?" Marcus demanded. "Was he stabbed? Or strangled? Or drowned? If he was drowned, that's really not so different from a shipwreck."

"He was poisoned," Felix said. "In order to cover up a scheme of corruption in the province he was governing."

Marcus let out a groan. "You win," he conceded. "You definitely win."

"Thank you." Felix accepted the macabre victory with a nod "Shall we turn from the topic of dead fathers back to our living mothers?"

Marcus rolled his eyes. "Just because *your* mother is interesting doesn't mean all of them are."

"Yours is smart, ambitious, hardworking, and kind." *Also beautiful, soft, and able to make me ache with just a glance.* "Do you know how easy it would have been for her to give all this up after your father died? I certainly tried my best to make her give up. I even proposed marriage to her. She would never have had to work a day in her life if she didn't want to. But she was determined to keep your father's business prospering, all to create a legacy for you. It wouldn't hurt to be kinder to her."

Marcus made a disgusted face. "You *proposed* to her?"

Felix should have known that was what the boy would take away from his speech about Lucretia's virtues. "A misguided attempt to sway her. She refused without a second thought."

Marcus made a noise of disgust. "You would have been my *stepfather*."

"As I said, it was a mistake."

Marcus shot him a sidelong glance. "She doesn't want to marry again, just so you know. I asked, after Father died. She said she had no use for a husband, so I wouldn't have to worry about being stuck with a stepfather."

Marcus's words sent an unexpected pang through him. But it shouldn't have surprised Felix that Lucretia wanted to keep her independence, especially after she rejected his proposal. She had everything she needed—income, a son, an occupation that seemed to bring her fulfillment. A husband would add nothing to her life.

It certainly didn't matter to Felix. Their arrangement had nothing to do with marriage. It was just business. But Marcus's words sat heavy in Felix's stomach nevertheless.

When Felix returned home after the boxing lesson, his steward greeted him with a letter, bound in a tight scroll and sealed with wax. He recognized that seal; the tiny image of a rearing horse indicated that the letter hailed from his mother and horse-obsessed stepfather.

"Thank you," he murmured, and took the letter to his study to read it. He broke the seal to find a short message in his mother's neat handwriting.

*From Volusia to her son Lucius:*

*We have the most wonderful news! Your sister has been blessed with a healthy baby girl. We are going to spend a few weeks with Herminia and Fulvius. It would be so splendid if you came to visit to meet your new niece. We would all love to see you; it's been too long. Are you married yet? Being a grandmother is delightful so far, and I would appreciate another grandchild sooner rather than later…*

The rest of the letter consisted of updates on the various foals that had been born on their farm, which Felix skimmed.

He was happy for his half-sister, though the difference in their ages meant that they weren't especially close. Herminia was ten years younger, born after his mother's marriage to Maximus. Herminia had been married two years ago, at the age of seventeen, to a prosperous farmer only a short trip from his parents' estate.

Well, he would have to make the journey out to see them. He wouldn't ignore a summons like this from his mother—though it was framed as a request—and in truth it had been too long since seeing his family.

The prospect of a journey reminded him of his earlier plan to search for Lucretia's guardian, who supposedly lived near his family. That felt like another life, when he had still been trying to undermine her. So much had changed since then, and he was grateful he'd never needed to enact that part of his scheme against her.

He'd leave the day after tomorrow. He had a meeting arranged with Lucretia for tomorrow night, and that would give him enough time to make sure Siro and Paulinus were apprised of anything they might need to manage in his absence.

# CHAPTER 23

"Y ou're leaving?" Lucretia asked when Felix told her of his upcoming journey. They were, once again, sequestered in his dining room, accompanied only by a few steaming platters of food and a pair of gently flickering candelabra. "For how long?"

He shouldn't have been so gratified at the disappointment in her voice. "Two weeks or so, if there are no delays. It should take about three days to reach my sister's home. She and her husband live near my mother and stepfather, outside of Spoletium. Are you familiar with the area?"

He couldn't help asking: if her guardian lived near there, she must know something of the vicinity.

But she shook her head. "No, my family is from the south. I've never been that far inland."

Well, *that* was somewhat interesting. He stopped himself from prying further. Given their truce, it was of no concern to him.

Besides, she was now lifting her dress to her waist, which thoroughly distracted him from all thoughts of Spoletium or guardians or anything but the fast-growing ache in his cock.

She slid into his lap, soft thighs clasping his hips. His hands sank into the flesh of her bottom, pulling her closer.

"Mm," she breathed, giving a little rub against him which made him groan. "I think you're ready for a more advanced lesson."

"Advanced...?" His mouth went dry at her words and her closeness. *Could this be...did she mean...*

He'd been growing increasingly desperate to bed her, to know what it felt like to slide into the tight, slick clasp of her body. He hadn't wanted to press her on it; he understood she might prefer to avoid that particular act due to the risk of pregnancy.

She dragged a finger down his lips. "Utilizing these."

"We've already covered kissing." He extended his tongue to lick the tip of her finger.

A pleasing flush rose to her cheeks. "Utilizing these...somewhere else." Her gaze swept downward, and he started to understand.

"You want me to kiss you...here?" He palmed the warm place between her legs, which made her arch against his hand.

She nodded, hands tightening on his shoulders.

Despite the immediate surge of interest that made his cock twitch, he hesitated. "Is that, er, something people do? Something men do?" Though he wasn't personally experienced in these matters, he had listened to other men discuss their carnal endeavors. He'd gotten the impression that using one's mouth to pleasure another, whether male or female, was something only slaves or courtesans did.

Lucretia raised an eyebrow. "It can be something *you* do."

"But is it, I mean, proper?"

She gave him a cheeky grin. "I'm not sure anything we've done is considered proper. Are you looking for special dispensation from Caesar Augustus himself?"

"You know what I mean."

"I don't, actually. Tell me." She climbed off his lap, coming to sit on the couch next to him.

He shrugged, embarrassment crawling over his skin. "I've heard people say it will give you bad breath or rot your teeth."

She chuckled. "Did you ever notice that Cornelius's teeth were particularly affected?"

"*He* did that?"

"Occasionally."

"Hmm." Felix reevaluated what he'd heard about performing such acts. He'd never known anyone who actually admitted to it, but he'd always respected Cornelius. And perhaps he felt a tiny jolt of competitiveness toward Lucretia's dead husband, over something entirely different from their old business rivalry... "I suppose we could try it."

His hesitant words belied his eagerness. Once, after being inside her, he'd furtively tasted his fingers, and the sweet, musky savor sent a pang of desire straight to his groin.

She rolled her eyes as she lay back on the couch. "If you don't like it, we need not continue."

"I have a feeling I'll like it," he muttered, half to himself as her legs spread before him.

He was familiar with the sight of her quim by now, but it never failed to scramble his mind and reduce his thoughts to little more than pulsing need. He trailed his fingers up the insides of her silky thighs, relishing her shiver as he did so. He loved eliciting reactions from her—a shiver, a sigh, a catch of her breath...

"You know the basic principles," she said, her voice taking on that husky tone he'd learned meant she was aroused. "You just need to apply them in a different way."

He attempted to clear his mind of the haze of lust and focus on the task at hand. These lessons were made markedly more difficult than any other subject he'd tried to learn by the constant throbbing in his groin, the itch of desire crawling over every bit of his skin.

He forced himself to survey her beautiful, pink quim with as much academic detachment as he could muster. He knew what to do with his hands to make her shudder and quake. He only had to figure out how to replicate that with his mouth, his lips, his tongue.

He leaned close, inhaling her drugging fragrance. Oh, that was good. Why were other men so determined to warn each other off this singular pleasure?

His tongue flicked out and licked down one of her folds. She let out a sigh, and one of her hands caressed the back of his head, fingers tangling in his hair. He continued exploring her with his mouth, reveling in the plush softness and heady taste of her.

His tongue found her entrance, and he couldn't resist lapping at the dampness that had already gathered. She shifted beneath him, thighs clasping on either side of his head. In this position, his entire universe was consumed by her—her feel, her smell, her taste. Nothing else existed but the way she twitched and gasped, and his urge to drive her higher, higher until she gave in to the frenzy of pleasure.

"Up," she demanded, voice breathy but insistent. "Move up."

He chuckled against her. He knew exactly what she wanted, and he loved when she got like this—an enticing combination of begging and commanding.

For now, he decided to give her what she wanted. Or at least attempt to, given his untested skills in this area.

He dragged his mouth higher, finding the swollen nub at her center. He swirled his tongue around it, clumsily attempting to replicate how his fingers moved against her. "Like that?" he murmured.

"Try using your lips instead." Her fingers wove in and out of his hair, the sensation soothing and stimulating at the same time.

He closed his lips around her, drawing her into his mouth.

"Yes," she hissed. "Like that."

Felix braced his hands around her thighs as he continued to work her with gentle suction. He experimented with swiping his tongue over her at the same time and was rewarded with a moan.

He kept doing that, and her hand in his hair clenched tighter and tighter.

Felix lifted his head. "Am I doing it right?" He was fairly sure he was, but it was always satisfying to hear her say it.

"Don't stop," she panted, so he put his mouth back to work.

Soon, she was shuddering beneath him, hips writhing and bucking. He had to curl a hand around her thigh to hold her in place. "Yes," he growled. "Come for me, Lucretia."

She moaned his name as the climax took her, and the sound sent a burst of possessive pride through him. He would never get tired of satisfying her—not if their arrangement lasted for months, or years.

Her grasp on his hair loosened, and her hand fell slack against the cushion. She was breathing hard, flushed, her lips parted and her eyes glazed with residual pleasure. Felix drew her skirt back over her legs so she wouldn't get cold.

Instinct urged him to gather her into his arms, but he hesitated. They'd briefly embraced that way after their last encounter, until she gently rebuffed him when he'd asked her to stay the night. He wouldn't make that mistake again, but he still longed for her closeness, especially knowing they were about to be parted for at least two weeks.

The prospect of weeks without her eroded his restraint. He lay down on the couch next to her, then slid an arm around her waist and gathered her to him. She curled into him, resting her head on his chest, her weight warm and limp.

He let out a long, slow sigh. Suddenly, going on this trip was the last thing in the world he wanted to do. If it had been a business trip, he would have found a reason to delay or sent Siro in his place. He had a duty to his family, though, and he did want to celebrate the birth of his niece. But at this moment, with Lucretia's warmth surrounding him, her scent imprinted into his mind, the thought of two weeks without her felt impossible.

# CHAPTER 24

A FEW DAYS LATER, Felix arrived at his half-sister's farming estate in central Italy. Fields of barley, millet, and other crops stretched over the rolling hills, with fruit trees planted in neat rows near the villa and outbuildings.

He dismounted from his horse and wiped sweat from his brow. Since moving to the coast, he always forgot how much hotter it felt inland, even on a relatively mild day. In Ostia, the cooling sea breeze was a constant presence.

He gave his horse to a stablehand, then entered the villa while another servant ran off to announce his presence.

His sister's husband, Fulvius, received him a few moments later. Fulvius, around Felix's age, was easy-going and good-humored, and today he appeared to be practically buoyant as Felix congratulated him on his new daughter. Fulvius showed him to the sunny garden at the back of the house where Herminia sat with the baby.

"Lucius!" Herminia looked as if she was about to jump to her feet before remembering the squirming baby in her arms. She had their mother's delicate features and dark golden hair, paired with Maximus's lively brown eyes. "Oh, I wasn't sure you would come!"

She held out an arm to him, and he accepted the half-embrace, pressing a quick kiss to her forehead. "It's not every day one gains a niece," he said. "Congratulations." He surveyed the infant. "She looks very, er..." His brain flicked through several possible adjectives, trying to determine the most fitting compliment for a baby. "Healthy?"

"You should hear her cry." Herminia smiled indulgently down at the baby. "The midwife said she had the strongest lungs she'd ever heard!"

"How...nice."

"Do you want to hold her?" Herminia proffered the baby, which gazed at Felix with blue eyes that somehow managed to seem doubtful.

Felix had never held a baby before, and he had a feeling that if he did, she would soon demonstrate those healthy lungs. "Perhaps later."

Herminia returned the baby to her shoulder. "I need to feed her soon. Mother and Father were just taking a stroll through the orchard. You should go find them. They'll be so pleased to see you!"

"I'll do that." He nodded to her and the baby, then proceeded out the back of the garden toward the orchards.

He walked along the neat rows of plum and peach trees. The fruit was in season at this time of summer, but most of these trees appeared to have already been harvested. Felix managed to find one plum that hadn't yet been plucked, and stretched his arm up into the branches to grab it.

He didn't bite into it, but tossed it in his hand as he walked. Marcus was especially fond of plums—not that there seemed to be any food he disliked—so Felix would bring the fruit back to Ostia as a present for the boy, and an apology for being away so long.

He took a deep breath of the fresh country air. It was like a different world out here, a peaceful haven compared to bustling, crowded Ostia. But Ostia had an energy, a vibrancy that he couldn't stay away from for long.

It also had Lucretia and Marcus. Somehow he already missed them both.

Ahead, he heard the sound of footsteps brushing over grass and the murmur of quiet conversation—his mother's light voice mixed with his stepfather's deeper tones.

A booming laugh broke out, scattering a flock of birds from a nearby tree. Yes, that was definitely his stepfather: loud and uncouth as always.

His parents came into view on the path ahead of him, their backs to him. His stepfather's arm was wrapped around his mother's waist, and she laid her head on his shoulder as they walked.

Felix cleared his throat. His mother, Volusia, stopped short and turned around. Her eyes widened when she saw him. "Oh, Lucius! You came!"

She crossed the short distance to him and enfolded him in a tight yet decorous hug.

"Why is everyone so surprised that I'm here?" he asked as he withdrew from the embrace.

"Because you might as well live in India for how often you visit!" Maximus, his stepfather, gave Felix a good-natured punch on the arm that sent Felix stumbling into the trunk of a peach tree.

"Ouch," Felix muttered, rubbing his arm. "Well, I was actually planning an earlier visit. There was a business associate in this region whom I was going to meet. But plans changed." *In that I decided not to pursue my campaign against Lucretia by persuading her guardian to drop his support.*

"Oh? Who was that?" Mother looped her arm through his as they ambled down the row of trees. "I wonder if we know him."

"It was a man named Manilius Cotta."

Mother frowned. "If I'm not mistaken, I believe that man is dead."

Felix drew to an abrupt halt. "Dead? It must have been very recent." *Does Lucretia know? She must not.*

Maximus shook his head. "At least five years ago. He left no heirs, so his estate was sold to another family."

Felix couldn't bring himself to move. Dead for five years? It was impossible. There must be some mistake.

"How did you arrange a meeting with this man, if he's been dead for five years?" Mother asked.

"I—I was given his name by another." Felix struggled to summon a façade of calmness. "Perhaps a miscommunication." What did this mean? Several possible conclusions jumped into his brain, tangling themselves in a web of confused suspicion.

His mother was asking how long his journey had taken, so he forced himself to put the question of Lucretia's guardian from his mind—for the moment.

Felix managed to keep up polite conversation as they meandered through the orchard back to the house. Upon reaching the villa, he retreated to the bedroom he'd been assigned under the excuse that he wished to wash and change clothes after his long journey.

In the quiet room, he paced, his mind spinning. Lucretia's guardian was dead. Could Siro have given him the wrong name? It was possible, but Siro didn't make mistakes like that. Felix had to assume the name was correct.

If Lucretia's legal guardian had been dead for years, even before her husband's death, there was no way she didn't know of it.

Which meant she had arranged the situation exactly as she wanted.

When Cornelius had died, she must have decided to invent a guardian. She had no father, brothers, or uncles in Ostia or Rome. Manilius Cotta probably was her closest male relative before his death. And a distant relative who lived far from Ostia would suit her purposes very well.

In reality, the system of guardianship was not strictly tracked, so it was likely that no one had ever bothered to check. It was usually assumed that an independent woman could manage her affairs as she pleased, unless her guardian raised an explicit objection.

Which was exactly what Felix had been planning to convince Manilius Cotta to do.

But that was before their truce. So this new information, of course, didn't matter to Felix.

He sat on the bed, dropping his head into his hands. A headache pulsed in his temples. The room was so quiet his ears rang.

This could be damning for Lucretia if anyone were to find out. The rules around guardianship might not be closely monitored, but the fact that Lucretia had been brazen enough to invent a guardian would not go ignored. Women were supposed to appreciate such regulations, which existed to safeguard their interests and ensure no one took advantage of them. They were not supposed to flout the rules.

Lucretia's business operations would be considered unlawful. All her assets would be seized. It would ruin her. And all it would take was a whisper in the right magistrate's ear.

If Lucretia was removed, that would clear the way for Felix to attain unquestioned control over all shipping in Ostia, as he'd always intended.

*You have a truce,* he reminded himself. It was reprehensible to even consider betraying her, given their current arrangement.

He rose from the bed and resumed pacing, hoping the orderly movements would bring some logic to the chaos of his mind.

As far as he could tell, he had three options.

One, he could anonymously reveal her secret to the magistrates. She and Marcus would lose everything. But she might never find out it was Felix who had destroyed her.

That option seemed cowardly, and besides, Lucretia was too smart not to realize that her old rival had finally vanquished her. He would lose her, even if he gained everything else.

The second option was to tell her of his discovery. To convince her it was in her interest to transfer all her operations to his control, before anyone else should discover her secret. Perhaps they could come to an amicable agreement. Perhaps he would be able to keep her in the bargain.

*You think she'll consent to sleeping with you after you blackmail her? Idiot.*

The third option was both the easiest and the hardest: do nothing. Say nothing, either to a magistrate or to Lucretia. Pretend none of this had ever happened. Go on with their highly enjoyable carnal explorations, and maintain their truce in Ostia.

Part of him—the ambitious, greedy, scheming part—was shocked he could even consider this option. Two months ago, he would have been gleefully running to the nearest magistrate to expose and ruin her.

But much had changed. His gaze lit on the plum he'd pilfered from the orchard for Marcus. Her son would despise him if Felix took any action against Lucretia. And Lucretia—

Nausea spiraled in his stomach as he contemplated betraying her.

Something about this situation felt different than any of the other efforts he'd undertaken against her.

With a jolt, he realized why: it wasn't *fair*. This dilemma wouldn't exist for any other business rival—any *male* business rival. But because the world had decided that women required legal guardians in order to run businesses or manage property, he now had a unique opportunity to demolish everything she'd worked for.

For some reason, his mind went back to his first meeting with Marcus, that three-on-one beating in the alley. There was nothing wrong with schoolboys scuffling with one another, but Felix had intervened because it wasn't a *fair* fight. There was no possible way Marcus could win against three bigger, stronger boys.

Just like there was no possible way Lucretia could win against a society that believed she required guardianship.

He picked up the plum, its smooth skin cool against his hand. The decision settled into place in his mind.

Lucretia didn't deserve to be beaten like this. If their truce ran its course and their rivalry renewed, he would eventually best her.

But he would do it in a fair fight.

# CHAPTER 25

T ALKING AND LAUGHTER filled Lucretia's ears as she sat
on a high-up seat at the circus. The long oval racetrack
stretched below her. She and Marcus had found seats bordering
one of the four corners. That was the best spot, according to Marcus, as watching the chariots navigating the tight angle provided
a great deal of thrill and potential for crashes.

Lucretia didn't particularly wish to watch a chariot crash,
but Marcus loved the excitement. Since Felix was still visiting
his family, Marcus had some extra time after school, so she'd
offered to take him to the races. It was their first mother-son
outing since…since before Cornelius died, she realized. They'd
occasionally gone to the races as a family and had even taken
Marcus to the great Circus Maximus in Rome a few times. She
still remembered how he'd shrieked with delight at the size of
the racetrack—much bigger than the one here in Ostia—and the
speed with which the chariots flew around it.

Now, before the race began, Marcus had gone to purchase
some food from one of the vendors that paced the stands, so for
the moment, she was alone. She wondered what Felix was doing
now, if the weather inland was as pleasant as it was in Ostia today.
The sun burned bright, but the sea breeze provided welcome
relief.

Somehow, she missed Felix. Her thoughts had turned to him many times over the past several days he'd been away. Her nights felt empty without the prospect of their lessons, and her body missed his touch, the single-minded way he pleasured her.

Her desires had been running rampant since he'd been away. Usually, one or two efficient climaxes were enough to satisfy her for a week. But lately, she'd been indulging in pleasure first thing upon waking and again before she went to sleep. Even so, her efforts did little to curb her thoughts of him. It was as if her body wanted *him* alone, not just simple physical satisfaction, and the ache wouldn't be quelled until she felt his hands on her skin once more.

She didn't like feeling this way: so helpless, so dependent.

Marcus returned, laden with food, so she turned her thoughts away from her troublesome attachment to Felix. "What did you find?"

He sat on the bench next to her and laid down the food between them. "I got meatballs. Crispy chickpeas. And a slice of savillum!"

"My favorite." She reached for the honeyed cheesecake, wrapped in a thin napkin, and took a bite. They still had at least a quarter of an hour before the race began, as Marcus had insisted on arriving early to get the best seats.

Marcus stuffed a handful of fried chickpeas in his mouth and crunched happily. "I wagered the leftover coins on the Blue team. You know, Felix was explaining ship financing to me, and it seems sort of similar to betting on racing. You're just betting that a ship won't sink so you get paid. Maybe one day, if I ever win a really big bet, I'll start making ship loans."

Lucretia couldn't recall the last time Marcus had spoken so many words in a row to her. "I'm glad you're enjoying your lessons with him."

"He's very smart. And he says I'm getting better at boxing."

"I'm sure you are. You've been very diligent about continuing your training while he's been away. He'll be impressed when he returns, no doubt."

Marcus turned his attention to the skewer full of greasy meatballs and bit off a whole one. He chewed avidly, swallowed, then gave her a sidelong glance. "You know…" He hesitated, contemplating a second meatball.

"What?" Lucretia took a delicate bite of the dense, sweet savillum.

"I think Felix *likes* you."

She nearly dropped the cheesecake. "I—he—well…" She struggled to address this conjecture. "What makes you say that?"

Marcus shrugged. "The other day he was saying all sorts of things about how smart and hardworking and talented you are. And then he said he'd proposed to you months ago—"

"That was nothing," Lucretia said firmly. "A foolish business proposition, which I rejected."

"I know. But then I mentioned how you said you never wanted to marry again and, I don't know, he looked…sad or something."

Lucretia absorbed this new information in silence for a long moment. Was it possible…? No, Marcus must have misjudged that conversation. "I'm sure it was nothing."

"You see him a lot, don't you?" Marcus said, his tone taking on an accusatory edge. "You have a lot of dinners with him lately."

"Those are business." Guilt filled her at the lie, and she couldn't meet his gaze.

"Do you…like him?" her son asked. "I mean, he's not exactly ugly, is he? I assume ladies, er, find him appealing—"

"Marcus!" She had to put a firm stop to this conversation. "Felix and I have a business arrangement. Nothing more." She wrapped an arm around his shoulders. "I promised you when your father died that I would not marry again. I have no interest in Felix of that sort." That, at least, was true; though she desired Felix, marriage was the furthest thing from her mind.

"Good," Marcus said, gathering another handful of chickpeas. "Because I like Felix, but I wouldn't want him as a *stepfather*."

"Understood." She pulled him closer, expecting him to wriggle away.

Instead, he laid his head on her shoulder—just for a moment, but it was enough to make Lucretia catch her breath. Warmth flooded her, chasing away all thoughts of Felix and whether or not he liked her or she liked him.

By the time she recovered, Marcus had already pulled away.

Lucretia gave his shoulder one extra squeeze before releasing him. "Goodness, that boxing practice is fleshing you out, isn't it? You're going to have a legion of girls chasing after you before you know it."

"Mother!" he groaned, and Lucretia chuckled.

Below them in the circus, the chariot teams started to emerge, and the crowd roared. Lucretia turned her attention to the race, but the whole time, she could feel a little spot of warmth on her shoulder where Marcus had rested his head.

On the second day of his visit, Felix rode to the former house of Manilius Cotta, having gotten directions from his mother. There, he spoke with the current owner and verified that Cotta was indeed deceased, with no known heirs. When Siro visited, the property owner had been away, so Siro must not have realized the man wasn't whom he was seeking.

Despite himself, Felix was impressed at Lucretia's audacity. She must have known that if her invented guardian were discovered, everything she'd worked for would be lost. But she had taken the risk in order to hold onto her independence, to ensure she wouldn't have to answer to anyone. She was fearless.

Felix returned to Herminia's house as the sun was setting, sore and dusty after another long day on horseback. He washed, changed his clothes, then joined his family for dinner. The dining room of this house was small, on the verge of feeling cramped with only the five of them seated on the couches around the table. The walls were painted a plain light green, no murals or other decorations adorning them. Out here in the country, they had no need to show off with oversized dining rooms or elaborate ornamentation.

"How was your errand?" Mother asked as Felix lowered himself onto an empty couch.

"It was as you said," Felix replied. "The gentleman I'd been told of is deceased. But it doesn't matter."

Maximus was holding the baby, nestled in the crook of his burly arm, to give Herminia and Fulvius a reprieve while they ate on the other side of the table. Felix was half-surprised Herminia would trust her oafish father with something as delicate as a baby, but the little girl cooed happily as Maximus's large finger tickled her stomach.

Mother reached over to adjust a fold of the baby's swaddling, smiling down at the infant. "Being a grandmother is marvelous. All the fun of having a baby without any of the real work." She gave Felix a pointed look. "I bet little Fulvia would love to have a cousin close to her own age."

Felix poured himself a large measure of wine.

"There must be many girls in Ostia who would leap at the chance to marry a man as successful and handsome and smart as you," Mother continued.

"I'm too busy to marry," he said automatically. It was the same response he'd given each of the many times his mother had brought up his status as a bachelor.

"You'll always be busy," she chided.

"I'll get around to it one day." He'd always planned to marry eventually. Having a wife was useful in many respects—a hostess for social engagements, someone to manage the household, a mother for his heirs. But none of those things had ever seemed particularly pressing to accomplish.

Maximus switched the baby to his other arm. "You could always do what I did. Marry a woman who already has a child. Takes some of the pressure off. It's an excellent shortcut."

Felix raised his eyebrows. "If I recall, Herminia was born almost exactly nine months after your marriage."

"Yes, but there wasn't any *pressure*." Maximus grinned.

Felix snorted. His mind immediately went to Lucretia and Marcus. Marcus would be a worthy heir; after all, he was already set to inherit Lucretia's business. But there was no point in considering that, as Lucretia would never marry again.

His thoughts must have shown on his face, for Mother leaned closer. "Is there really no girl who has caught your interest, in all this time? The girls in Ostia can't be that unappealing, can they?"

Felix hesitated. He didn't like to lie to his mother, but he also didn't want to reveal the depths of his futile obsession with Lucretia.

Mother cocked her head. "Is it someone unsuitable? A girl whose father hates you? Or is she married? Or, no, she's a Vestal Virgin—"

"She's not a Vestal Virgin!" Felix spluttered, before realizing his mother was chuckling.

Maximus guffawed too, which nettled Felix to his core.

"So there *is* someone," Mother said smugly.

"There's a girl?" Herminia piped up from where she and Fulvius enjoyed their dinner across the table. "Now this is exciting. Fulvius, Lucius has a girl!"

"Praise Juno." Fulvius lifted his wine cup skyward and drank deep.

Felix shot them all a glare without any real heat. "I don't *have a girl*." He let out a resigned sigh. "If you must know, there is a widow of my acquaintance whom I...admire deeply. From a distance." His family didn't need to know that lately, "from a distance" meant face-deep in Lucretia's quim.

"Admire deeply," Herminia murmured, a jubilant light in her eyes.

"From a distance?" Mother demanded. "If you like her, and she's widowed, why not pursue her?"

"It's not that simple," Felix muttered.

Maximus nudged Felix's mother with his shoulder. "Widows make excellent prospects, you know."

Fulvius and Herminia chortled. Felix glowered into his wine cup and refused to say another word.

After dinner, Felix retreated to his room to prepare for bed, wearied from his travels to the late Manilius Cotta's estate and the revelations of the last two days.

A soft knock came at his door. "Lucius?"

His mother's voice. "Come in," he called.

She slipped into the room, closing the door behind her. "I hope we weren't too intrusive earlier. About your personal affairs."

Felix gave her a placatory smile as he searched for a fresh tunic to wear to bed. "It was no more than I expected. Probably what I deserve, having been absent for so long."

She returned his smile. "You seem…somewhat different these days. Max noticed it too."

*Different?* "I did pick up a bit of a tan on my journey here, if that's what you're referring to."

"No, it's not that." She sat on the edge of the bed, patting the spot next to her.

He came to sit beside her. Their shoulders brushed, and he was reminded of the days of his youth when she occasionally observed his lessons, sitting beside him as his tutor quizzed him on this or that. He'd always been driven to impress her, and her smile or words of praise would buoy him for the rest of the day.

"There is a certain softness about you," she continued. "An ease that I haven't noticed in a long time. Since…" Her voice trailed off.

He let the silence lapse for a moment. He was fairly sure he knew what she was going to say. "Since?" he prodded gently.

"Since I told you the truth about how your father died." She laid a hand on his arm, turning to face him. Her eyes were wide, her gaze anxious and beseeching. "For years I've wondered if I made the right choice by telling you when I did. Maybe I should have told you straightaway. Or maybe I never should have told you at all. You were always a serious boy, but after that…you changed."

She'd never said this to him before, but maybe she was right. He just hadn't been able to notice it for himself. Hearing the truth of how his father died had stripped away the final layers of his childhood innocence. It had disabused him of any notions about honor or decency. It had torn him from the path he thought he'd pursue, pushing him toward something entirely different.

He never would have met Lucretia if he'd followed in his father's footsteps, Felix realized with a jolt.

He clasped his mother's hand. "You made the right choice." Felix understood why she'd kept it from him until he was old enough to understand, why she'd wanted to give him a childhood free from such darkness.

Some of the anxiety faded from her gaze. "Thank you," she murmured. Her tone lightened. "Anyway, I wondered if the lady you spoke of at dinner might have something to do with this recent change. You seem…happier."

"I-I don't know," he stammered, caught off guard. It hadn't occurred to him that Lucretia might have changed him in ways he'd never have noticed. His mind flashed back to that day at the beach, the shipwreck, when he'd turned away from chasing a thief to help Lucretia. He'd soothed her fears, even though it was in his interest for her to succumb to them. Then, just yesterday, he'd decided to let go of something that could vanquish her once and for all.

Because he no longer wanted to vanquish her. He wanted *her*.

But she didn't want him. She might enjoy their evenings together, but that was as far as it went. "It doesn't matter," he muttered. "She does not wish to marry again."

"Did she say this to you?" Mother asked.

"Well...no," Felix admitted. "I heard it secondhand."

"Until she says it to you, don't assume anything. Perhaps she's not yet ready to move on, but if you make your interest clear, she may come back to you when she is ready." Mother gave him a significant look, then rose from the bed and kissed him on the forehead. "I'll leave you to rest. You must be tired."

After she left, Felix mulled over her words. His mother made an interesting point. Marcus was the one who had said Lucretia didn't plan to marry again. Perhaps Lucretia had only told him that when Cornelius's death was still fresh, to reassure the boy that nothing else would change so suddenly. Perhaps, now that time had passed, she might change her mind, might even consider Felix as a husband.

A sudden surge of hope filled him from head to toe. Marrying Lucretia could allow them to combine their business interests. She could be the perfect partner, both romantic and commercial.

He could protect her, too; as her husband, he'd assume the role of guardian she'd fabricated. That way, no one would ever find out about her subterfuge.

Would she accept him, though? The question loomed large in his mind. What if she didn't want him the way he wanted her? What if she only wanted their nights together, their lessons?

Felix had not made it to where he was by taking foolish risks. This situation was no different. So he'd wait, gather as much information as he could, and act only once he was sure of success.

# Chapter 26

"WELCOME BACK," LUCRETIA GREETED Felix as she entered his dining room a few days after his return. She'd tried not to seem too eager to see him, waiting several days after he sent word of his arrival back in Ostia to arrange their next meeting. Now, setting eyes upon him for the first time in two weeks, she wanted to run into his arms, but held back and greeted him with a decorous nod.

"How was your sister's baby?" she asked, stretching out on the dining couch beside him.

He shrugged. "She eats, sleeps, cries, and burps, so I gather she is quite the success."

Despite his nonchalant words, his eyes lit with warmth as he spoke of his new niece. Lucretia smiled. "Did you enjoy the countryside?"

Another shrug. "It's pleasant enough, but the quiet is almost deafening. It hurts my head. Sometimes the loudest thing is the breeze ruffling the leaves in the trees."

"You prefer the dulcet tones of sailors swearing at each other in the harbor?"

He shot her a quick grin. "I do." He poured her a cup of wine and passed her a tray of poached fish. "Speaking of the harbor…there is something I wished to ask you."

Lucretia froze in the midst of serving herself a portion of fish. Something to ask her? Her mind shot back to the conversation with Marcus about marriage and Felix and *liking* each other..."Oh?" she said, the syllable unsteady.

He glanced at her as he filled his own plate with roasted duck. "While I was gone, Siro received some correspondence from one of my key suppliers in Cyrene that he's trying to hike his prices on me. So I thought some in-person negotiation might be the most efficient solution. It's only about a nine day sail from here. I would like to invite Marcus to join me, if you are agreeable. We would leave next month. I expect we'd be gone for four weeks."

"*Oh.*" Relief coursed through her that the question wasn't what she feared. But the relief was chased by a suffocating anxiety at the thought of Marcus on a ship voyage. She sat up, food abandoned. "A nine day sail? That's quite far. He's never been away from home. And what if something should happen? What if he should get sick, or injured, or homesick, or what if he doesn't like the food—"

Felix took her shoulders in a gentle grip. "Breathe, Lucretia."

She gulped in a breath, let it out, then took another one, slower this time. The way he was holding her reminded her of that day on the beach after the shipwreck, when she'd been spiraling into guilt-ridden agitation. He had soothed her, even though they were still enemies then.

She met his eyes, and their cool grayness calmed her, like a cloudy sky after a raging tempest. "I don't know if I can let him go," she confessed.

He rubbed his hands up and down her arms in a comforting rhythm. "Marcus is almost a man. It would be good for him to see something of the world. I think the trip would teach him a great deal."

"I know." She had to think of what was best for Marcus, not fall prey to her own fears.

"Do you trust me to look after him?"

She let out a deep exhale. "I do."

"So…do I have your consent?"

She closed her eyes. Images of all the terrible things that could happen on this voyage flitted behind her eyelids, so she opened her eyes, anchoring on Felix's face. She tried to think of all the ships that arrived safely in Ostia harbor, day after day. All the sailors that spent their lives voyaging from one port to another.

Marcus would be safe with Felix, and the voyage would be good for him. "Yes," she finally said.

"Thank you." His hands didn't leave her shoulders. To her surprise, he drew her toward him for an embrace, his arms wrapping around her body.

Another calming breath left her lungs, and she hugged him back. For all they'd done together, she and Felix had never actually embraced like this. It felt so good to lay her head on his shoulder and be enveloped in the heat of his body.

"I know that was difficult for you," he said, voice low and tender. "I hope you know, I don't take your trust in me lightly."

Warmth kindled in her chest, chasing away the last traces of anxiety. "I hope you know, if anything happens to Marcus, I will curse you a thousand times over."

He chuckled, the sound vibrating through her. "I'd expect nothing less."

She drew back from the embrace, smiling up at him. The feeling of his strong arms around her made desire swell. Her body had hungered for him these past two weeks, and she couldn't deny her appetite any longer. "Now, since you've been gone for so long, I think a review of our previous lesson is in order." She pivoted to rest her foot on the surface of the couch, then took a handful of her dress and lifted it to expose one calf.

His eyes tracked her movements, and a greedy grin lifted the corners of his mouth. "There's only so much one can accomplish with independent study." He reached out to grab her dress, yanking it up to her hips.

She giggled and parted her legs, allowing her head to fall back as he lowered his mouth between her thighs.

Felix's fists thumped against the sand-filled leather bag swinging in front of him. Marcus was due to meet him here shortly, but for now, Felix was alone, which gave his mind plenty of freedom to wander.

Ever since Felix returned from his trip to his family, the question of marrying Lucretia loomed large in his mind. The more he thought about it, the more he was sure he wanted her as his wife. He wanted all of her—from her intelligence and her business expertise to her carnal knowledge and tempting curves.

He had always known he would marry eventually, but whenever he pictured his future wife, it was a vague, blurry image of a quiet, dutiful woman who would manage his household and raise his children. Someone conventional, unchallenging, easy to like, if not love. He had never dared to imagine a woman like Lucretia.

There was Marcus to consider too. Felix had grown fonder of the boy than he ever expected when Marcus first wheedled him into giving boxing lessons. He could easily imagine adopting Marcus as his heir, if Lucretia didn't wish to have more children or if the gods didn't bless them with a son.

But no matter Felix's feelings, he was still uncertain of Lucretia's desires. Would she even entertain a proposal from him? What if she refused him for the second time?

Her rejection of his first proposal had been merely a snag in his old plans to overtake her business operations. But if she refused him again, when he truly wanted to marry her for *her*, not just her ships, it would crush him.

The thought of it now, of her possible rejection, was enough to make his stomach churn.

He stepped back from the bag, breathing hard, and passed a linen-wrapped hand over his face to wipe the sweat from his brow.

He wasn't brave enough to face the risk of Lucretia turning him down. What if she felt nothing for him? She clearly enjoyed their sexual exploration, but what if that was as far as it went for her?

He could have sworn he detected something deeper upon his return. She had seemed genuinely happy to see him, and she'd agreed to trust him with Marcus's safety on their upcoming voyage. That had to mean something. But what if it wasn't enough?

In this situation, too much boldness could ruin everything. A circumspect approach would be more prudent. So he would wait, try to suss out if she harbored any deeper feelings toward him. Once he was sure, once he was *certain*, he could attempt another proposal.

If she did reject him, it would fully cement his bachelorhood. He would find someone to adopt as his heir in the coming decades; perhaps Herminia would have a son. But if Lucretia didn't want to be his wife, he had no interest in anyone else.

# CHAPTER 27

"I HAVE A QUESTION for you," Lucretia said as she joined Felix for another dinner. They'd eaten first this time and spent the whole dinner talking. Felix had explained the route he and Marcus would take on their journey to Cyrene, coming up in three weeks, which led into a discussion of which wares were better acquired in Cyrene versus Alexandria.

But now, as their plates emptied, her mind turned to a different subject.

"Oh?" Felix said, tipping back his cup to drink the last of his wine.

"You have been excelling in your lessons," she began with a smile.

He shot her an intolerably smug grin. "I have, haven't I?"

She rolled her eyes. He was getting almost too good at pleasuring her, and he knew it. But this next thing she wanted to broach would no doubt require more instruction.

"I wondered if you might…that is, I'm not sure if…we haven't yet tried…" She flushed as the words tangled themselves in her mind. Why was she getting so flustered? She was the experienced one. She should not be rendered stammering and hesitant by the simple mention of…

He raised an eyebrow. "Yes?"

She took a deep breath and forced the words out. "If you wish to, er, attempt copulation, I think we could try that."

His pupils dilated, darkening his eyes to charcoal. "Are you sure?"

"I'm not the virgin here," she rejoined shortly. "It's nothing to me, so of course I'm sure."

*It's nothing to me.* That was a lie. Doing this with Felix would be much more meaningful than she let on. After all, Cornelius was the only man she had ever lain with, and that was a matter of protocol. It was right and proper for a husband and wife to lie together, to share the marital bed and conceive children.

But if she were to lie with Felix, that would have nothing to do with propriety. It would be entirely about want, about desire. It would be something selfish, something for her alone.

"In that case," Felix said, "I would be pleased to *attempt copulation* with you, Lucretia." A small smile played around his lips. "Though I hope I'm suitably experienced now that the stipulation of 'attempt' is not necessary."

"It's a different skillset," she warned him. "And for this, we may be better served in a bed. We've defiled these couches enough, I think."

He snorted. "I've had to start taking my other meals in the atrium due to all the associations this room has taken on." He rose from the couch and extended a hand to her.

She allowed him to help her to her feet. The firm press of his hand on hers sent a shiver down her arm. "I hope you won't have to start sleeping elsewhere after this."

With a chuckle, he led her from the room.

Felix's heart pounded as he escorted Lucretia to his bedroom. How many times had he longed for her in his bed, thirsted to be inside of her, for her to fully consume him?

He could hardly believe it was about to happen. Surely, at any moment, she would change her mind, think better of her plan.

But they reached the door to his bedroom without incident, and then he was closing the door behind them and she was still next to him, her hand in his. She hadn't disappeared in a puff of smoke or turned into a bird or otherwise escaped.

He lit a few lamps to brighten the space as she looked around. There wasn't much for her to see, as he spent little time in here: a comfortable bed against one wall, made up with a blue blanket and an assortment of pillows. A chest of drawers by the opposite wall, and a table and single chair which he used to shave.

She inhaled deeply, then walked over to the chest of drawers and opened the top one, in which lay several neatly folded tunics. She reached in and withdrew a dried green sprig of herbs. "Marjoram," she said, holding it up. "I was right. I thought I smelled that on you from time to time."

*She noticed my scent?* "Do you like it?"

She brought the sprig to her nose and took another deep breath. "I can't smell it without thinking of you."

Warmth bloomed inside him.

She returned the marjoram stem to the drawer and closed the distance between them. She glanced up at his face, then down, then around the room, shifting from foot to foot. Was it possible…could she be nervous? Despite her indifferent words in the dining room?

If she was nervous, that made two of them. As much as he wanted this, as much as desire was already coursing through him, he couldn't seem to steady his breathing or quell the tremor in his palms. It wasn't just the physical act that made his stomach tighten. He felt as if he were about to give her something he'd never be able to retrieve, a piece of himself that would be hers forever.

It was an unaccustomed feeling; he'd made a career out of exchanging, negotiating, trading one thing for another. Money for ships, one shipload of goods for another. Never before had he given part of himself with no hope of getting it back.

"One thing first," she said, meeting his eyes once more. "I have no wish to risk a pregnancy, so you'll need to withdraw. I don't expect you to master the timing right away, so for the first few times, I will be atop you. We will go slowly until you've acquired the necessary control."

Her words were as brisk and pragmatic as when Siro delivered a briefing, but the image of Lucretia riding him, soft thighs clasping his hips, her ample breasts bouncing, sent a burst of heat straight to his cock. "Very well."

He couldn't wait another moment before sliding his arms around her waist and pulling her close. "Does copulation usually begin with kissing?" he murmured, lowering his head to the curve of her neck.

She ran her fingers through his hair. "It can." Her voice trembled.

He kissed her neck, sucking the silky skin of her throat into his mouth until she gasped.

He pressed his body harder against her, which caused them to stumble back, until the wall stopped them. She knotted her fingers in his hair and pulled his head up, seeking his mouth. Their lips met in a messy tangle. She wrapped one leg around his, curving her body along his with delicious friction.

"Does copulation usually involve…" He paused to catch his breath, dizzied from the heady pleasure of kissing her. "A wall?" He wasn't entirely sure how the logistics would work, but his body was issuing a firm demand for him to ruck up her dress and sink into her then and there.

She giggled. "That's an advanced technique."

"What about…" Next to them was his chest of drawers, so he grabbed her around the waist and set her atop it. "A chest of drawers?"

She giggled again, wrapping her legs around his hips. "Let's master the bed first."

"As you wish." He lifted her from the chest and carried her over to the bed. He dumped her onto the mattress on her back, which earned him an indignant squeal.

He covered her mouth with another kiss, cutting off the sound, as he climbed on top of her. His hands worked efficiently to strip her of her dress, and a few moments later she was lying naked in his bed. He sat back on his heels to survey the sight, burning the image into his memory. A flush crept from her cheeks over her neck and collarbone, echoing the pink of her nipples. She looked as tempting as a nymph who had somehow found her way into a mortal's bed.

He did away with his tunic, tossing the bundle of cloth to the floor. Her gaze roved over his bare body, an amber heat lighting in her hazel eyes.

Her hand traced down her stomach to brush the reddish curls between her legs. "You'll need to use the skills from our previous lessons to make me ready."

He grinned, hoping he didn't look too much like a cat presented with a fat, shiny fish. "With pleasure."

He slid a hand down her thigh, and her legs parted for him, revealing those plush pink folds already shimmering with moisture. If he wasn't mistaken, she was well on the way to being ready without a single touch.

But he would not neglect such a pleasurable duty. He dragged his fingers over her, relishing how she twitched and squirmed. "You want to be ready...here?" He pressed one finger inside her.

Her head fell back with a sigh. "Yes."

"Ready to take my cock?" He slid his finger deeper, then added another.

She let out a soft moan. "I never taught you to talk that way."

"Some things don't need to be taught." He worked his fingers in and out, feeling how her tight muscles slowly relaxed around him. What would that warm, wet heat feel like wrapped around his cock? It seemed inconceivable that he might be moments away from finding out.

He spared a moment to briefly compare the thickness of his fingers to that of his cock, then slid a third finger into her.

"Oh!" Her hips flexed, and he matched the movement, finding the rhythm she liked.

With his free hand, he stroked the sensitive bud at the top of her sex. "Am I meant to make you climax before the act?"

"Not necessarily." Her voice was breathless, the words garbled.

"Good." He moved his fingers in a few light, teasing circles. "I want you desperate. Aching. I want to feel what it's like to be inside you when you're frantic with want." *Like me.* He increased the pace and pressure of his movements. Her muscles gave a spasmodic twitch around his fingers, and he slowed.

"Felix!" she moaned. "I'm ready. I'm ready now."

He gave her quim a pensive look. "I'm not sure. I think you require more preparation. You taught me not to rush, remember?" He played her with his fingers again, driving her pleasure high and then backing off when he felt her muscles begin to tense.

She let out a frustrated hiss. "I've taught you much too well."

He chuckled, but allowed her to sit up.

With surprising force, she pushed him flat on the bed and climbed on top of him, palms braced on his chest. His hands grazed her thighs as he looked up at her. She was as magnificent as he had imagined—all flushed curves and hazel eyes burning with lust.

She wrapped her hand around his cock, which gave a demanding throb that made Felix catch his breath. "Are you ready?" she asked.

"Yes," he hissed.

She anchored her hand at the base of his cock, then moved herself above him. Felix wanted to watch exactly how she positioned herself, but his eyes fluttered shut as soon as he felt the warm heat of her enveloping him.

His fingers sank into the flesh of her hips, gripping her as if that was the only thing tethering him to reality. She lowered herself slowly. She was somehow pleasurably slick and achingly tight at the same time, the sensation like nothing he had ever felt.

She settled all the way onto him with a little sigh. His hips flexed of their own accord, driving into her. "Fuck, Lucretia," he breathed. Now he understood why she wished to be on top their first time; he was already perilously close to losing control, and if he was atop her, he wasn't sure he'd be able to stop at the requisite moment.

"Good so far?" she murmured. She wiggled her hips, working him deeper.

He groaned. "Very good." The words were hideously inadequate, but he was fast losing his ability to compose a rational thought.

She leaned into her hands, still braced on his chest, and moved her hips up and down. The rhythm was slow, tantalizing, the friction delicious.

A familiar tingling pressure built at the base of his spine. He tightened his grip on her hips. "Lucretia," he ground out. "You may want to s-slow down..."

She ceased the motion. "Already?" She let out a dark, smug chuckle that did nothing to calm his ardor. "Perhaps we should return the focus to me, then." She removed one hand from his chest and slid it between her legs. Her back arched, hips angling forward as she touched herself. Each movement, no matter how small, sent stabs of pleasure through him. And when her muscles twitched around his cock—he had to bite his lip.

Given his tormenting of her earlier, it took little time for her to lose herself in pleasure. "Fuck," he grunted through gritted teeth as she shuddered atop him. Her quim was clenching in a way that seemed designed to make him lose control, and the writhing movements of her hips didn't help.

But somehow, he managed to hold on, and when the climax left her, she gazed down at him with a satisfied smile.

"That nearly killed me," he growled.

Her smile widened into a grin. "I'm sorry," she said with mock pity. "Will this make it up to you?" She leaned forward onto her hands and began to ride him. Once she established a slow, deliberate rhythm, it was easier to anticipate the movements, to breathe through them as he grew accustomed to the sensation. He wanted to make this last as long as possible, so he strove to gather every ragged thread of control he could.

But when she did something—he wasn't sure what—that changed the angle of connection and sent him even deeper into her, he knew all hope was lost. "Lucretia!" he managed.

The urgency in his voice must have been enough to warn her. She pulled herself off of him, and the absence of her warmth made him groan in near-anguish. It didn't last for long, though: a moment later, her mouth clasped around the head of his cock, her hand stroking the shaft.

The sight of her full, pink lips wrapped around his cock was enough to undo him once and for all. Finally, he allowed the pleasure to swell and burst, emptying himself into her waiting mouth. He might have cried out her name, or a curse, or an appeal to the gods—he wasn't sure.

The climax receded, and he was left panting and dizzied, trying fruitlessly to catch his breath. Lucretia settled herself next to him, running a soothing hand up and down his chest. "You're trembling," she murmured.

That made sense, given that he felt as if his soul had been ripped from his body, taken a quick journey to Elysium, and then been reattached.

She propped herself up on one elbow to survey him. "Was it all right? Your first time?"

"Dis," he swore. "If I'd known it could be that good…why did I wait so long?"

She chuckled. "You were waiting for me, weren't you? It may have disappointed with another." She lay back down next to him, stretching a warm arm over his shoulders.

"Did you find it passable?" He assumed mediocrity was the most he could hope for at this point, but he was determined to reach excellence with some practice.

"You lasted longer than I expected, for what it's worth." She nestled her head into his chest. "It was very passable." Her fingers stroked a sensitive place on his neck, which made his depleted cock give a twitch. "If you're able to try again in a bit, we may have the opportunity for some…lengthier practice."

"Give me a quarter of an hour," he said with fierce determination.

She laughed, the sound husky in his ear. "I'll find a water clock and hold you to that."

# CHAPTER 28

F ELIX HELD TO HIS word, which led to a much lengthier session that left both of them exhausted. He tried to convince her to stay the night, as he wanted nothing more than to fall asleep with her in his arms, but she wished to get home to Marcus, so he escorted her back and then returned home.

Heavy satisfaction weighed down his limbs as he traversed the streets between their houses. Dusk had fallen, late at this time of summer, and everyone's work was done for the day. Laughter and music echoed from the taverns he passed, and lights glowed from houses and apartment buildings as families gathered to share an evening meal together.

At that moment, he realized he would love nothing more than to return home to Lucretia and Marcus after the end of a tiring day. Lucretia, if she wished to keep up her work, would have had a long day of her own, and a picture rose in his mind: the two of them relaxing on a dining couch together, feeding each other morsels of food with weary contentment. Could there be anything better?

But tonight, he had to return to his lonely house, empty but for his unobtrusive staff.

His mind ran over the events of the earlier evening. He had been looking for a sign that Lucretia felt something deeper than lust for him. Had she given it to him tonight? Surely she wouldn't have let *anyone* do what they had just done, agreement or no. Surely she had offered this because she harbored a true attachment to him.

Even something as small as her appreciation of the marjoram with which he scented his clothes reinforced his conjecture. Suddenly, his mind was made up: he was going to propose to Lucretia.

Again.

At the end of a productive day of work, Lucretia returned home as the shadows began to lengthen in late afternoon. She visited the kitchen to obtain a pre-dinner snack and then planned to catch up on some weaving before the sunlight disappeared.

Only yesterday, she had finally divested Felix of his virginity. Already, she was eager to have him again. Not tonight, unfortunately, but they had another meeting set up for tomorrow evening. She couldn't wait to continue her debauching of him.

As she sat at her loom in the atrium, where the light was greatest, a knock came at the front door. Her household was busy with other tasks and Marcus had gone to the races with his friends after school—a rare break from his apprenticeship—so she rose and answered the knock herself.

Felix stood outside her house. "Good afternoon, Lucretia."

Lucretia blinked for a moment, taken aback, but stood aside to let him in. "Good afternoon."

This was strange. Felix had never visited her home. Was something wrong? Perhaps he'd had ill news from his family—could something be amiss with his sister or the new baby?

But he didn't look as if anything was wrong. Wearing a tunic of emerald green that looked very pleasing against his fair skin and dark hair, he followed his greeting with a smile. His bearing was relaxed, but there was an eager intensity to his eyes. This visit was odd, but it didn't seem to signal any mishap.

Seeing him here, looking composed and dignified to a fault, reminded her how undone and disheveled he'd been after their coupling. Cheeks flushed, hair tousled, barely able to form a coherent sentence...It had given her great pleasure to render him so thoroughly defiled.

"This is a surprise," Lucretia said. "You couldn't wait another day to see me?"

He slid his arms around her waist and pulled her close. "I couldn't." He lowered his head to kiss her, which she permitted for only a moment before breaking away.

"I'm in the middle of things," she chided teasingly. "You think you can just show up at my house, give me one charming smile, and I'll fall into bed with you?"

"You think my smile is charming?" He brushed his lips over her throat, making her shiver.

"Only as of recently. I used to find it irritatingly conceited."

He chuckled. His hands wandered up her torso to palm her breasts, fingers deftly locating her nipples.

She wanted to slap his hands away, but his light stroking of her nipples sent tingles straight to her quim, and it was difficult to think. Perhaps she could spare the time for a brief tumble…maybe she could teach him a new position…

"You've never visited me at home before," she said.

"Well, this is not a business matter, and I thought it more appropriate to see you here," he murmured, breath tickling the crook of her neck.

She curled one leg around him, drawing him close enough to feel his growing arousal against her. "Oh?"

The noise of the front door opening made her break off. A shock of horror ran through her. *Marcus. Oh no. Oh no.*

She jumped away from Felix as fast as she could, disentangling their bodies and putting distance between them.

But the front door was only a few arms' lengths away, and Marcus was already entering the atrium.

He stopped short as Lucretia was in the midst of righting the fallen sleeve of her dress.

"Marcus!" she gasped, trying to force her voice to sound light and cheerful. Instead, it came out shrill, with a distinctly guilty edge.

By the confused, horrified look on Marcus's face, she knew he had seen them. Or at least seen enough. Lucretia tried fruitlessly to summon the words to explain, but nothing came out.

Marcus's eyes flicked between Lucretia and Felix, who had retreated a few steps, as if trying to fade into the background. His gaze settled on Felix. He marched forward, drew back his right arm, and landed a vicious punch to Felix's nose.

The impact sent Felix reeling backward, hitting the floor hard on his backside as he clutched his nose with one hand.

"Marcus!" Lucretia exclaimed. "What have you done?"

Marcus rounded on her, fists clenched and eyes blazing with fury. "I saw him!" he spat. "I saw his hands all over you—"

"Fucking Dis!" Felix groaned, still on the floor, his hands quickly becoming slippery with blood.

"Watch your mouth," Lucretia snapped. "I hope you don't regularly use that language around my son."

Felix shot Marcus a baleful glare. "Only when he *breaks my fucking nose.*"

Lucretia returned her attention to Marcus, attempting to soothe his rage. "Sweetheart, I don't know what you think you saw, but—"

"Don't lie to him, Lucretia," Felix interrupted. "Marcus, it was exactly what you saw. I love your mother, and I came to ask her to marry me."

*Love. Marry?* There wasn't enough time for his words to sink in.

"Marry?" Marcus yelled. He launched himself at Felix again, and Lucretia had to grab the neck of his tunic to stymie another attack, her head spinning from everything happening at once.

"Marcus. Calm down." She kept a firm grip on her son's tunic. He was probably more than capable of breaking her hold on him, but despite his anger, he allowed her to restrain him.

When he stilled, she released his tunic and clasped his shoulders, forcing him to meet her eyes. "Please let me speak with Felix in private. I will handle this."

"But he said he wants to marry—"

"I will handle it," she repeated, firming her voice. "Please go to your room."

"Fine," Marcus muttered. He gave Felix one last threatening scowl, then left the atrium.

Lucretia turned to Felix. "Let's get you cleaned up." *And then we can talk.*

The ruckus had drawn several servants to the atrium, and Lucretia asked for cloth and hot water to be brought to the dining room. Felix rose to his feet, one hand still clasping his nose, and she led him to the dining room.

"Surely you've had a broken nose before, with all the boxing you do," she said as she dampened a cloth and helped him clean his bloodied hands. Anything to avoid talking about what he'd said earlier.

"Only once." He gingerly poked his nose with his index finger, then winced. "There is a tacit agreement among those who box for recreation to avoid any permanently damaging shots, to the best of our ability." He sighed. "I suppose I only have myself to blame, teaching him to throw a punch like that."

Together, they mopped up the majority of the blood, and Felix held a clean cloth to his nose to staunch any further bleeding, but it seemed to have slowed. The front of his tunic, however, was saturated.

"I can give you one of Cornelius's old tunics to wear home, if you wish," Lucretia said. "So you don't look like the victim of an attempted murder."

"Thank you, but I'm not ready to leave yet." He reached for one of her hands. "I meant what I said to Marcus. I came here to ask you to marry me."

"Felix," she murmured, unable to meet his gaze. "I don't know—I don't think I can—"

"Hear me out before you say anything." He tightened his grip on her hand, as if worried she would pull it away. "We could be the perfect team, Lucretia. Between your network in the western Mediterranean and mine in the east, we could have everything we've ever wanted."

She raised an eyebrow. "Everything *you* ever wanted. I never thirsted for total control. I am happy with the way things are." Exerting gentle force, she withdrew her hand from his grasp. "We've covered this ground before, Felix. I have no wish to marry, and certainly not for mercenary reasons."

"It's not mercenary," Felix objected. "I *love* you, Lucretia."

That word sent a flutter through her, but she ignored it. "You love my ships. That's what you've always wanted. I have no desire to give up my independence to a husband, even you. Nothing has changed."

"Everything has changed!" He leaned close to her, lowering his voice even though they were the only two in the room. "Lucretia, I *know*. I know about your guardian. I found out when I tried to visit him on my trip to—"

Lucretia shot to her feet, fists clenching. "*What?*"

When Cornelius died and she took over his business operations, she had decided to take a calculated risk—giving the authorities the name of a deceased male relative to serve as her guardian. She even went so far as to forge a letter from the man, indicating his acceptance of the role and his assent to her conducting her business as she saw fit. No one had ever bothered to check, just as she expected.

No one, except Felix.

He rose too. "I found out, and I didn't say a word. If I hadn't changed—if you hadn't changed me—do you think I would have kept silent?"

Lucretia's head spun. She backed toward the wall and braced an arm against it. Felix took a step toward her, concern flickering across his bruised face, but she held out a hand. "Don't touch me."

"Don't you see what I'm telling you?" he demanded. "I will keep your secrets."

She exhaled a long, shaky breath. "How did you find out?" Her voice was flat, too shocked even to summon the energy to rage at him.

Felix shifted, crossing and uncrossing his arms. "Long ago—before our truce—I set Siro to find out who your legal guardian was. It was underhanded, I know, but my intent was to convince him to withdraw his consent for you to manage your business."

She felt as if she'd been punched in the stomach. "You—you would have done that to me?" She couldn't even look at him. This man she'd grown to trust, to *like*—he had plotted against her to that extent? Nausea swirled in her gut, and she swallowed hard.

"That was before," he insisted. "Before our truce. We were both sabotaging each other, remember?"

She shook her head. "You were trying to ruin me. I was only defending myself."

"Well, yes," he admitted. "But then, like I said, I found out your guardian didn't exist, and I said nothing."

Her hand, braced against the wall, curled into a fist. "You said you discovered that on your trip to visit your sister. But that was *after* our truce. So why were you trying to locate my guardian then?" She drew in a sharp breath through her teeth.

"You never intended to hold to the truce. You wanted to destroy me regardless."

"No, I didn't—" Felix reached for her, but she shoved him away. "That's my point. I said nothing."

"You should never have found out in the first place!" she shouted. "You should never have been looking!"

He flinched. "Perhaps that's true. But you're not hearing what I'm saying. I love you, Lucretia. You're the only woman I have ever wanted."

"You have a strange way of showing it," she spat. "Let's say I agree to marry you. I give it a month before you try to convince me that it would be safer for me to transfer all my assets into your name. Just in case someone should find out about my guardian, even though I'm married now—they could still make trouble. Still question everything I've worked for. So of course it would be safest to give you full control. Which is what you always wanted, isn't it?"

His mouth opened and closed. The lack of an instant denial sent a stab of pain through her heart.

"I-I wasn't thinking that far ahead—" he stammered.

"Liar," she snarled. "You do nothing if it doesn't benefit you. I bet even with Marcus, you thought giving him boxing lessons would reveal something you could use against me."

"No!" he protested.

She ignored him. "I know you will hold this secret over my head for the rest of our lives, whether I am married to you or not. So let me maintain what little independence I have managed to scrape together."

His jaw worked, as if he was trying to summon more words.

She didn't let him. "We have nothing more to say to each other. *Ever.*"

His shoulders slumped, and he turned and left the dining room. Dimly, she heard the front door open and close as he let himself out.

The sound sent a pang of loss through her, turning her rage to a deep melancholy. She lowered herself to sit on the nearest couch. Felix's betrayal seemed to have sapped all her energy.

She should have known better than to think she and Felix could be anything more than rivals. He couldn't stop himself from trying to win, at any cost. He might believe he loved her; their couplings had grievously muddied the waters there. But a man who loved her wouldn't scheme against her, wouldn't use her most carefully kept secret to try to manipulate her into marriage.

Felix loved no one but himself, and she would not allow herself to forget it again.

# CHAPTER 29

FELIX TRAVERSED THE STREETS in a fog. The ache in his nose was nothing compared to the searing pain in his chest.

How had that gone so terribly wrong?

Lucretia hadn't *listened* to him, that was how. She hadn't heard how much he loved her, how he wanted them to be together forever.

No—she had heard him. She had just heard all the things he didn't want her to.

She heard how he'd schemed against her. How he'd disregarded the terms of their truce. How he'd bragged about *not* doing something reprehensible.

He could explain it away as just business, but he would be lying to himself. It hadn't been just business with Lucretia for a long time, despite both of their best efforts to pretend otherwise.

And now he'd ruined everything.

Instead of going home, he walked to the harbor. He stood on one of the piers, feeling the sea breeze whip at his bloodied clothing. A spray of salty water from a wave hitting the side of the pier stung his eyes.

Further out in the harbor, large ships—several of them his—sat at anchor in the deeper water. Little boats ferried goods and people to and from the ships. Smaller vessels were docked at the various piers dotting the edge of the harbor, each with a hive of activity surrounding it as goods were loaded, unloaded, inspected, and haggled over before being transported down the Tiber toward Rome.

*This* was what he'd worked for—this relentless cycle of buying and selling, profit and risk. He'd been willing to sacrifice so much for a chance at a bit more money in his coffers. He had betrayed Lucretia, the woman he loved, out of nothing but greed and the desire to win.

Now, he would have gladly given up all his ships if he could take back what he'd done.

But there was no way to undo something so heinous. His greed had ruined everything between them.

Maybe she was right: how could he be certain that one day, sooner or later, he wouldn't have tried to persuade her to transfer all of her assets to his control? That hadn't been his motivation to marry her, but he knew himself well enough to know it wouldn't have been long before the idea occurred to him. He might not have been able to resist the prospect of getting everything he wanted: Lucretia as his wife *and* control over her ships.

That was why he'd stammered and hesitated at her accusation. He hadn't been able to summon an instant, convincing denial because as soon as she'd raised it, he knew it sounded exactly like something he would do.

Lucretia deserved better than him. She deserved a man who would support her, not scheme against her. If he truly loved her, then he had to recognize he wasn't right for her. This was one scenario where there was no way to win, nothing he could plan or scheme or negotiate to get what he wanted. For the first time, he'd lost.

After Felix left, Lucretia took a moment to gather herself. She could feel the heavy pressure of tears building in her nose and behind her eyes, but she staved them off. Felix didn't deserve her tears.

She intended to go speak to Marcus, but he beat her to it. His head poked around the doorframe of the dining room. "He left?" Marcus asked.

Lucretia wiped a hand hastily over her eyes. "Yes."

Marcus entered the room with hesitant steps. "I heard yelling."

"Yes," she said again. "I rejected his proposal."

"Oh," Marcus said, relief coloring his voice. "Well, everything's all right then, isn't it?"

She forced a smile, rising to her feet. "Yes. Everything's all right." Marcus didn't need to know of everything else that had transpired between her and Felix. "But you shouldn't have hit him, even so."

He adopted a look of wide-eyed innocence. "Shouldn't I have?"

She shook her head firmly. "It was impulsive and reckless. You can't go around punching people with no provocation."

"There was provocation!" Marcus objected indignantly. "He was *touching* you and—"

Lucretia folded her arms over her chest. "Did I ask for your help?"

"Well, no, but—"

"Did I look distressed at the time?"

He chewed his lip. "I-I didn't notice—"

"Exactly," she said. "You didn't take the time to suitably assess the situation. The impulse to defend someone is all well and good, but it must be properly applied. If you're going to learn to fight, you also need to learn when to do nothing."

Marcus listened to her words without meeting her gaze. "I thought I was helping," he said in a small voice.

"I know." She stepped forward and folded him into her arms. Felix was nothing to her anymore. Marcus was all that truly mattered.

He allowed the embrace and even hugged her back for a brief moment before withdrawing.

"We needn't worry about it any more," she said, giving him a gentle smile. "It's over." The words sat like lead in her stomach, but she refused to let her smile waver.

Felix jumped to his feet in surprise when Marcus trotted into his office the following afternoon. The boy looked so carefree, Felix wondered if he'd forgotten about the events of yesterday.

"Marcus," Felix managed through the astonishment. "What are you doing here?"

Marcus shrugged and seated himself in the chair opposite Felix's desk with languid ease. "I usually come here after school, if we're not meeting at the gymnasium."

"But—yesterday—"

"Mother told me what happened. She rejected your proposal. So that's that."

Felix held a deep envy of the boy's nonchalance about the situation, though it was clear that Lucretia had only given Marcus the abridged version. Felix had a feeling that if Marcus knew everything, his healing nose would rapidly be under renewed attack. "Does your mother know you're here?"

"Dunno. She didn't tell me not to come."

*She likely thought she didn't have to.* "I'm not sure she would be happy with you being here."

Marcus ignored him, instead surveying Felix's bruised face. Felix knew it was a rather hideous sight: a black eye had bloomed overnight, and his nose was puffy and tender.

"I'm sorry about your nose," Marcus said. "I shouldn't have hit you."

Felix accepted the apology with a nod. "For what it's worth, it was a well-executed punch. Though I'd have preferred a different target."

Marcus beamed at the praise. "Do you think I can start fighting real people at the gymnasium now?"

Thus far, Felix had only permitted Marcus to practice on the leather boxing bags with occasional matches against Felix himself, fearing that another opponent would pummel the boy into the dust. "Perhaps. But I'm not sure our lessons should continue."

Marcus nodded. "Right, we have to prepare for our trip. I can't believe we leave next week!"

Felix pressed his lips together. He hadn't thought this would be a conversation he needed to have with Marcus, but clearly Lucretia had been very generous with her version of yesterday's events. "Marcus, I don't think you can accompany me to Cyrene anymore."

His face dropped. "But...why?"

Felix's insides twisted. Marcus had been so excited about this trip, and it pained him to take it away. "I have a feeling your mother will no longer want you to come."

"But she said I could," Marcus insisted. "She agreed to it. Remember?"

"Yes, but that was before...all of this. I believe her rejection of my proposal served to implicitly withdraw her consent."

Marcus absorbed this with a long, considering look. "Do *you* still want me to come?"

Felix knew he should refuse, so at least then Lucretia wouldn't be the sole villain in this scenario. But he couldn't bring himself to distress Marcus, to break the trust that had been growing between them. Besides, Felix also had been looking forward to the trip. There were so many things he could teach Marcus, so many opportunities to broaden his knowledge.

"I do want you to come," he finally admitted. "But you need to discuss it once more with your mother."

"Fine." Marcus let out a resigned sigh. "I'll do that."

"Good." Felix knew that, if given the opportunity, Lucretia would firmly forbid Marcus from ever seeing Felix again, much less going on a long journey together. So this would likely be their last time together. Another pang of regret hit him. His actions had deprived him not just of Lucretia, but of Marcus as well.

# CHAPTER 30

"**Y**OU WANT TO WHAT?" Lucretia demanded as Marcus faced her in their garden. Her loom sat between them, linen fabric stretched across its warp threads. She was taking a break from work to weave some cloth, as Marcus would need new tunics soon with the way he was growing.

Marcus set his jaw in a familiar stubborn expression. "I want to go to Cyrene with Felix. You already said I could."

"That was *before*." Until now, she hadn't even realized she should have forbid Marcus from seeing Felix again. She had assumed Marcus wouldn't even have wanted to continue his apprenticeship, but he must have a more forgiving nature than she realized—especially as he knew only a fraction of the truth.

"All he did was propose. He's done it before, hasn't he? Why does anything have to change?" He threw up his hands.

Her heart clenched at the gesture of frustration. That was exactly what Cornelius used to do whenever he was fed up with something, whether it was a delayed shipment, an uncooperative supplier, or an invitation to a dinner party he didn't want to attend.

"If Father was here," Marcus continued, "I wouldn't have to go with Felix in the first place. He would have taken me."

A hard ball of sorrow settled in the pit of her stomach. Finally, she started to understand that this might be about more than just the prospect of an exciting journey. If she forbade Marcus from going on this trip, or indeed from continuing his apprenticeship with Felix, she would force him to lose another relationship, just like he'd lost his father. Of course, his relationship with Felix was nothing like that of a father, but it was still a relationship. They seemed to have become something close to friends.

She had to admit that he'd been thriving under Felix's influence. He wasn't stealing money or getting into fights—perhaps now because the other boys knew he could fight back. He was learning the business he would eventually inherit from her. And there had been moments of warmth between them that she'd been missing since he was a child. He'd been adrift since his father died, and something about Felix seemed finally to have settled him.

She focused on finishing her current row of weaving. The problem was, she no longer trusted Felix, and thus couldn't bring herself to let Marcus go off with him for weeks in a strange land.

Then again, trusting Felix with her heart was an altogether different matter than trusting him with her son's safety. Perhaps, no matter what had happened between them, Felix could still be a careful steward with Marcus's wellbeing.

Her original reasons for agreeing to the trip came back to her. It would be an invaluable learning opportunity for Marcus, and it could only benefit him to increase his experience of the world. She couldn't deny him that just because of her falling out with Felix.

She chewed her lip as she untangled a small knot in her yarn, considering.

Marcus gave an impatient huff. "Well?"

She summoned a stern look. "Leave it with me for a day. I will let you know what I decide."

The next day, Lucretia looped her arm through Dihya's as they walked away from their office. Their homes were in the same direction for several blocks before their paths would diverge. Twilight had fallen, but the sun's warmth hadn't yet abandoned the air.

Lucretia's other arm supported a basket piled high with delicacies from Caeso. He knew the broad strokes of her rift with Felix, and he'd insisted on plying her with his finest wares, assuring her that good bread and pastries could heal any wound.

"Caeso was much too kind," she said as she adjusted the weight of the basket.

Dihya shot her a sympathetic glance as they rounded a corner. "He only wants to help. And I fear the only way he knows how to help is by stuffing you with baked goods." Dihya raised her eyebrows. "Unless you want me to have him poison Felix? That option is still on the table, you know. I really think Caeso would do it this time."

Lucretia chuckled. "Thank you, but no. Felix doesn't deserve that."

"I disagree," Dihya muttered darkly.

Thinking of Felix made her stomach tighten, as if in anticipation of pain. She'd be happy never to lay eyes on him again, but after the conversation with Marcus yesterday, she knew she had to see him at least once more. She needed to discuss the matter of the journey face to face. That was the only way she'd know for sure if Felix could still be trusted with Marcus.

But for the moment, she allowed herself to think of pleasanter matters. "Have you set a date for the wedding yet?"

"We have!" Dihya's hand gave an excited bounce where it rested on Lucretia's arm. "Two months from now, the tenth of October. I don't mind waiting. It will give me time to weave my bridal garments, and we need to find somewhere new to live. Both of our apartments are too small for three people. Caeso wants to buy a house. He's been saving money!"

Lucretia smiled at the elation in her friend's voice. "That's wonderful."

"I met his mother for the first time the other day." Dihya's mouth twisted in distaste. "Horrid woman. She looked down her nose at me the entire time. You should have seen the look on her face when I spoke a word or two in Berber to Tadla in front of her." Dihya gave an irritated shudder. "If anyone needs poisoning, it's her."

Lucretia snorted. "I'll make sure to keep her occupied at the wedding so you don't have to speak to her."

"You have my blessing to lock her in a closet," Dihya pronounced.

They'd reached the street where their paths parted, so Lucretia bid Dihya goodbye with a kiss on the cheek. Beneath her happiness for Dihya, a trace of melancholy lingered. Dihya had found a new love, someone who treasured her. Whereas Lucretia had only managed to get her heart broken by a man she never should have become entangled with.

And now she had to see that man once again, which was the last thing she wanted to do.

Lucretia went home, dropped off the weighty basket of baked goods, then continued reluctantly to Felix's house. Better to get this encounter over with.

A few moments after she knocked on Felix's door, a servant pulled it open, recognized her, and offered to show her in, but she refused. "I would like to meet with Lucius Avitus Felix outside." His house held far too many memories that would only cloud her judgment.

The young man nodded and withdrew.

When the door opened next, Felix was there. It had only been two days since they last parted, but the sight of him still sent a pang through her. His nose and left eye were mottled with purple-yellow bruises, and Lucretia suppressed a wince.

He surveyed her with his old aloofness, his gray eyes remaining dispassionate and chilled. No warmth sparked in his gaze, and his expression was as blank and implacable as a concrete wall. "You refuse to step foot in my house?"

She met his coolness with as much tranquility as she could muster. "It's a pleasant evening. I thought it better to take a walk." At least, if they were walking, she wouldn't have to look directly at him.

"Very well." He left the house, closing the door behind him. "What do you want?"

Her shoulders tensed at his rudeness as they began to walk. He was the one who had transgressed—he had some gall to address her so brusquely. "You must know Marcus still wishes to go to Cyrene with you."

"I assume you have forbidden it?" His voice was clipped, as if every syllable cost him something.

She shot him a sidelong glance as they turned a corner. They had set no destination, but by some unspoken agreement they seemed to be heading in the direction of the harbor. "Not yet. I don't wish Marcus to suffer because of our…disagreement." *Because you betrayed me, and broke my heart.*

"You are…a good mother," he said in a begrudging tone.

She ruthlessly quashed the warmth that rose within her at the compliment. Felix's opinions on her parenting meant nothing to her. "I need to know, first, if you even want him to accompany you. Or to continue his apprenticeship at all. If you don't wish to have anything more to do with him, tell me honestly, and I'll put a stop to it." *Even if Marcus hates me for it.*

Felix was silent for a moment as they navigated a cluster of people queuing at a food stall. The scent of spiced meat wafted through the air, tickling her nostrils.

"He's making good progress," he finally said. "It would be a waste to stop now."

"I can tell he's making progress in boxing, if nothing else," she said with a tiny smile he wouldn't be able to see. "I did reprimand him for hitting you." *Though you may have deserved it.*

"He apologized."

His curt, icy tone irritated her. It made her feel driven to charm and smile, to soften and placate him, though he deserved none of her warmth or smiles. He should be groveling on his knees for what he'd done. But he seemed to feel no remorse.

They reached the harbor, where merchants and sailors hurried to finish the day's work before dark, and walked out along one of the long jetties that extended into the water.

At the end of it, Lucretia turned to face Felix. "Can I still trust you to take care of him?" Her eyes searched his face, seeking any scrap of benevolence. She leaned back against the flimsy wooden rail behind her, which served as an insubstantial barrier between the wooden dock and the water beneath.

"You can," he said. "I'll swear an oath to any god you choose not to let any harm come to him."

She considered for a moment, leaning her weight more fully against the rickety wood behind her.

The wood creaked, groaned, and then suddenly disappeared. Lucretia barely had time to take a breath before her body lurched backward toward the water. Her arms flailed.

Felix's hand caught her forearm, tugging her upright, away from the edge of the dock. Her body collided with his, and his arms braced her shoulders, steadying her. A rush of warmth flooded her, but she couldn't luxuriate in the pleasure of his touch. That was all over.

"Someone should really fix that," she murmured breathlessly as she found her footing and stepped away from him.

"I'll have a word with the harbor authorities." A strange instability colored his voice.

She glanced up at him. His icy mask had slipped, and he was gazing down at her with the intensity she remembered from their lessons, as if she was the only thing in the world that mattered to him. Sorrow, pain, and regret swirled in his gray eyes, the emotion so piercing it took her breath away.

Then he dropped his hands from her shoulders, and the emotion vanished, replaced by cool blankness. She realized his ungracious manner was hiding a deep well of pain. He did feel remorse about what happened between them. He just didn't know how to acknowledge it.

Her gut told her that Marcus would be safe with him. Marcus had been longing for this trip, and it would be cruel to deprive him of it.

"Marcus may join you," she finally said. "But I'm going to require that oath first."

# CHAPTER 31

FELIX THOUGHT MARCUS'S NECK was at risk of breaking from how quickly he was turning his head in every direction, trying to absorb all of the sights in Cyrene. Different languages flew all around them in the harbor district: Greek, Latin with several different accents, Aramaic, Punic, Coptic, and even something that might have been Gaulish. A hot, dry breeze blew over them, a reminder of the endless desert that lay to the south. But here on the coast, the land was green, with mountains in the distance overlooking the sea.

The nine-day voyage had passed smoothly. They'd stopped in Regium, at the southernmost tip of the Italian peninsula, to resupply, then left Italy behind to cross the great expanse of sea southwest to Cyrene. Marcus experienced some seasickness at the beginning of their journey, but rallied quickly and soon struck up several friendships with the sailors. They taught him how to harness the angle of the wind to attain the most efficient speed and how all of the various lines and ropes worked. He took to it with great enthusiasm. Felix worried the boy might have discovered a new passion. Lucretia might not be pleased if her son chose to spend his life on the seas.

His mind had returned to Lucretia with unrelenting frequency during their trip. There was little else to think about during the

long days of staring at nothing but an expanse of blue-gray water.
He knew he should have apologized to her—or at least tried to—at
their last meeting, but really, what was the point? It wouldn't
fix what he had done. It wouldn't make her love him. It would
only assuage his own guilt, and he didn't deserve to seek her
forgiveness.

The best thing he could do for her was guide Marcus's growth
and learning, to give her a son worthy of inheriting what she
built.

Marcus had disappeared into the crowds ahead of him, but now
reappeared, doubling back at a jog. "There's a ship over there
carrying silk from Serica!" he exclaimed. "Can we go see it? I've
never seen a Serican person before."

"The crew won't be from Serica," Felix said, to Marcus's disappointment. "The goods will have changed hands in India, then
Parthia, then sailed here from Syria. But we can take a look." Silk
had one of the highest profit margins of all luxury goods due to
its rarity. No one but the people of its far eastern country knew
how it was produced, and its fineness was highly sought by the
wealthy.

Marcus led him to the ship. A crowd milled around the dock
next to the gangplank which led onto the vessel, and even more
people clustered on the deck. It seemed to be one of the more
popular cargoes in the harbor, and Felix would have some competition if he hoped to purchase any.

They eased their way through the crowd and onto the ship.
The wares must be held below deck, and a steady stream of people
filtered down the narrow stairs. "Let's wait for the crowd to thin."
Felix pulled Marcus over to an unoccupied spot by the mast.

"See?" Felix said in a low voice, directing Marcus's gaze toward the sailors dotted around the deck. "The crew is not from Serica."

Marcus absorbed this with a nod. "Well, they must be from somewhere rough. They look as if they've seen some excitement."

Marcus was right; though every crew had its share of grizzled members, it seemed that each sailor on deck displayed an assortment of scars and the remnants of past broken noses. Felix's own nose, still healing, throbbed in sympathy. The crew member nearest Felix sported a tattoo on his forehead of the Greek letter *delta*, marking him as a former slave, tattooed either in punishment for disobedience or after an escape attempt.

It wasn't unusual to have a crew comprised of men with fraught pasts.

The more unusual thing was the way the sailors were positioned, which Felix noticed as his gaze passed over each of them. They seemed to be stationed at regular intervals around the deck railing. Many had their hands on the weapons tucked into their belts, and they surveyed the crowds on deck with forbidding glares, as if the people aboard were not merchants wanting to buy their cargo but their enemies in some way.

On the dock, another set of crew members shepherded more and more people aboard.

A trickle of unease ran down Felix's spine, a gut feeling he couldn't quite find a reason for. "Marcus," he murmured. "I think we should disembark."

"We haven't even seen the silk yet," Marcus protested.

Felix hesitated, his gaze sweeping over the deck as he tried to assess the situation. Perhaps he was overreacting, but his intuition was sending up a flare that something wasn't right. He didn't want to reveal his worries to Marcus in case the boy panicked, especially if he was wrong and there was nothing amiss. "We can come back later if they're still here."

Felix took a step toward the gangplank, but there were too many people in the way, having just been shoved aboard by two crew members—crew members who were now working to remove that very gangplank.

Breath stuttered in Felix's throat as the reality of the situation crashed over him. "Hey!" he shouted at the sailors.

His shout drew the attention of the others on deck, who looked to the gangplank and realized that their mode of exit was being removed.

The brawny and menacing sailors jumped into action. Several let down the lines that held the sails, causing the huge swaths of canvas to unfurl. Others dealt with anyone protesting, doling punches and drawing their swords, daggers, or clubs.

"*Fuck*," Felix hissed.

If he wasn't mistaken, they were in the process of being kidnapped by pirates.

He had heard of events like this before: pirates were known to lure unsuspecting people onto their ship at a port, then sail away before anyone could escape. Their victims would be sold into slavery for a tidy profit.

"What's going on?" Marcus demanded, his voice wavering with fear.

*Lucretia is going to gut me if these pirates don't do it first.*

He had to master himself. There was no time for panic. Felix grabbed Marcus's elbow, mind racing. The ship had already pulled back from the dock, putting distance between them and land. Chaos reigned on the deck as people panicked.

Most of the turmoil was concentrated on the side of the boat closest to the dock. The stern of the ship was comparatively empty. Felix dragged Marcus to an empty spot by the railing. They were already at least thirty feet from the dock, the gap widening by the moment.

A sailor spotted them and started toward them, perhaps guessing what Felix was about to do. There was only a moment in which to act, so Felix wasted no time in shoving Marcus hard over the railing.

With a shocked yell, the boy fell into the water, disappearing briefly beneath the surface. "Swim!" Felix shouted when Marcus's head reappeared, arms flailing. He'd seen Marcus swim in the pool at the gymnasium, and knew he was more than capable of covering the short distance back to the dock.

Felix moved to leap after him, but an iron hand closed over his shoulder, and a fist smashed into his gut.

# CHAPTER 32

F ELIX COLLAPSED TO THE deck, choking and gasping for air.
The sailor who had punched him hauled him to his feet,
then began to drag him toward the stairs that led below deck.

"Wait," Felix gasped. He forced air to enter his lungs and
spoke Greek, as it was more common in this part of the world.
"I am a Roman citizen." His voice was weak and breathless. "A
*wealthy* Roman citizen."

The pirate paused. "How wealthy?" His Greek had the lilt of
an unfamiliar accent.

Calculations ran through Felix's mind at lightning speed.
Of course everyone knew the story of the young Gaius Julius
Caesar having been kidnapped by pirates fifty years ago. The
pirates had demanded a ransom of twenty talents of silver, and
Caesar had insisted on it being increased to fifty, to reflect his
position in one of the best families of Rome.

Felix didn't have fifty talents, so he'd use the pirates' original
ransom demand of twenty as a starting point. Felix estimated
that he was worth about half of a Julius Caesar, as his own
lineage was not quite as vaunted, so that would come out to
about ten talents. But that was fifty years ago, and he would
need to account for inflation, so perhaps twelve talents was an
appropriate offer.

"I will pay twelve talents of silver for my safe release," he finally said.

He knew he'd offered the right number when the pirate's eyes lit with greed. "Where is your money?"

"Ostia," Felix answered.

The pirate glowered. "Too far. We are bound for Crete."

"Fifteen talents, then," Felix said desperately. He could go no higher; fifteen talents would empty his accounts. But if he ended up in Crete, a notorious haven for pirates, he'd be sold into slavery and might never make it back to Italy. More calculations rushed through his brain. "You just captured, what, two dozen people? They'll sell for five hundred denarii each, on average. So that's about twelve thousand denarii for selling all these people."

He paused a moment, as the pirate's eyes were glazing over during his calculations. "In contrast, one talent of silver is worth six thousand denarii on its own. And I am offering you fifteen talents."

Felix waited for the numbers to sink in. Handing over fifteen talents of silver would very nearly bankrupt him. It would wipe out the entire fortune he had built over the years of his business. He might have to sell a few ships to cover costs until he could rebuild.

But his choice was clear: give up his fortune, or lose his freedom.

Nine very unpleasant days later, the pirate ship pulled into a secluded cove south of Ostia. Felix surveyed the rocky coast with exhausted relief. He had been treated better than the rest of the pirates' victims, those destined for slavery. Felix had been kept on his own in a different part of the hold and even allowed up to the deck for fresh air once or twice a day. Now, he stood against the rail, the breeze on his face a welcome relief from the fetid, airless hold.

Pirates now weren't as massive of a problem as they used to be, before Felix's birth. He had heard stories of how they used to effectively rule the Mediterranean, making trade nearly impossible and travel a serious peril. Pompeius Magnus had led a successful campaign against the pirates about forty years ago, but the great general hadn't fully rid the Mediterranean of their incursions—he only reined them in.

The unfortunate truth was that Rome needed the pirates to a certain degree. Pirates provided a steady flow of slaves, and slaves were essential to the functioning of the state's economy. So the pirates were allowed to operate, as long as they didn't become too bothersome.

At least Marcus had been spared this. If Marcus had boarded their ship and returned immediately, he must be almost about to arrive in Ostia as well. Felix hoped Lucretia wouldn't be too furious with him. He had, after all, saved Marcus.

As Felix lingered on the deck, the man he'd come to know as the leader of the pirates approached him. He bore a mangled scar on his left cheek, which Felix suspected was the result of attempting to cover up a slave brand. "Where will we find your money?" the captain asked, speaking Greek.

"Let me write a message to my secretary, Siro," Felix replied. "I can give directions on where to find him. He will only supply the money if given a message in my own hand."

The captain grunted, then shouted an order to another pirate nearby. A few moments later, a wax tablet and writing stylus were brought.

Felix balanced the tablet on the rail to write a short message.

*Lucius Avitus Felix to Siro—Unfortunately I ran afoul of pirates in Cyrene. Marcus is safe, should be back in Ostia any day now. I have agreed on a ransom of fifteen talents of silver for my release. Please assemble the money accordingly.*

He gave the message to one of the pirates, with instructions on how to find Siro. Luckily, Siro was well known in the port, and nearly anyone would be able to point him out.

The messenger rowed to shore in a small boat, and Felix sat back to wait. His mind turned to Lucretia, as it never failed to do. He would see her again, and Marcus. He would have the chance to beg for her forgiveness, as he should have done earlier. She might not forgive him, but at least he could try.

He thought of the people who'd been captured along with him, who didn't have fifteen talents of silver to ransom themselves. They all had friends, families, lovers whom they would never see again.

An unfamiliar feeling welled in his chest. It wasn't fair that his money had saved him from such a fate, but that was how the world worked.

Unless…there was a way for his money to save more than just him.

His mind went back to the shipwreck he'd visited with Lucretia. She had insisted on him setting aside money for those left widowed or orphaned by his sailors' deaths. She cared about people, even those she'd never met. If she were here, she'd no doubt be compelled to help the other captives in any way she could.

The pirate captain was still out on deck, so Felix waved a hand to get his attention.

"When my money arrives," Felix said once the man approached, "I want you to free everyone. Let them all go in Ostia." The pirate began to snarl a denial, but Felix kept talking. "I know, I know, you want to sell them in Crete. But the most you'll be able to get for them is twelve thousand altogether. I'm paying fifteen talents. Which is ninety thousand denarii. That's a fine deal for twenty or so people."

The captain narrowed his eyes.

Felix pressed his advantage. "Imagine sailing away from Ostia with an empty hold. No captives to feed. Free to follow the wind wherever you wish. You could do another round of plundering in the time it would have taken you to get to Crete and complete twenty sales. And you never know, a few people might die between here and Crete, so you'd lose out on that revenue." Felix lifted his chin, attempting to look as aloof as if he were negotiating for a shipment of spices, not the freedom of nearly two dozen people. "Do we have a deal?"

The captain surveyed him for one more moment, then gave a brusque nod. "We have a deal."

Felix couldn't help feeling proud of himself as he waited for the money to arrive. If he wanted Lucretia to forgive him, this would have to be a mark in his favor. He'd done a selfless thing, saving an entire ship full of people from slavery.

Siro would have received the message by now. His secretary would no doubt be concerned at this development, but Felix knew he'd handle the matter with his usual diligence and efficiency. Felix probably had about half of the money in his coffers at home, which Siro had access to. For the rest, Siro would merely have to go to the temple bank and—

A horrible realization hit Felix with an icy punch to the gut. He froze, mind racing, unable to breathe. His knuckles whitened as his fingers dug into the wooden rail.

Siro wouldn't be able to withdraw the money from the temple bank. In the interest of security, Felix had given strict instructions to the priests who guarded their patrons' deposits not to let anyone but Felix himself touch his money. Even someone he trusted as much as Siro would not be allowed to withdraw a single denarius.

He struggled to pull in a breath, lungs straining.

Siro wouldn't be able to access Felix's fortune. He wouldn't be able to assemble the full ransom.

*You fucking idiot. Why didn't you think of that before? Why didn't you try to negotiate a smaller ransom?*

In the immediate aftermath of his kidnapping, he'd been too focused on negotiating the amount that would see him freed. He hadn't thought through the logistics of assembling the money. A foolish, fatal oversight.

He forced himself to exhale. Surely there was some way around this. Siro was resourceful. He would convince the priests to make an exception. Or perhaps, if he couldn't, the pirates would be satisfied with a smaller amount...

Nausea roiled in his stomach, even more so than when trapped in the hold as the ship rose and fell with the waves. Pirates weren't known for their lenience. He had promised them fifteen talents. And if he didn't pay—would they execute him in retaliation? Throw him overboard?

To make matters worse, due to his brief impulse of empathy and selflessness, it wasn't just himself this mistake condemned. All the other captives had their chance at freedom snatched back.

Now he was even more grateful Marcus had not been caught up in all this. Lucretia would have cast enough curses on him to follow his soul to the underworld and torment him for eternity.

He was never going to see Lucretia again. Pain erupted in his chest at the thought, and he curled his arms around himself, sinking to the wooden boards, his back against the rail.

He loved her, and he would spend the rest of his miserable and possibly very short life regretting the choices that had ruined everything between them. Maybe, if he had just been able to bring himself to apologize before he left—but he'd been too stubborn, too conceited to beg for the forgiveness he didn't deserve.

He swallowed down the bile that rose in his throat at the thought of the future that awaited him. He was so close. His fortune, the only thing that could save him from death or slavery, was mere miles away. But it was as useless as if it were made of dung.

# CHAPTER 33

AN URGENT KNOCKING CAME at the door to Lucretia's office. Dihya had just stepped out to fetch some lunch for them both—from Caeso's stall, of course—so Lucretia went to the front room to answer the door.

Felix's secretary, Siro, waited outside, hands clasped around a wax tablet. A distraught expression marred his usually reserved countenance. "Forgive me, lady, I didn't know who else to come to."

Lucretia let him in, unease swirling in her stomach. "What is it?"

Siro swallowed hard. "It seems Felix has been kidnapped by pirates." He kept talking, but the words muddled together in Lucretia's mind.

*Pirates. Kidnapped.* "Marcus," she managed in a strangled gasp. "Is my son—"

"He writes that Marcus is safe," Siro said hastily, holding out the tablet. "I'm not sure exactly what happened, but—"

"Give me that." Lucretia snatched the wax tablet and read over the few lines inscribed in Felix's handwriting. *Marcus is safe, should be back in Ostia any day now.* She read that line three times, burning the words into her mind.

*Marcus is safe.* The jolt of terror left her body in a rush. She leaned against Dihya's desk, legs trembling. *Marcus is safe.*

She let out a shaky breath, handing the tablet back. "If this isn't about my son, then why have you come?" *Marcus may be safe, but Felix…* She shrugged off her worry. Felix was no longer her concern.

Siro twisted his fingers together over the tablet. "It's the ransom they're demanding. Felix has about half of it in his coffers at home. But the rest…it's secured at the temple bank. The priests won't let me touch it. Even after I tried to explain what had happened. I showed them the letter. They wouldn't relent!" Anxiety tightened his voice.

Lucretia crossed her arms over her chest, affecting nonchalance despite the unease twisting in her stomach at the thought of Felix's predicament. "So what am I meant to do about it?"

"Well, I thought you might be able to lend the money," Siro said, meeting her eyes with a beseeching gaze. "Felix would repay it in full immediately upon his release, of course."

She pressed her lips together. "You must know what has transpired between me and Felix."

Siro glanced away. "I have pieced together certain details. My employer's private affairs are not my business, of course."

Lucretia took a step toward him, abandoning the support of the desk. "I think they were your business at one point. You must have helped him dig into my secrets. Did you investigate my guardian for him?"

Siro rotated the wax tablet in his hands. "I followed my employer's instructions, lady."

"So you know he was trying to ruin me. To destroy everything I've worked for, to discredit everything I've done, purely because I happen to be a woman." She lifted her chin. "And you think I would spend a single denarius for his benefit?"

"Please, lady," Siro said. "His freedom, perhaps even his life, is at stake!"

"He was willing to gamble my freedom for his own greed," she snapped. "Perhaps he deserves to feel what it's like to lose everything."

"You cannot truly plan to abandon him to such a fate," Siro insisted. "Whatever he planned to do to you, it did not amount to slavery or death."

Siro had a point there. Could she live with herself if she condemned him to such a fate? She thought of Marcus. He cared for Felix; he would want her to do what she could to save him.

"How much is the ransom?" The number must have been in the letter, but she'd been so consumed with worry for Marcus that it escaped her.

"Fifteen talents," Siro replied.

"Fifteen!" she gasped. "Does Felix have that much money?"

Siro nodded. "As I said, split between his home and the temple bank."

"Fifteen talents," she repeated in awe. It was a titanic sum. Felix was wealthier than she'd realized.

"He has seven at home. I need eight to fulfill the ransom."

She let out a short, humorless laugh. "Well, I don't have eight talents." No matter if Felix deserved her help or not, she didn't have the power to save him. The realization should have soothed her; she no longer had to decide if he was worthy of saving.

Instead, it sent a strange pang through her, thorny with emotions she couldn't name.

Siro's face fell. "I see. I-I suppose I'll have to think of something else." He turned to leave, shoulders slumped.

"How long did they give you?" Lucretia asked. "Maybe...maybe I can think of something." It was only for Marcus's sake that she would try.

He turned back as he opened the door. "The pirate who delivered the message gave me a deadline of sunset the day after tomorrow."

*Not much time.* "All right."

Siro left.

*Kidnapped by pirates.* The reality of the situation sunk in. And somehow Marcus hadn't also been caught? No doubt her son would have a story to tell.

A fresh wave of worry spiraled in her stomach. Felix had said Marcus was safe, but she couldn't truly relax until he was back here, until she could see with her own eyes that he was well. Hopefully, Felix was right that Marcus would return any day now, and she could find out the truth of what had befallen them.

Dihya returned, carrying a basket laden with baked delicacies that Lucretia now had no stomach for. "Hello, I picked up some—" Dihya stopped short as she caught sight of Lucretia's face. "What's happened?"

In a few words, Lucretia told her of Siro's visit and the news he'd brought.

"Well," Dihya said, eyes wide. "I suppose that's a certain kind of justice for what Felix did, isn't it?"

"What should I do?" Lucretia asked. "Does he even deserve my help?"

Dihya considered for a moment. "That fate is not one I would condemn anyone to lightly. Even my enemy. Even Felix."

Lucretia nodded. Dihya, as a freedwoman, knew the painful reality of what Felix faced far better than Lucretia did.

"And, not that I would ever defend him, but to be fair, he didn't actually *do* anything to you," Dihya continued. "He thought about it—he planned it—but he didn't go through with it, did he?"

"You're right," Lucretia admitted. Perhaps she had been judging him too harshly. "He thought better of it in the end."

Dihya tapped her fingers on her desk, considering. "If the situation was reversed, what would Felix do for you?"

The answer struck Lucretia like a blow to the chest. If she had been kidnapped by pirates, she knew with bone-deep certainty that Felix would not rest until she was safe. He would scour the Mediterranean to bring her home. He would use every last resource at his disposal to rescue her.

Her eyes filled with tears. "He would do whatever it took," she whispered through a tight throat.

"So maybe you have your answer," Dihya murmured.

Lucretia took in a shaky breath. "I know."

She had two days to raise eight talents of silver, or Felix would be lost forever.

Lucretia spent a sleepless night worrying for Marcus. Her son was on a ship with strangers, traversing the open sea. She would have given anything—her ships, her house, even her life—to have him back safe. But she was powerless.

She forced herself to look at the situation with a shred of rationality. Marcus might be separated from Felix, but he must be on the same ship he'd departed on, with the same crew. Not strangers. He was no longer a child, but nearly a man. He could look after himself to a reasonable extent. With luck, his ship might be approaching the harbor even now. At first light, she'd go to the harbor, and she wouldn't leave until she found him. She'd come back every day until he returned.

When she managed to untangle herself from her worries about Marcus, her mind turned to conjuring a plan to save Felix. She knew she wouldn't be able to sleep until Marcus was back with her, so she might as well use the time to think of something.

By morning, Lucretia had a fragment of an idea. Or rather, she knew exactly what she could do to save Felix. She only had a fragment of confidence that it wasn't utter idiocy.

She was just preparing to set out for the harbor to await Marcus's return when her son stepped through the front door. Relief choked her, cutting off her breath and filling her eyes with tears.

She ran to him and swept him into a tight embrace. "Oh, Marcus! I heard what happened to Felix—are you all right?" She pulled back from the embrace to look him over anxiously. He didn't look to be injured, and he had even acquired a golden tan over his skin.

"You know about the pirates?" Marcus demanded. "How did you find out?"

"They issued a ransom demand to Siro," Lucretia said, stroking his cheek to reassure herself that he was real, that he was truly standing before her, alive and unharmed. "They must be anchored somewhere close by."

"So he'll be saved!" A relieved smile lit Marcus's face. "I-I didn't know what would happen to him after they took him. I thought they might have killed him!"

"That would have been very wasteful." Lucretia led Marcus to a bench on the edge of the atrium, where they could sit and talk. "Pirates want either money or slaves, which they can turn into money. Now, will you tell me what happened?"

Marcus relayed the story of how they had boarded a ship supposedly carrying a cargo of Serican silk. "It was all my fault," he said, voice tight with anguish. "I insisted we go aboard. If I hadn't been so *stupid*, none of this would have happened!"

She put an arm around him and drew him against her. "You had no way of knowing, sweetheart. What happened after you went aboard?"

"Well, we were waiting on deck for the crowds to thin. Felix started to get nervous about something. He said we should leave, but I didn't know why. And then before we could get off the ship, the gangplank was gone and we were setting sail."

Lucretia inhaled a shocked breath. "And then?"

Marcus closed his eyes, as if recalling the exact moment. "Felix dragged me over to the side of the ship and threw me overboard."

"He did *what?*"

"We weren't far from the dock," Marcus explained. "It was easy to swim. I thought he was coming after me, but I looked back and I couldn't see him anywhere. They must have caught him."

"Blessed Orbona," she murmured, sending a fervent prayer of thanks to the goddess of children for safeguarding her son. She added one to Neptune for good measure, since the incident had occurred at sea.

"But he's going to be all right, isn't he?" Marcus asked. "The ransom will be paid, and he'll be freed?"

Lucretia hesitated. "There is an issue with the ransom. Felix has the money, but about half of it is in the temple bank, and no one but him can withdraw it."

Marcus's eyes widened. "We have to do something! He wouldn't have been there if it wasn't for me. And he saved me."

Lucretia nodded. The pieces of her plan fell into place in her mind. After hearing Marcus's story, she saw that Felix had sacrificed himself to save her son. Thus, Lucretia would do whatever it took to free him, even if it might cost her everything. "I have a plan." She gave Marcus one more hug and kiss on the cheek. "You go to the kitchens and get some food in you. You must be hungry and tired after such a journey. I must pay a visit to Publius Calpurnius Lentulus."

# CHAPTER 34

F ELIX SAT WITH HIS knees tucked to his chest in his spot
in the hold, surrounded by sealed amphorae and crates
of provisions. The boat rocked gently beneath him as they
bobbed at anchor near Ostia.

Dread laid like a heavy stone in his stomach. Each hour that
passed was one less hour of life as he knew it. He knew the
pirates had given Siro a deadline of two days to provide the
money. He also knew there would be no money, and his life
as a free man was over.

He pondered the fate that awaited him, assuming he sur-
vived the pirates' displeasure at the lack of ransom. He was
educated, so he'd likely be sold as a scribe or secretary. At least
he'd avoid the sort of menial, backbreaking labor others might
be destined for.

Could he parlay his boxing experience into being sold as a
gladiator? That would either lead to a quick, merciful death, or,
if he was successful, he might be able to earn enough money to
buy his freedom and find his way back to Ostia, and Lucretia.

That idea had promise. A gladiator trainee would fetch
the pirates a higher price than a scribe. He didn't fancy the
prospect of risking his life in the arena, but it might be his best
shot.

He shook his head. Winning his freedom as a gladiator was a ludicrous idea. He was destined for a life of drudgery as a scribe or something similar.

And his prospects as a slave didn't matter if the pirates decided to kill him in retaliation for wasting their time with the promise of a ransom that never arrived.

He hoped Siro wouldn't feel too guilty about failing to gather the money. It wasn't his fault, and Felix wished he could see him just for a moment to tell him so.

At the thought of everyone he would never see again, his chest ached. He would never see his family again: his mother, his boorish but warmhearted stepfather, his half-sister. They would all grieve his loss. He would never get to watch his niece grow up. And Lucretia and Marcus—the thought of them made his throat tighten painfully.

He would never get to apologize to Lucretia. He should have done it the last time he saw her, when they'd walked to the harbor.

How stupid he had been. He should have thrown himself at her feet and begged for her forgiveness. Now he would never have the chance to tell her how foolish he'd been, how he'd let his greed and desire to win blight everything of real importance.

He closed his eyes, blocking out his dismal surroundings. He conjured the image of her face, pretending he could bask in the warmth of her hazel eyes and the sunlight of her smile once more. He remembered the melody of her laugh, the cool way she challenged him, her utter boldness in flouting the law with her invented guardian.

Now, when he was on the verge of losing everything, his success in business was meaningless. It was Lucretia who loomed large in his mind. She was what he longed for. She was the only thing that truly mattered.

Lucretia arrived at the home of Publius Calpurnius Lentulus, her biggest investor, and awaited him in the atrium. When he joined her, he greeted her with a kiss on both cheeks.

"Lucretia, how nice to see you. How is young Marcus these days?"

"Very well," she answered. "He's taken up boxing recently, and I fear his shoulders are about to outgrow all of his tunics."

Lentulus chuckled as he led her into his study to sit. "Boxing, eh? A wholesome activity for a young man."

She sat in the chair he proffered. "Forgive me for my bluntness, but I come to you on a matter of some urgency. I must ask a great favor."

He sat behind his desk, leaning forward as interest and concern mingled on his lined face. "Oh?"

"I require a large sum of ready coin. I would ask you for a loan of eight talents of silver. It will be repaid within the week."

Lentulus's gray eyebrows shot up. "Eight talents? What could you possibly need that for?"

She briefly relayed the details of Felix's capture by pirates and Marcus's near escape.

Lentulus frowned. "Lucius Avitus Felix is your enemy, is he not? If I recall, but a few months ago he was doing everything in his power to ruin you. Including trying to convince me to sell him my stake in your operations."

"Yes," she admitted. "But things recently changed. We agreed on a truce, a condition of which was that he would apprentice Marcus."

"A truce?" Lentulus repeated. "Why would he have agreed to such a thing?"

Lucretia strove to keep her face neutral. "Forgive me, but the terms of our agreement are confidential."

"I see." Lentulus leaned back in his chair and surveyed her. "So you want my money to free Felix from the pirates. And he will repay it immediately upon being released."

Lucretia nodded. "With whatever interest you deem fair."

"It is a significant sum," Lentulus said. "And a risky proposition. Pirates are unpredictable and underhanded. They could take the money and refuse to release him."

"I know," Lucretia admitted. "But I fear this is our only hope."

Lentulus took another moment to consider, while Lucretia waited, hiding the anxious twisting of her fingers beneath the fold of her palla in her lap.

"I would require significant collateral to make such a loan," he finally said. "You know there is little I wouldn't do to help you, Lucretia, but when it comes to a loan of this magnitude, I must be prudent."

"Of course," Lucretia replied. She had been prepared for this. Lentulus would have been a fool not to require collateral. But this was the most painful part of her plan. At first, she had thought to offer her house as collateral. But the house did not technically belong to her; after Cornelius's death, it passed to Marcus, held in trust by Lucretia until he came of age. Besides, even if she could, she would have hesitated to risk losing the very roof over their heads.

There was only one other thing of value which she owned.

"I will offer my ships as collateral," she said. The words hung in the air, ominous as a thundercloud. If anything went wrong with the exchange of ransom, she would lose everything. But somehow, she was willing to make the gamble if it could see Felix freed.

Lentulus's brow furrowed. "Are you sure?"

She nodded. "I'm sure."

Lentulus sighed. "I want you to know, as your friend, I advise against all of this. I would sooner have you leave Felix to his fate and go on with your life. Don't take such a risk."

"I appreciate your counsel, but my decision is made." Felix had sacrificed himself to save Marcus, and for that, she owed him anything she could do to save him.

It was only in return for Marcus's safety, she told herself. Not because she wanted to see him again. Not because she longed for his touch, for the devotion in his gaze when he looked at her. He had betrayed her, hadn't even apologized for it, and she would not forgive so easily.

"Very well." Lentulus reached for a blank piece of papyrus. "Let us draw up the terms."

The next day, Lucretia met Siro at Felix's home as the eight talents of silver were delivered, escorted by a guard of six men. The crates of coin joined the further seven talents withdrawn from Felix's own coffers.

It had taken longer than she hoped for Lentulus to gather and send over the money, and the day was already half gone. The sunset deadline loomed large in her mind. They would have to move fast to make it.

Lucretia stared at the mountain of wealth before her. It was a true fortune. One talent was roughly half a man's weight, so the fifteen talents came out to about seven or eight men in silver.

Siro stood beside her as they watched the crates of coin be loaded into the house. "I'm not sure what you did to achieve this, lady, but you have my eternal gratitude. And Felix's as well, I'm sure."

She refrained from telling Siro what she had staked to attain this much coin. Nerves spiraled in her belly as she surveyed the massive fortune. If anything went wrong today, she would lose everything.

She tried to distract herself by focusing on the logistics of the day. "Is everything prepared?" she asked.

Siro nodded. "I have hired two boats that will transport the silver, along with the guard, down the coast to where the pirate vessel waits. The man who delivered Felix's message gave me clear directions."

"Will we make it in time?"

Siro raised his gaze skyward. "With Neptune's blessing, yes. I will accompany one of the boats." He paused.

"And I will join the other."

"Felix would wish me to warn you that it may be dangerous. One never knows with pirates."

Lucretia raised her chin. "I would tell Felix that as half of that silver is mine, I will see it safely delivered."

Siro dipped his head. "Of course, lady. We will both accompany the ransom."

"And then we'll bring him home," she murmured.

# CHAPTER 35

A s afternoon set in on the second day of the ransom
deadline, Felix allowed himself to abandon any scrap of
hope he'd been clinging to. The sun dipped closer to the horizon
with each passing moment. The pirates grew restless. They didn't
relish sitting at anchor for this long, doing nothing, and in his
moments on deck he overheard some low conversations in which
they debated leaving early.

If Felix had maintained any hope of the money arriving, he
would have interjected that organizing a sum of money as large
as fifteen talents took time. A guard would have to be hired, and
it would have to be transported in separate carts if going by land
or separate boats if by sea, due to the weight of the metal.

But he knew there would be no money. His time as a free man
was running out, the last drops of water slipping through the
water clock.

Now, in his spot in the bow hold, he heard raised voices from
the deck, and an increased pattern of footfalls sounded on the
wood over his head. It was difficult to tell the hour down here in
the dark, but he bet that either sunset had arrived, or the pirates
had given up and decided to leave early.

Footsteps thumped on the ladder that led below deck. A moment later, Felix squinted as one of the pirates entered the hold

with a flickering lantern. Felix braced himself, expecting to be thrown into the aft hold with the rest of the captives.

The pirate hauled Felix to his feet and dragged him into the small corridor that separated the bow and aft holds. But instead of thrusting him into the aft hold, the pirate shoved him up the ladder.

"What's going on?" Felix asked in Greek as he climbed, his weakened muscles protesting the effort.

Maybe they weren't moving him into the other hold. Perhaps this was the moment the pirates decided to exact retribution for wasting their time. Maybe their frustration had outweighed their greed and they were about to slit his throat. He imagined his blood spilling out onto the deck, his lifeless body splashing into the water, quickly sinking beneath the waves.

A shiver of dread ran through him, and he stumbled on the ladder before catching himself, his hands shaking where they gripped the wooden rungs. He drew in a deep breath—perhaps one of his last—and forced himself to be calm. There was honor in facing death with equanimity, like the defeated generals who chose to fall on their swords rather than be slaughtered or captured by an enemy. If the only remaining thing in his control was giving himself an honorable death, he'd do it.

"Your money is here. Finally," the pirate growled as he followed Felix up the ladder.

"What?" The pooling dread ignited into shock. Felix climbed faster, emerging onto the deck to squint in the light of a brilliant sunset.

It was impossible. Perhaps Siro hoped to convince the pirates to accept a smaller ransom, but Felix knew that wouldn't end well.

Felix hurried to the rail, and what he saw on the water below made his heart stop for a moment. Two small boats bobbed on the waves, each riding low in the water, laden with crate after crate. Siro was in one of the boats, nearest the ship. And in the boat further back…there was a woman. A palla covered her head, but the wind caught it, tugging it back.

Golden rays of light shone on auburn hair. Felix's breath stuttered in his throat as a fresh surge of shock flooded his body. *Lucretia. She was here? And how—?*

Eyes moving with frantic speed, he counted the crates. Enough to make up fifteen talents of silver. *How? How did they manage it?*

Siro waved to him. "Good afternoon, sir," he called, sounding for all the world as if he was greeting Felix on any other day. "Are you all right?"

"Fine," Felix replied. "Is it—is it all there?"

Siro patted the crate closest to him. "Fifteen talents, as request-ed."

"But—how?"

Siro glanced back at Lucretia, who had risen to her feet despite the swaying boat. "I'm not entirely sure myself, sir."

As soon as Lucretia saw Felix's pale face appear over the rail of the pirate ship, she shot to her feet. The boat lurched beneath her.

"Sit down!" barked the boat's pilot, who had sailed them the distance from Ostia to this hidden cove.

Lucretia ignored him, focusing only on Felix.

This whole time, she had known intellectually what happened to him. He'd been kidnapped by pirates, which was a risk for those who traveled by sea.

But now, seeing him aboard the pirate ship, a bolt of visceral understanding shot through her in a dizzying rush. He'd been taken captive, held on this ship in probably very uncomfortable accommodations, in danger every moment of being sold into slavery.

And that was what he had saved Marcus from. In the brief moment he had to act, he'd thought first of Marcus's safety and lost his own chance at escape.

Her heart splintered as she fully realized what he had sacrificed.

Then, their eyes met, and her heart knitted back together. A smile grew on her face, despite the circumstances.

He gave her a searching frown, his eyes skimming from her to the crates of silver. Likely he was trying to figure out how they managed to raise the entire sum. That would have to be a story for later.

While she'd been gawking at him, Siro, in the other boat, was busily negotiating with the pirates, arranging for half of the silver to be hauled aboard before Felix's release. The pirate crew set up a system of ropes and pulleys which lowered down a wooden platform, onto which they could secure a crate.

It seemed to take forever for the first seven crates of silver to be hauled up. Lucretia couldn't see much from down here, but it appeared the pirates were opening each crate as it arrived to verify that the contents were all silver before sending the platform back down to retrieve the next crate—just in case Siro had tried to adulterate the silver with something else.

Finally, Siro's boat had been emptied of its half of the ransom. A rope ladder swung down over the side of the ship. Lucretia held her breath as Felix climbed down, one rung at a time. He seemed to be uninjured, which was better than she might have hoped, but no doubt he was exhausted from the ordeal.

She let out her breath as Felix's feet touched the deck of Siro's boat. He released the ladder and turned to greet Siro, speaking words she couldn't hear and clasping his secretary's arms with a weary smile.

Siro's boat rowed away from the pirate vessel, and Lucretia's progressed forward, preparing to deliver the second half of the ransom.

Felix said something to the pilot of the other boat, who maneuvered so their boat pulled up alongside Lucretia's, a handsbreadth of space between them. With surprising agility, Felix hopped over the gap into her boat.

His arms were around her before she could even take a breath. "Felix," she gasped, hardly able to believe this was real. After what happened between them, she never would have imagined that she'd be here, hugging him as if her life depended on it.

"I'm sorry," he whispered in her ear, his voice rough and unsteady.

"For what?" She drew back to look at him, verifying her earlier assessment that he was overall uninjured, despite the deep shadows beneath his eyes.

"Firstly, because I fear I smell terrible."

She laughed. He did, but she didn't care. "Your staff will have a bath waiting upon our return."

"Praise Vesta." He lifted his eyes skyward with a smile.

Their boat had reached the side of the pirate ship, and the process of unloading and hauling up the crates of silver recommenced. To stay out of the way, Lucretia led Felix to the aft of the boat, where they could sit on a narrow bench.

Instead of sitting beside her, Felix dropped to his knees in front of her. "I must also apologize for how I schemed against you." He clasped her hands. "My greatest fear on that ship was that I would never get the chance to tell you how wrong I was, or to ask for your forgiveness. I don't deserve it, but I want you to know how deeply I regret betraying you."

She stroked the back of one of his hands. "It has been pointed out to me that you didn't actually go through with your plan against me. You thought better of it on your own, didn't you?"

"I should never have investigated your guardian. Not after our truce."

"No," she agreed. "But you also risked everything—your life, your freedom—for Marcus's sake. He told me what you did. You saved him and ruined your own chance of escape."

"I was hardly thinking at the time. It was not a fully considered decision."

"That's my point," she said. "When presented with an instant to make a life or death decision, your gut instinct was to sacrifice yourself to save my son. If that's not worthy of forgiveness, then I don't know what is."

He blinked up at her, his gray eyes wide and disbelieving. "Do you mean…"

She pulled him up to sit beside her. "I forgive you, Felix," she whispered. The words felt as much like a blessing for herself as for him. They eased the knot of tension wound tight inside her and filled her with a warm sense that finally, the broken pieces of her world were shifting back into place.

She drew him into another embrace, gentler than their previous frantic one. His arms skimmed over her back, a hand coming up to cradle her head reverently, as if she was the most precious thing in the world.

"Thank you," he whispered. Then he pulled back, as if a sudden thought had seized him. "Lucretia, how did you get this much money? I know Siro wouldn't have been able to retrieve it from the temple bank."

Her heart squeezed as she realized he must have believed his rescue would be stymied by their inability to access his fortune. How hopeless he must have been, waiting powerlessly for the deadline to expire and his fate to be sealed.

"I obtained a loan," she replied. "Publius Calpurnius Lentulus was good enough to understand the circumstances and come to my aid. Though there will be substantial interest, I fear."

"He loaned you eight talents of silver? I can't believe anyone would undertake such a risk, interest or no."

Lucretia hesitated. Should she reveal how far she had been prepared to go to see him freed? Or should she brush it off as an act of kindness on Lentulus's part?

*Tell him*, she decided. He deserved to know how much he meant to her. "I did offer significant collateral."

"Your house?" he demanded. "You risked your home—on me?"

She shook her head. "The house belongs to Marcus. I put up my ships."

He stared at her, utter incredulity stark on every plane of his face. "Why, by the furthest reaches of Dis, would you risk such a thing?"

She smiled tremulously. "Because I love you."

"You love me," he repeated, as if he didn't understand the words.

"Despite my better judgment, I fear." Her smile grew. Warmth filled her, so strong it chased away the chill of the sea air, which grew cooler every moment after sunset. "I love you, Felix."

His gray eyes searched her face, as if waiting for her to laugh and reveal it was all a prank. She gave him a few moments for the truth of her words to sink in.

"I love you too," he finally whispered, and pressed his lips to her forehead.

# CHAPTER 36

B Y THE TIME THEY reached Ostia harbor, night had fallen. Lanterns swinging on the boat lit their way to the dock. The craft bumped gently against the wooden pier and the pilot tied a line to secure them. Lucretia rose to exit, eager to be on land, but Felix paused to speak to the pilot.

"Would you make one more trip out?" he asked. "I arranged for the other captives to be freed as well, and I expect about half of them are in the second boat behind us. But the rest will require transport."

The pilot frowned. "I've only been paid for the one trip. But…" He looked Felix over. "I suppose I wouldn't mind being owed a favor by Lucius Avitus Felix."

Felix grinned and clapped him on the shoulder. "You have my gratitude."

Lucretia blinked at him. "What do you mean, you arranged for the other captives to be freed?"

Felix climbed off the boat and held out a hand to her. "Exactly that. I negotiated for everyone to be freed. Of course, that was before I realized the issue with the ransom money."

Lucretia clasped his hand, grateful for the support as she stepped over the gap between the boat and the dock. Her mind whirled. Felix, one of the most self-serving people she had ever known, had not only sacrificed himself to save her son, but had also negotiated for the release of an entire shipload of captives? His rescue of Marcus could be explained by his affection for her son, but those other people were strangers to him.

"*Why?*" she demanded in shock.

He gave her a long look as the boat behind them pulled away from the dock. "Because I couldn't live with the thought of never seeing you again, and I realized every person on that ship must have someone they felt the same about."

She let out her breath in a shuddering rush. Before she could say anything further, a figure hurried down the dock toward them.

"Marcus!" Lucretia exclaimed. She wanted to chide him for being out alone at night, but bit back the impulse. Of course he'd want to witness Felix's safe return.

"You're back!" Marcus said.

"Clearly there was no cause to worry, thanks to your mother," Felix said. "Was your journey from Cyrene smooth?"

Marcus nodded. He hesitated for a moment, then launched himself into Felix's arms, wrapping him in a hug that made Lucretia's heart clench in mingled joy and pain. It reminded her of the unrestrained, exuberant hugs Marcus used to give his father when he was younger.

Felix returned the hug for a moment before Marcus pulled back, wrinkling his nose. "Is that what pirates smell like?"

Felix chuckled. "I suppose so."

"What were they like? Were they ferocious? Did they slaughter anyone? Are they cannibals?" Marcus's eyes lit with interest.

"Marcus!" Lucretia scolded. "Felix does not wish to discuss such things."

"It's all right," Felix said with a laugh. "Though in truth, it was rather boring, all things considered."

Marcus made a noise of disappointment.

"Come, let's be on our way," Lucretia said. "Marcus, you'll return home, and then I'll see Felix to his house and make sure he's taken care of."

"Can't I come with you?" Marcus asked.

"Felix needs to rest," Lucretia said sternly. "You'll keep him up half the night with questions about the pirates. Don't pretend you wouldn't."

Marcus gave her a look of begrudging concession. "Fine."

"Meet me at the gymnasium tomorrow after you're done with school," Felix said.

Lucretia raised her eyebrows in disbelief. "You mean to exercise? Don't you wish to take a few days to rest?"

Felix flexed one arm experimentally. "I've spent the last nine days sitting on a ship doing nothing. Marcus may actually have a chance of beating me in my current state."

Marcus let out a gleeful laugh, and Lucretia sighed. "Very well."

They saw Marcus home, and then made their way to Felix's house. As she expected, his staff had a hot bath waiting for him, and he disappeared to wash and change his clothes while the kitchen prepared dinner.

He looked much restored after the bath, and he ravenously tucked into the expansive spread laid out in the dining room. Once she saw the food, Lucretia realized she hadn't eaten all day, and she joined him in demolishing an embarrassing amount of the excellent fare.

"I will repay Lentulus first thing tomorrow morning," Felix said as he polished off a second duck leg.

Lucretia loaded up her plate with wine-poached pears. "Will losing all that money hurt you?"

"I won't be begging on the street, if that's what you mean. But I will need to scale back my operations temporarily, until my capital is rebuilt. I'll have to delay my planned expansion to other ports."

"So you'll stay in Ostia." She shot him a coy sidelong glance. "A terrible fate."

He met her gaze with a crooked half-smile. "Devastating."

They resumed eating in companionable silence. Finally, Felix pushed back his third empty plate with a sigh of defeat. "That's about all I can manage."

"Are you very tired?" She would leave if he wished to rest, but being alone with him in the dining room where they had spent so many intimate moments was causing a different kind of appetite to flare. Now that he was safe, and now that she had forgiven him, all she wanted was to fall into bed with him, to truly reunite and repair their relationship.

"Not very," he replied. "I think I should be, but I feel strangely invigorated."

"Good," she said. "May I take you to bed, Felix?"

His eyebrows shot up—clearly that was the last thing he expected her to say. Then the surprise faded, and a lascivious gleam took its place in his eyes. "You may."

She stood and took his hand, pulling him to his feet. They left the dining room, heading for his bedroom. As soon as the door closed behind them, Lucretia busied herself in pulling off his tunic. The fresh clothes smelled strongly of marjoram, and Lucretia took a deep breath, filling her lungs with his scent. She had missed that.

Her hands skimmed down his body, luxuriating in the feel of him beneath her fingers. He was a trifle thinner than she recollected, but no doubt a few good meals would remedy that in short order.

His cock, thankfully, hadn't been affected by his ordeal, and it was as robust as she remembered. She curled her fingers around it, feeling it twitch and stiffen against her palm.

"I forgot how good that feels," Felix hissed. "How good *you* feel."

He reached for the shoulder of her dress, but she caught his hand and moved it away. "Not yet." She gently guided him over to the bed, where she sat him on the edge of it.

Then, she sank to her knees between his thighs and took him into her mouth.

He let out a strangled groan as her lips slid down his length. "Wh-what lesson is this meant to—" He broke off in a gasp as her tongue swirled around the head of his cock. "Teach me?"

She pulled her mouth off of him. "No lesson," she murmured, giving him a languorous stroke with her hand. Tonight was different, not about lessons, but about celebrating the fact that they were alive, and together, and loved each other. "Well, perhaps the lesson is how to endure this without spilling in my mouth."

"You don't want that?" His voice became hoarse as she resumed the play of her lips and tongue over him. He laid his hand on the back of her head, a caress.

"Not there. Not today." She took him as deep as she was able, filling her mouth with his girth. The feel of him in her mouth, against her tongue, made her quim pulse in yearning.

His sharp gasp rewarded her effort, along with the spasmodic tightening of his hand in her hair. "I fear—I fear I'm going to fail your lesson."

She withdrew, arching an eyebrow at him. "So soon?"

He scowled. "You know what you do to me."

She rose to her feet and shed her dress in one quick movement, then climbed into bed. His eyes darkened with hunger as she pulled him down to lie next to her. The feeling of her bare skin against his was a warm, gentle pleasure like no other.

He put his hand on her hip, starting to draw her on top of him, but she shook her head. "I want you like this," she said, maneuvering herself beneath him. Tonight, she wanted to feel completely possessed, taken by him.

He settled his weight over her with a sigh, the thickness of his arousal pressing against her core in a way that made her want to squirm. "You said a certain level of control was required for this position," he said, dropping a kiss on her collarbone. "I warn you, I don't have it."

"Don't worry about that tonight. I know my courses and the chance of conception is minimal." She skimmed her fingernails down his lean back, and he shuddered.

"Are you sure?"

She nodded, tightening her thighs around his hips. She was ready, aching for him. "Forget control. Just take me. Please," she added, in case he needed further convincing.

He made a low sound of pleasure. "I like the sound of that." His hand trailed down her neck, coming to rest possessively at the base of her throat. "Beg for me, Lucretia."

Her pride flared momentarily in resistance, but he nudged his hips against hers, causing his cock to give a tempting push against her entrance. Simple need burned away the vestiges of her pride. "I want you inside me, Felix. Please, I want to feel you lose yourself, I want you to—"

"Fuck," he rasped. "Are you ready, Lucretia? Ready now?" Even as he spoke, he was adjusting his position, a hand wrapped around his cock to guide it into her.

She nodded with voracious eagerness, unable to form more words. There was a moment of fumbling as they found the right angle, and then she gripped his shoulders hard as he slid into her. "Oh!"

He froze. "Did I go too fast?" His voice was strangled, breathless in her ear.

She shook her head, relaxing her grasp on his shoulders to give his back a reassuring stroke. "Let me take all of you."

He rooted himself deep inside her with another muttered curse. Then he drew back and thrust, the powerful movement driving her halfway across the bed.

She giggled and held on, arms and legs wrapping tight around him, as he took his pleasure. This was what she wanted—to make him lose control, abandon all traces of composure, to think only of his satisfaction. With moans and gasps, she encouraged him to take her harder, faster, to use her exactly as she wished.

"Yes," she breathed. "Just like that."

His climax seemed to burst as quick and sudden as a summer rainstorm, passing through him in wracking waves. He moaned her name, one hand clenching on her hip so tightly she wouldn't be surprised if it bruised.

When it left him, he rolled off her and collapsed onto his back. He seemed incapable of speech, so she laid her head on his shoulder and rubbed her hand over his chest, feeling the rapid thumping of his heart.

Gradually, it slowed. She expected him to fall asleep after all he'd endured, but his hand came up to stroke her hair. "Lucretia," he murmured. "For the third time, will you *finally, please* marry me?"

She propped herself on her elbow to survey him. After their confessions of love earlier, she'd anticipated this question. And she knew exactly what her answer would be.

"No." She couldn't stop a smile from spreading over her face. "I will not marry you, Felix."

*"What?"* He shot into a sitting position, heat flaring in his eyes. "Now is not the time for jokes."

She schooled her face into a more serious expression. "I'm not joking." She sat up and reached for his hand, twining his fingers with hers. "I love you, Felix. But I don't need a husband. And Marcus has made it very clear he doesn't want a stepfather, despite his affection for you."

He opened his mouth, but she held up a hand and continued speaking. "A husband holds no benefit to me, but a business partner might. I think we are better suited as colleagues and lovers, rather than husband and wife. At least for now. You know we'd be stronger if we combine our efforts, instead of working against each other."

He narrowed his eyes, disbelief mingling with irritation. "You're actually refusing my proposal? For the third time?"

She nodded. "But I'm not refusing *you*. I want you, by day and by night." An unpleasant thought occurred to her, one that turned her stomach but that she had to voice. "However, if you prefer to have a wife who can give you children that bear your name, I won't stand in your way."

He glanced away from her, and she held her breath. What if she had misjudged his desires? What if what he truly wanted was a traditional marriage with a wife who would keep his house and bear his children?

Felix met her gaze once more. The momentary frustration faded from his eyes, replaced with a steady acceptance. "I thought I made it clear. *You* are the only woman I have ever wanted, or will ever want. If this is how you'll have me, then I accept."

Warmth surged inside her, and she raised their twined hands to kiss his fingers.

"As for a child," he continued, "that is easily solved. If my sister ever has a son, I can settle my estate on him. But until then, I'll designate Marcus as my heir. We need not be married for that."

Tears pricked at her eyes. "You would do that?"

"Of course," he said, as if he thought nothing of it. "Who else?"

"Oh, Felix," she whispered, and wrapped her arms around him. Together, they tumbled from their sitting positions to lie flat on the bed, holding each other tight.

They were quiet for a moment, until Felix let out a low chuckle in her ear.

"What's so funny?" she asked.

He traced a finger along her cheek, tender and reverent. "In one day, I've lost nearly my entire fortune. If an oracle had told me this would happen, I would only have imagined the utter devastation I'd feel. But I find that I've gained something far more precious." He dropped a kiss on the tip of her nose. "I would spend the rest of my life without a single denarius to my name, if that's what it took to keep you by my side."

She closed her eyes and smiled. "Luckily, I do not plan to live a destitute life. We'll rebuild your fortune. Together."

"*Our* fortune," he said, and sealed his words with a kiss.

# Epilogue

*One year later*

LUCRETIA RESTED HER HANDS on the rail of the ship as the port of Alexandria came into view on the horizon. The deck rolled gently beneath her feet, but after two weeks of sea travel, she hardly noticed it. The first few days had been an utter misery of seasickness, but after many prayers to Neptune and Amphitrite for mercy, her body had eventually become accustomed to the ceaseless motion.

It wasn't just seasickness that plagued her in those early days. At first, anxiety had been a constant thrum in her chest, a twisting in her stomach. She'd cursed herself for allowing Felix and Marcus to convince her to come on this trip to Alexandria. Every sway of the ship portended sinking, and every time they caught sight of another sail in the distance, it was pirates.

At least if they died, she reasoned in her darkest moments, the three of them would die together.

But the ship hadn't sunk, they hadn't even seen any bad weather, and no pirates were to be found. Felix had been a steady presence at her side, a reassuring voice in her ear whenever her worries threatened to overwhelm her.

As one uneventful day followed another, the tension in her chest eased, and she no longer spent every waking moment consumed with worry about shipwrecks or pirates or storms.

Marcus's enthusiasm had also helped. It was hard to be anxious when her son's eyes glowed with delight as he learned a new knot or wheedled the captain into teaching him a new navigational technique.

Though Marcus remained a somewhat ambivalent student when it came to learning the nuances of trade and commerce, he'd taken to sailing with an enthusiasm that reminded her of Cornelius. She sensed he'd found his passion, though she might have wished his interest stayed with chariot racing or something else that would keep him on land.

Dihya and Siro had remained behind in Ostia to manage affairs while Lucretia and Felix were gone. Their working relationship was tumultuous but somehow efficient, and Caeso's baked goods smoothed over many a quarrel between the two deputies. Dihya and Caeso had married the previous autumn as planned, and Dihya was now several joyful months into a pregnancy. Lucretia smiled as she imagined how big her friend would be upon their return.

Felix, beside her at the rail, wrapped an arm around her waist. His fair skin had acquired a glow of color from the trip, and the wind whipped at his dark hair. "Almost there," he murmured as he gazed out at the approaching land.

"The first thing I'm going to do is buy a hat." Instead of an even, golden tan like Felix, Lucretia's skin had gained a disagreeable array of freckles over the two weeks of being out on the sunny deck. "And perhaps some cosmetics."

Felix chuckled. "If you cover up those freckles, I won't know where to kiss you." He had developed an irritating habit of kissing each new freckle as it appeared.

She scowled. "I can live with that."

He pulled her closer, speaking low in her ear. "The first free afternoon we have, I'm going to rent a pleasure boat and take you out on it. Just the two of us. And then I'm going to strip you bare in the sunlight so your entire body gets covered in freckles. That way I'll have *plenty* of places to kiss."

A tendril of heat wound through her at his words. Despite her dislike of the freckles, he presented an appealing picture. Privacy had been at a minimum aboard the ship. They were lucky to have their own cabin, as opposed to sleeping in a tent on deck like the crew and Marcus, but it directly bordered the captain's cabin. By the volume of the captain's snoring audible in their cabin, Lucretia knew he'd be able to hear anything and everything they did. To spare the poor man, they had refrained from indulging in each other.

After two weeks of such restraint, desire was a nearly constant tickle under her skin. And by the way Felix was holding her, she could tell he felt it too.

The crew was already making preparations to dock, adjusting the sails and doing indecipherable things with the various piles of rope that lay around the deck. Marcus was at the aft of the ship, hovering at the captain's shoulder as he surveyed the operations. So no one was paying them any attention as Felix moved behind her, laying his hands next to hers where they braced on the rail. His body pressed against her from shoulder to hip.

"Imagine being taken like this," he whispered, breath tickling her neck. "On a boat by ourselves, nothing but the open sea for company."

She gave an unsteady laugh as warmth gathered between her thighs. "I fear Neptune would be watching, if no one else."

"He can watch if he likes." He lowered his head to kiss the curve of her neck.

The touch made her arch against him, and her bottom bumped the swelling thickness of his cock. Her mouth went dry with want. "Felix," she hissed, resisting the urge to rub against him. "Not here."

He let out a growl of displeasure, but released her, moving to stand more decorously next to her. He rested his elbow on the rail. Beyond, the Egyptian coast drew closer with every moment. Lucretia could make out the curve of the harbor, marked by the famously towering lighthouse on an island just offshore.

They'd separated not a moment too soon, for Marcus came jogging toward them. "Captain says we should be docking in an hour or so," he relayed, excitement lighting his hazel eyes. "We're to enter the harbor under oar power, rather than sails, to have more control over the approach."

"Excellent," Lucretia said, smiling at him. Over the past year, Marcus had learned to tolerate her relationship with Felix, as long as she held to her promise that Felix wouldn't become his stepfather. The arrangement suited Lucretia perfectly; Felix and Marcus were much better suited as apprentice and teacher rather than father and son, and the three of them got along better than she ever could have imagined.

Gone were the days of Marcus's surly, sulking behavior. He seemed to grow inches every week, and boxing had taught him discipline and control. His knowledge of business and trade was increasing every day, thanks to Felix's thorough tutelage.

An hour later, as promised, their ship docked in the harbor of Alexandria. As Lucretia stepped off the gangplank, the boards of the pier seemed to lurch beneath her feet. She grabbed at Felix, and he wrapped a steadying arm around her waist. Marcus was already halfway down the dock, eager to explore a new city.

"Careful," Felix said. "Your legs are used to the movement of the ship. The solid ground will feel unstable for a while."

She leaned into his secure hold. "I suppose I'll just have to make sure there's a strong, handsome man within grabbing distance until I acclimate."

Felix chuckled. His fingers spread wider where they grasped her body, turning his hold from supportive to suggestive. "I've been *aching* to be grabbed at by you."

Lucretia grinned at him, looping her arms around his neck. A rush of gratitude washed over her as she gazed at him. She had everything she'd ever wanted: a profitable business, a son who had found happiness and stability, and a shrewd business partner.

And Felix was more than just a business partner. He was by her side during the day as they coordinated shipments or inventoried cargo or updated their accounts. And though they remained unmarried, Felix spent nearly every night in her bed, pleasuring her with his usual meticulous attention.

After two weeks of abstinence, she was in dire need of some of that meticulous attention. She stood on her tiptoes and lifted her mouth to his ear. "Let's see about that private boat, shall we?"

A spark of hunger flared in his gray eyes. He gave a low, rumbling laugh, then took her hand and led her down the dock.

Thank you for reading! If you enjoyed Felix and Lucretia's story, please consider leaving a review wherever you found this book.

Want more of the Roman Heirs universe? Scan below or head to jennabigelow.com/fortune for a free prequel novella, *The Merchant Match.*

# Also by Jenna Bigelow

## The Imperial Games series

Set in the early days of Caligula's reign, the Imperial Games series follows three gladiators during a stretch of games held to celebrate the new emperor's accession. Win or lose, one thing is sure: love will be found where they least expect it.

### Gladiator's Embrace (Book 1)

A retired gladiator reluctantly returns to the arena for one last series of fights, only to fall for his manager's ambitious niece when she hires him to train the up-and-coming gladiator she's taken on.

### Gladiator's Beloved (Book 2)

She's Rome's most feared female gladiator. He's the emperor's personal physician, commanded to heal her latest injury. Sparks fly when they're together, until the machinations of the imperial court threaten to tear them apart.

## *Gladiator's Touch* (Book 3)

A former Vestal Virgin seeks out the gladiator-turned-sculptor whose life she spared. He wants nothing to do with her after she ended his fighting career, but the heat that blossoms between them is impossible to escape.

# THE ROMAN HEIRS SERIES

The Roman Heirs series follows the love stories of three generations of an unconventional family in the last decades of the Roman Republic. There's a politically motivated marriage of convenience, forbidden pining between a soldier and a governor's wife, and a pair of business rivals who somehow find themselves trading sex lessons for a truce.

## *The Merchant Match* (free prequel novella)

After gaining her freedom from slavery, Gaia will do whatever it takes to build a new future for herself and her son—even infiltrate a dinner party under an assumed identity to extort money from her former mistress. There, she meets Herminius, a wealthy merchant in search of a respectable bride. Despite her subterfuge, Gaia can't ignore the heat that sparks between them. She knows she should keep her distance, but what's the point of freedom if she can't enjoy the pleasurable attentions of a man who makes her heart flutter every time they touch?

## *The Tribune Temptation* (Book 1)

In the cutthroat world of Roman politics, family is everything. Aelius, a freed slave turned ambitious politician, enters into a marriage of convenience with a disgraced patrician divorcee, hoping her powerful family name will bolster his chances in his next election. Prickly one moment and icy the next, Crispina is determined to keep her charming husband at a distance. That is, until Aelius undertakes a campaign to win not just the city's vote, but his wife's heart.

## *The Legionary Seduction* (Book 2)

Max joined the Roman army in search of glory and adventure, but soon finds himself stuck in the provinces, unable to land even one promotion. During a stint on guard duty at the new governor's residence, he comes face-to-face with Volusia, the girl he loved ten years ago. Only now, she's married to the governor. But when her husband mysteriously dies and she suspects foul play, the only person Volusia dares trust is Max, and she begs him to help investigate. Their love is strong, but can it withstand a killer's blade?

## *The Fortune Flirtation* (Book 3)

After losing her husband to a shipwreck, Lucretia has devoted herself to keeping his shipping business afloat. Felix, her scheming rival, strives for a monopoly on trade, which requires seizing Lucretia's ships for himself. Unfortunately for Felix, it's not just her ships he desires. Even worse, he's been too busy building his business empire to dally with women...*ever*. When Lucretia discovers both how much he wants her *and* that he's as inexperienced as a Vestal Virgin, she decides to use this to her advantage—proposing a truce in exchange for initiating Felix into the ways of the flesh.

## OTHER WORKS

### *A Princess's Ransom (Tales of Timeless Romance* anthology)

After the sack of Rome, Galla Placidia, the emperor's sister, becomes the Goths' most valuable hostage. While awaiting ransom, the ambitious princess, tired of living in her brother's shadow, realizes the Goths could be the key to the power she craves. Allying with the Goths could also allow her to indulge her forbidden attraction to her captor—the stoic, noble, and irritatingly handsome Athaulf. Placidia must decide how far she'll go to secure both the man and the future she desires, and if she's willing to turn her back on Rome forever.

# ACKNOWLEDGEMENTS

As the Roman Heirs series comes to an end, I wanted to thank all the readers who have taken a chance on a new author writing in a less frequently explored setting. I'm so grateful to every single person who has read, reviewed, recommended, or otherwise shouted about my work. I wasn't sure what to expect when taking the plunge to publish my novels, but the support and enthusiasm from readers has made it all worth it.

Thank you to fellow authors Anne Knight, Rachel Fitzjames, and A.M. Weald for their insight on earlier drafts of this story, and to editor Emily Keyes for helping to further bring my vision to life.

Finally, thank you to Frankie, my husband, proofreader, and relentless cheerleader. As I write this, it's a few days from the 10th anniversary of our first date. It's been the best decade ever, and I can't wait for many more.

# ABOUT THE AUTHOR

Jenna Bigelow is a historical romance author based in Wilmington, DE. She has eleven years of Latin classes under her belt, as well as a minor in Classical Culture and Society. When not writing, she enjoys sewing, especially recreating historical fashions of the 18th and 19th centuries. She thinks about the Roman Empire every day.

Connect with Jenna at her website, jennabigelow.com, or on Instagram/Threads at @jennabigelowwrites.